To Eric and Kim,
Thank you guys so much. I wouldn't be here without friends like y'all. I love you guys. Tony

THE GARRISON
DOCTRINE

BY
ANTHONY JEMISON

Bloomington, IN Milton Keynes, UK

authorHOUSE

AuthorHouse™
1663 Liberty Drive, Suite 200
Bloomington, IN 47403
www.authorhouse.com
Phone: 1-800-839-8640

AuthorHouse™ UK Ltd.
500 Avebury Boulevard
Central Milton Keynes, MK9 2BE
www.authorhouse.co.uk
Phone: 08001974150

First published by AuthorHouse 12/30/05

ISBN: 1-4208-9368-8 (sc)

Printed in the United States of America
Bloomington, Indiana

This book is printed on acid-free paper.

To Shawnol, my one and only

One

"Sir Arthur it is time," the young man signaled. He like the nine others, four men, five women, was dressed in a white silk tunic; his forehead adorned with black ash in the form of two small letters: **cc**. The cavernous basement of Sir Arthur's country estate, set on twenty acres, outside of London was dark and drafty, the stonewalls cold to the touch, but that would change. The nine men and women were each handed a candle by Sir Arthur and they formed a circle. They placed the candles at their feet and then knelt down in front of the flickering light; holding hands they began to sway; their shadows dancing against the walls. In unison they chanted, their voices consumed with lust: *"We kneel in reverence to Aristippus; we kneel in reverence to the supremacy of pleasure, May we go forth we the Chamber of Cyrenaic."*

They stood up and each man paired with a woman, they all removed their tunics and each man placed the woman he was paired with on one of the five stone tables that sat side by side in the center of the room. The men embraced the women, and they chanted, *"It is pleasure we seek, it is pleasure*

1

we desire, it is pleasure we obey." They repeated the chant over and over, working themselves up to a fever pitch, their bodies drenched with sweat, the stonewalls vibrating, thundering. Then they traded places on the five tables, with the men lying flat on their backs as the women straddled them. The women clasped hands and in unison swayed rhythmically in a circular motion. As the intensity of their movements increased both the men and women screamed: *"It is the union of pleasure."* After they finished, they gathered in a circle and Sir Arthur placed a gold tipped sword in the center of the circle. Each person picked up the sword, raised it above his head, and then slowly lowered the sword towards the stomach, slightly piercing the bellybutton, so that a trickle of blood was released. After each person finished, Sir Arthur placed the sword back in the center of the circle, knelt down and picked up a leather satchel. He opened it slowly and retrieved what was inside. The nine touched what was in Sir Arthur's hand, then knelt down and bowed their heads. Sir Arthur spoke: *"This that I possess in my hands is the symbol of power and unity, it is our greatest strength and it must be protected from the hands of evil. The piercing of our stomachs signifies a solemn oath that the Chamber will not reveal knowledge of its existence until the appointed time; do you swear to this oath?"*

"We do." They responded.

"Then it is complete."

London, England, 1499

Jeremiah Pratt and Richard Black were nervous, but supremely confident that they were doing the right thing, after all they surmised, *it is God's will*. The two men didn't say a word to each other as they journeyed from Jeremiah's downtown quarters to Deptford, a section of London where men such as themselves, normally stood out like sore thumbs. Tonight they looked like the town's regular inhabitants, traders, pirates, soldiers; their disguises not too overdone as to stand out. The night air was crisp, unusually crisp for mid June, but weather was the last thing on their minds. This evening was a long time coming and not without risk. If they were discovered their deaths would be a foregone conclusion. Jeremiah and Richard smiled as they reached their destination, an old stone tavern, whose claim to fame was good liquor, loose women and a spectacular roof top view of the Greenwich Palace. The tavern was lively and raucous as usual but drinking and loose women were not on Richard and Jeremiah's agenda. The two men bypassed the front entrance and slipped around the back, to the cellar door, which was locked. Jeremiah reached into his trousers and retrieved a skeleton key. He turned the lock clockwise and slowly pulled the door open. Richard lit the candle that he was carrying and they climbed down the steps. The stone cellar was dank and musty but it was suitable for their purposes. The two men changed into long black silk robes and waited. Like clockwork they heard banging on the cellar door; a double knock, then a series of staccato knocks, four in all, which signified it was other members of the brotherhood.

When Jeremiah Pratt closed the door and locked it from the inside, the others, seven women and five men, changed into black robes as well and each was given a black candle, which each placed by his feet. On the floor was a single black chalk mark, which stretched the length of the cellar. Each person stood behind the line looking straight ahead. Jeremiah Pratt then spoke: *"For twenty-six years we have served the Chamber of Cyrenaic but Sir Arthur has failed us. He has failed to see the vision of God, the vision that reveals that we are the one and only true religion, so we must take matters into our own hands, forge our own destiny. Truth has been revealed to us by the great teacher Arete and it is our duty to use truth to wipe out all who speak that which is other than truth, so tonight we begin. Tonight, we* the Light of Hellas take a solemn vow to destroy the enemy, the pagan leaders of the world's great religions, whom are nothing but hypocrisy masquerading as truth. Lies, they speak lies, and we will unburden the world of their deception, so that all mankind will be enlightened with truth, and we will reign supreme. But man is an unbelieving creature, he must see before he will trust, so we must obtain the one thing that will convince these feeble creatures that we have been ordained by God; we must possess the sacred artifact."

"*The sacred artifact,*" they chanted softly.

Then each person picked up his candle with his left hand and quickly skimmed the top of the flame with the index finger of his right hand. Jeremiah Pratt then spoke.

"*We must never reveal our existence and we must continue in the Chamber. Do you swear to do so?*"

"*We swear.*"

"*To power and truth.*"

"*To power and truth,*" They chanted in unison.

London England, November 1, 1503

"*A secret brotherhood called the Light of Hellas?*" Sir Arthur Garrison asked for the third time.

"Yes, they've taken the teachings of," Sir Arthur interrupted his nephew.

"Yes Charles I know who they've taken the teachings from. These lunatics have disgraced the name of Arete; they've distorted all that she and her father, our leader Aristippus stood for. How dare they use her teachings to justify their insanity? Did you know that the epitaph on her tomb describes her as 'The splendor of Greece, with the beauty of Helen, the virtue of Therma, Aristippus, the soul of Socrates and the tongue of

Homer' did you know that Charles?" Sir Arthur was pacing the floor, his anger reaching the boiling point.

"Yes," answered young Charles. But Sir Arthur didn't hear him. He couldn't believe what he was hearing; *not Jeremiah Pratt and Richard Black!* They were part of the upper legion, trustworthy and loyal men who had proven their worth to the Chamber. He was hearing the unthinkable. Not only had they betrayed the Chamber but they were also planning to *murder* the leaders of the world's great religions and steal the sacred artifact. Sir Arthur had to sit down because his head was spinning. He looked intently at Charles; his debt to the young man could never be repaid. How Charles came across this information, he didn't want to know. But what he did know was that he had to stop them and he knew just what to do.

A remote wooded area some fifty miles outside of London, England, November 8, 1503

"There, it is finished," Sir Arthur Garrison said to Charles as the smoke raised behind him, creating a bluish-gray haze, a menacing contradiction to the otherwise bright blue sky, a blue the color akin to the magnificent waters seen only in the Caribbean. Charles stared straight ahead, his olive green eyes conveying a hybrid of emotions, ranging from guilt to triumph. Yes it is finished he thought, but at what cost? Sir Arthur placed his arm around his nephew, but the young man flinched. Sir Arthur rose and walked about two feet to retrieve a worn leather satchel. The smoke was getting heavier and the nauseating stench of the two dead bodies was becoming stronger so much so that he could feel the sensation of vomit rising in his belly. He handed the satchel to Charles, who took it gingerly.

"I wish there could have been another way, and I regret not telling you of my plans but we both know what would've happened if I'd allowed them to live."

"Yes Sir Arthur I know this, but murder is against the tenets of the Chamber and."

"Yes what is it Charles?" Sir Arthur felt deep compassion for his young nephew. Taking a life, even when it is justified, is not an easy thing to digest, he lamented silently.

'It's just that, well I know they had to die, they betrayed us, but to actually take a life, does something to a man's soul, but rest assured I will not fail you, I will complete what must be done."

"I knew that you would."

"What we did does it trouble you at all?" Charles asked Sir Arthur.

"Yes it does, very deeply. My soul will go to hell for what I've done, but sacrifice has been the cornerstone of man's existence; the few for the greater good. I must look at it that way and so must you."

"But what does it matter. You heard what Jeremiah Pratt said as he was dying: *Our deaths mean nothing, the legacy of the brotherhood will be carried forward, and it is God's will.* So we haven't stopped a thing Sir Arthur."

"We have stood up to evil, God will do the rest. Now leave me to do what I must," Sir Arthur said softly.

"I will remember your words," Charles said with sadness. The sun would be setting soon, which meant only a few more hours of daylight; Charles would have to be leaving to get to the appointed destination before nightfall. As he thought about his impending journey a wave of sadness washed over him because he had just fellowshipped with his uncle for the last time.

"It is time," Sir Arthur said.

"I know." Said Charles, fighting back tears.

Sir Arthur reached into the suede satchel that was draped over his stooped shoulders and handed Charles a sheet of parchment paper. The bluish-gray haze had now completely enveloped the area, creating an eerie presence. The moment was not lost on either man, and for a second they stood completely silent and still. Sir Arthur then spoke, "*Charles you are the only one who has knowledge of the secret; you are the first gatekeeper. This document I give to you is the Chamber's legacy, guard it with your very life and ensure that you follow the path I have chosen, a path that will lead to the last and final gatekeeper, five hundred years from this very date.*" Charles stared solemnly at the document. He hugged Sir Arthur and then mounted his horse, the leather satchel strapped over his shoulder. He rode to a clearing, stopped his horse and looked back. He decided he didn't want to see what was to occur and took off; it wasn't the memory he wanted; that of his uncle, Sir Arthur Garrison taking his own life.

London, England, November 11, 1503

"*We must presume they are dead,*" said a slightly balding gentleman, perhaps in his early thirties. He was next in command in the event of the deaths of Jeremiah Pratt and Richard Black, a duty he assumed with honor, yet sadness. "*We must continue; the brotherhood is bigger than any one individual. We must fulfill our destiny. We must obey God's will.*"

"*God's will,* "The brotherhood chanted.

"*We must obtain the sacred artifact.*"

"*We must obtain the sacred artifact,*"They chanted.

Then the gentleman rose, pointed towards the heavens and exclaimed, "*To power and truth, to power and truth!*

London, England, November 11, 1503

Charles Garrison didn't relish what he had to do, but it had to be done. As he walked down the winding stone steps to the basement of his uncle's estate to tell the others in the upper legion the news about Sir Arthur, he took solace in the knowledge that the sacred artifact was still safe. When he reached the last step, he paused before he opened the door and said a silent prayer for the gatekeeper; *May you do what is righteous and just.*

Two

Where do tales of adventure begin, those extraordinary events, as my father so aptly states, that occur outside of the parameters of man's normal course of existence? They begin when you least expect it, when you're simply trying to maneuver through the vagaries of life, when the pulse of life is beating so fast that you can't catch your breath, when all you want to do is escape from the people you have to see, the phone calls you have to take, and the aggravation you have to deal with. That's how I was feeling on the day my adventure began, and despite the fact I'm a well-respected, well-liked and well-compensated college professor who is fortunate enough to be blessed with means, none of that meant a rat's ass. In fact status and possessions never mean anything in the game of life because life's circumstances are no respecter of person.

But let's stick to the story.

It was the fall of 2003 and I was sitting in my office preparing for another semester at Landon College, a small liberal arts college, located in my hometown, bucolic Landon, New York, a small bedroom community, some twenty miles north of New York City. Set on a wooded campus about ten minutes walking distance from downtown, Landon College, for the fourth year in a row, was voted the most beautiful campus in North America, a feat that everyone in our tiny village of eight thousand takes great pride in. I've been teaching Ancient Religious Studies at Landon for about eight years and even though I am privy to it's beauty every day, I never tire of the red brick circular cobblestone walkway that sits in the middle of the quad; the four main academic buildings that surround it, each an architectural work of art modeled after the ancient structures of Greece, Rome, Egypt and Russia; the turn of the century lamp posts which inundate the campus providing the most romantic location in town, to see them lit on a warm, breezy summer night is indescribable; the entrance to the library, adorned with matching marble lions, a replica of the New York Public Library, beautiful dogwoods that line both sides of the winding walkway that extends from the library to the student union, an ivy covered facility of brown brick, highlighted by a man made brook. I could go on and on, but I don't want to get sidetracked from the story.

I was sitting in my office, and though it was extremely warm I left the air conditioner off, preferring the natural coolant of the slight breeze that was blowing softly through my window. My office is fairly large and comfortable a perk I'm sure for being so wildly popular, a badge I wear proudly, but not vainly. I was putting the finishing touches on a syllabus that I'd be using for my class, which began in about thirty minutes, when the phone rang. *Kelly!* I sighed as I stared at the caller ID. *Why do I torture myself?* I started not to answer but if I didn't, she'd only keep calling until I did. Kelly is my on again, off again girlfriend and our relationship is highly dysfunctional and yet I stay in it; but more on that later.

"Alex," she bellowed. I could envision her pacing back and forth in her plush mid-town Manhattan law office, wearing out her cobalt blue Persian carpet, pacing, the way she does when she's in court interrogating a witness.

"Yes Kelly, what's bothering you now?" I asked staring out the window at the dogwoods swaying back and forth, their branches drinking in the cloudless, sun- drenched sky.

"Don't take that tone with me Alex Marshall."

"And what tone would that be, *Kelly?*" I ask, removing my glasses and placing them on my desk next to the syllabus.

"The one that says I'm working on your nerves."

"Well that wouldn't be an exaggeration Kelly. Right now, *you are*, working on my nerves. Look Kelly we've been over this already and right now I don't have time to talk about it again." Why do I continuously allow this to happen I asked myself for the umpteenth time?

"You do have time to talk; your class doesn't start for another thirty minutes; which is another thing."

"Kelly, not today." I replied.

"I just don't understand why you continue to teach at Landon College!" Every week she had to tell me how it didn't make any sense *for Dr. Alex Marshall a world renowned expert on ancient religion to teach and live in Landon, NY. You could make millions as a consultant or something. You're thirty-eight years old Alex, get a grip for Christ's sakes!* Yes I'm sought after and no I don't have to teach, but I do. I teach because I love what it does for me; I teach because I love these young minds that I encounter every year, young minds eager to learn, to grow; I teach because as trite as it may seem I want to give back to the little village north of Manhattan that nurtured me, that embraced me, that loved me unconditionally, the little village where everybody_knows everybody and knows each others business and no one seems to mind.

I teach at Landon College because Landon is my home, my roots; it's the Garret family's fall fish fry to welcome the students to a new semester, a tradition that dates back to the early nineteen hundreds; it's Mrs. Wilkins who babysat for my sister and I, whose grass I cut when I was teenager, whose grass I still cut from time to time, whose "I remember when" stories never grow old, especially when we're on her front sipping her mouth watering homemade lemonade; it's Mr. Dotson's deli on the corner of Main and Birchwood, still equipped with a working old fashioned soda fountain and the best corned beef sandwiches on the planet; it's the annual Landon Village Fair, a festive three day affair, culminating each night with everyone bringing their lawn chairs to the back of the deli to watch movies being projected on the wall. These are just a few of the reasons why I stay, why I never moved to the city, or Los Angeles, or Paris, or any of those places where a person of my stature is "supposed" to live. I've been an expert in my field for years but it wasn't something I set out to do. There's an old adage that says if you do the thing you're passionate about, if you're true to your purpose, then rewards will follow. That's what happened to me.

I am a scholar because it's my passion, borne as a child, when I was too slight to be taken seriously in sports; instead of sulking I became a scholar. I read voraciously, devouring everything I could in particular ancient religion and as a result became an expert in the field, a highly sought after commodity. *So of course I could leave Landon,* I reply every time Kelly asks the question. Every week she would badger me with this and each time I asked myself; why do you stay with her? *What's wrong with you?* Sometimes I'd perform this ritual in front of my bathroom mirror, as though the image looking back at me would answer. But all I got was a pair of brown eyes staring at me as though I were crazy.

"Alex, are you listening to me!" Of course I was; did I have a choice? If I hung up, she'd only call back.

"I'm not getting into this again nor am I getting into *the other reason* that you called."

"Alex!"

"There's nothing to talk about; my mind's made up." I said

scratching my head.

Silence. Now she's sitting down, her eyes boring a hole through the phone.

"Kelly, are you still there?" More silence.

"You're an asshole." She finally replies.

"Maybe so, but I'm not going, and you know why."

"Alex give it a rest, its old news."

"I'm not going."

"If you won't do this for me, then we're through, *for good*."

"Whatever Kelly."

"You're an asshole." Then she slammed down the phone.

She'll be over later tonight, I thought. It's always this way with us; we argue and then we make up.

I love Kelly dearly, but it seems as if we're always fighting. It's been that way for six years and despite my complaining I've come to the obvious conclusion that we're one of those couples who need conflict. Every time we break up I swear to myself this is it, but I just can't leave her. I need her too much. I need every thing imaginable about her; six years will do that to you. I need her smile. I need the way she laughs at funny movies. I need her strength and confidence. I need the way she brushes her hair before she goes to bed. I need the way she says "Whatever Alex." I need to hear her talk about her day in court. I need the way she drives like a bat out of hell. I need the way she supports what I do despite the fact that she complains about what I do. I know that sounds like an oxymoron, but it really isn't. And yes, I even need the way she calls me an "asshole". What I'm describing is as old as time itself. It's what defines a relationship; it's the subtle nuances that make what we have more than just a cliché. It's what couples that have been together for a long time mean when they talk about the 'little' things. It's the little things that keep Kelly and I together, despite the fights. It's also great sex, but great sex cannot sustain a relationship. Great sex alone isn't the reason that I've been faithful to Kelly. Great sex isn't the reason why Kelly is nice to my sister, even when she knows that my sister would prefer that I be with someone else. Great sex isn't the reason why I stayed with Kelly in the hospital, around the clock when her dad had a cancer scare two years ago. Great sex doesn't understand nor care about the meaning of true friendship, which Kelly and I have. What Kelly and I have is a real, gut level, honest-to-goodness relationship, warts and all, and at that particular moment it was all warts.

The phone rang again. I figured it was her calling back to continue reading me the riot act.

"Hello, Dr. Marshall?" His accent was English.

"Yes, how may I help you?"

"My name is Alistair Pratt. Do you have a moment?"

"Just a few I'm on my way to teach a class."

"Okay can you take those few moments to speak with me?"

"That depends." I said.

"On what may I ask?"

"On whether or not you are trying to sell me something."

"I assure you, that's not why I'm calling," he said cheerfully.

"Good", I said, glancing at my watch.

"I am an admirer of your work on ancient religion, Dr. Marshall."

"Thank you, forgive me if I seem abrupt but I've got a class to teach, is there something about religion that you wanted to discuss?"

"I've attended a few of your lectures and I'm quite impressed, but what really piqued my interest was your book on the Chamber of Cyrenaic."

"The Chamber of Cyrenaic?" About ten years ago I'd written a book entitled *The Legend of the Lost Chamber*. The Chamber of Cyrenaic was a secret society, founded by British nobleman Sir Arthur Garrison. Their name derived from the ancient Cyrenaic School of philosophical thought, which is rooted in the tenets of Hedonism, of which Sir Arthur was a staunch believer. Legend has it that their deaths were due to mass suicide and that they'd left behind a sacred artifact. It is believed that this artifact is of great historical and religious importance, but after years of research my efforts came up empty.

"Yes", I'm writing a book on military orders and secret societies, and I am having a devil of a time finding anything new on the Cyrenaic. Unfortunately your book is no longer in print, and I was hoping that you would be able to help me."

"If it's a copy you want I can send one to you."

"A copy of your book would be greatly appreciated, but I was hoping to impose on you for more than just your book."

"More? How so?" I asked, slightly intrigued.

"I would like to pick your brain, understand your thought process, as you wrote the book."

"What is it that you think I would be able to provide?"

"Your expertise."

"I wrote that book quite a few years ago. My memory has faded. I don't know how much help I could be Mr. Pratt."

"You will be compensated quite handsomely."

"It's not a question of money, besides; I didn't say that I wouldn't help you. I said that I didn't know how much I could help you."

"So will you help me?"

"Possibly. Let me give it some thought and get back to you. Can I have your number?"

"Certainly."

"I will have an answer for you by the end of the week."

"I'm looking forward to working with you Dr. Marshall."

"I haven't agreed."

"Wishful thinking on my part, I'm afraid," he said with a chuckle.

"Why is this so important to you, if you don't mind me asking?"

"No, I don't mind", he said pleasantly. As he was about to answer my other line was ringing. It was Kelly.

"I'm afraid I will have to wait for your answer. I have another call. I'll talk to you on Friday."

"Thank you for your time Dr. Marshall and goodbye". He hung up.

At the same time that Alex was speaking to Kelly, billionaire Alistair Pratt was making a call of his own from the penthouse of his Upper East-Side apartment, one of the many buildings he owned.

"Hello," said Lydia Sinclair, a willowy dark haired woman in her mid forties, whose unforgettable presence was signified by a long angular face and cold blue almond shaped eyes; which Lydia used to her advantage, to intimidate or to seduce, whichever the situation called for.

"I've made contact."

"Good."

"Good indeed," said Alistair, smiling as he hung up the phone; his thoughts rewinding to another time, where it all began.

"Daddy, it's my sixteenth birthday." Young Alistair reminded his father.

"Yes son I know sit down and I will tell you everything." Young Alistair did as he was told, his stomach churning. For as long as he could remember he'd waited for this day. His father cleared his throat and began." In the late fifteenth century Sir Arthur Garrison, a British nobleman, founded a secret society called the Chamber of Cyrenaic, of which our ancestor Lord Jeremiah

Pratt, and other prominent men and women were members. The brotherhood grew, but Sir Arthur was without vision, failing to embrace new ideas. In 1499, Jeremiah Pratt and Richard Black, while giving the appearance that they still embraced the tenets of the Chamber secretly established the Light of Hellas; named after the Greek philosopher Arete. The society grew and was poised to become a force of immense proportions, the wheels set in motion to change the face of mankind, but then Jeremiah Pratt and Richard Black disappeared, never to be seen again."

"What happened?"

"On November 8, 1503, Sir Arthur murdered them after he discovered they founded another society, one that he believed would supplant the Chamber. He wrongly assumed that with the deaths of Pratt and Black the Light of Hellas would disband, but he was wrong, the society became stronger than ever and in 2003 the world will see the vision of the brotherhood, we will retrieve the sacred artifact and the world will bow to power and truth."

"What happened to the sacred artifact?"

"Sir Arthur stole it from the Chamber."

"But if it belonged to the Chamber, why is it our legacy?"

"It was your ancestor Jeremiah Pratt and Richard Black who discovered it while members of the Chamber."

"Why didn't they take it when they left the Chamber?"

"It was heavily guarded; they would have been killed had they attempted to take it."

"Where is it now?"

"Sir Arthur made provisions for it to be transferred and that it is to resurface in the year 2003 to someone only known as the gatekeeper."

"Who will that be?"

"No one knows, only that it is believed that the gatekeeper will be the last known male survivor of a figure of supreme religious and historical importance, a figure whose name will not be revealed to you until your reign over the brotherhood begins."

"Why can't I know who it is now?"

"It is the way of the brotherhood my son."

"And when will my reign begin."

"When the brotherhood deems that you are ready."

"And when will that be?"

"I've said enough my son. Just know that you are our last hope, you must not fail."

"No sir, I won't."

No sir I won't, Alistair repeated aloud as he stared at the picture he carried around in his wallet of his dead father. It was his duty to fulfill the legacy of the brotherhood and he would not fail; would not be thwarted, as was Jeremiah Pratt. Nothing and no one could stop him, could stop *them*. Soon the world will know who we are; and when I am through, *will bow to us*. He stared again at his father's picture and he became angry; his father's legacy, the legacy of the brotherhood all changed because of one man. *Sir Arthur Garrison*. He slammed his fist into the wall, so hard that the glass from a framed original Monet shattered sending shards of glass flying around the room. A piece of glass lodged in his left arm, causing him to bleed. He ran his right thumb across the wound and pressed the blood to his lips. *Power and truth* he whispered; *I will not fail.*

"Alex, what took you so long to answer the phone?" Kelly asked irritably.

"I was on the other line. Why are you calling me anyway, if I recall you said that we were through?"

"Why do you have to be so difficult?"

"I'm not being difficult. If you cared for me as much as you say then you wouldn't badger me about going to this party. That's like me inviting you to something involving my sister. Since I know that you don't like her I wouldn't dream of doing that. All I'm asking for is the same consideration."

"*Your* sister and I, that's different and you know it."

"How?"

"Don't play games with me Alex; you know what I'm talking about."

"Helen Adamson," I said.

Silence.

Helen Adamson was my first love and she's my sister Carol's best friend. Helen and I dated in high school and college, but then Helen, left after graduation to take a job in Milan, and when she came back two years later, our relationship wasn't the same; but more on that later. My sister Carol believes that Helen and I are kindred spirits; that we belong together; but she says it won't happen until I let go of my unhealthy entanglement; those were her exact words, with Kelly. My sister means well; her desires for me are a continuation of her role as the great protector.

When I was younger, because I was so slight, Carol took it upon herself to protect me, even if that meant fighting boys. When I would get teased for always reading, Carol would defend me. As I got older, my features matured, I grew into myself, the girls started coming around. By the time I'd reached high school I'd been totally transformed physically. I was considered cute. I would hear the girls whisper about me; *that can't be the same Alex Marshall, my God he's gorgeous!* Of course I got a big head, it's only natural, but Carol was there to make sure I didn't become like my former tormentors. She had something to say about every girl I took out; that was until Helen and her family moved to Landon.

It was my junior year, Carol's last. Carol met Helen at field hockey tryouts. Carol was already on the team and was helping the coach, who happens to be our Aunt Margaret with tryouts. Helen made the team and her and Carol hit it off immediately. One day Carol invited Helen over for the specific purpose of hooking her up with me. I'd spoken to Helen on numerous occasions and I found her attractive, but at the time I'd had my eye on Taylor Wallace, a petite, pert breasted sophomore who would give me the "I'm ready" look. I was sitting on our front porch when Carol drove up with Helen. Helen is a striking woman, think of Audrey Hepburn with a bronze complexion and auburn hair. For a high school girl what stood out about Helen was her sense of fashion and style, which was more impressive than my sister; a feat hard to top. But it wasn't just her sense of style. Helen has an angelic spirit, she's one of those people who others call a "good person" and mean it from the depths of their soul. I was taken by Helen; smitten after our first conversation, and though my hormones were raging for Taylor Wallace, it was Helen I wanted. That evening we went on a double date with Carol and Richard Nichols, who has been her husband for the past twelve years. After that first date Helen and I were inseparable and after we graduated from college I thought we'd begin discussions about marriage, and then she hit me with Milan. Now mind you I knew about the offer, but I foolishly thought she would decline because she'd had offers from several top-notch fashion designers in New York City. The conversation is as vivid as if it'd happened yesterday. We were in Landon, strolling arm in arm through Landon Park. It was early June, a warm, breezy evening, the type New Yorkers cherish, a welcome respite from the oppressive heat that had held Landon hostage for the past couple of weeks.

"Alex this is Italy, Milan, surely you can understand that?"

"Yes, but I still don't want you to go, I know that's selfish but that's how I feel."

"I appreciate your honesty and trust me this decision isn't easy."

"I know."

"I don't think you do. I never thought I'd love someone the way I love you, nor did I think I'd ever be loved the way you love me, so leaving you for two years is going to be torture, but if I don't I'll always ask *what if* and even worse I may blame you."

"Helen I know, but two years is a long time to be without you."

"But you'll visit right? And I'll be home for Christmas."

"I love you so much," I said taking her in my arms and kissing her passionately right in front of the gazebo. Passersby applauded.

"Alex we'll be fine," she said. And that was that, we didn't talk about it anymore. She left and we did see each other during the two years, but when she came back, she'd changed. I can't quite say what it was, but she was different, and it was clear that we weren't going to make it. I knew something happened in Milan, an affair perhaps. Helen wouldn't say, but I knew something's wasn't being told. For the next couple of years we went through the motions, but it was clear that the death knell for our relationship tolled on that warm June evening. We didn't belabor the point, just said it wasn't working and promised to be friends; something which never works. Then she moved away again, this time to Los Angeles. We kept in touch, but not for long, each interval between calls, lengthening, each conversation less intimate, an exercise of awkward politeness, a requisite between ex-lovers who parted on amicable terms. She married and divorced and she and Carol kept in touch, as best friends do. Then about two years ago she came back.

She didn't tell me she was coming back and I suppose I didn't expect her to, though I admit that the fact that she didn't bothered me. When we finally saw each other, it was at the opening of her boutique, butterflies twinkled in my stomach, and my mouth was dry. I hadn't seen her in almost twelve years. She looked the same, of course the passage of time added a few wrinkles around the eyes, the hands; her hair was cut shorter, modernly stylish, befitting of her age, she was slimmer, but not freakishly thin, like some women in their mid-thirties who think they can recapture their younger years. You've seen them; they looked frail and washed out, too much treadmill, too many tanning beds. No she looked marvelous, regal, and an older version of the lithe seventeen year old I first fell in love with, way back in the dark ages of nineteen eighty-two. We spoke, the conversation stiff at first, warming to familiarity by evenings end. I told her all about Kelly, who thankfully couldn't attend, and she told me about her failed marriage, he "traded" her in for his twenty-two year old acupuncturist. We ended the evening by agreeing to keep in touch, but we didn't, though I often saw her around town; something that's inevitable in a small town. My sister says Helen came back because of me, says it's serendipity, says it can work if I'd only let Kelly go. Kelly knows that Carol feels this way.

"Kelly, Helen and I are old news, that's Carol's fantasy."

"I'm painfully aware of that Alex. You know sometimes I think the real reason you stay in Landon is because you want Helen back."

"That's not true Kelly."

"Do you still love her?"

"No."

"Liar."

"Dammit Kelly enough of this crap. Every week we go through this and I'm tired of it; it's like you want me to be with Helen. Are you trying to prove that I'll abandon you like your *mot--?*" I caught myself, but the damage was already done.

"You bastard," she screamed and then hung up. I'd messed up royally. I immediately called her back, but she wouldn't answer. I tried again, nothing but the machine. I felt bad.

I was wrong and I knew it. It's not that I don't empathize with her situation concerning her mother. It's just that I don't know what it's like to be in her shoes and so sometimes I'm not as compassionate as I should be. My mother has always been there for me and like anything that's a good thing, I sometimes take the fact that she has always been there for granted. Instead of listening to Kelly and letting her express her feelings about Helen, I automatically tried to make it seem as though it were an insecurity issue with her. An issue relating to her mother's abandonment; and that was wrong. No it was fucked up and that's because this has nothing to do with Kelly and her mom; this was about Helen and my unresolved feelings for her. Kelly hit a nerve, a raw deep-seated nerve that has ached for a long time. For years it was a dull ache, it was there, noticeable, but not prominent. As long as Helen was miles away in Los Angeles, I only thought about her in the abstract. Her image would pass through my head if I walked by one of our old haunts or if someone mentioned her name. I didn't think about her everyday, but she loomed like a shadow.

But when she moved back to Landon, things had changed; the shadow was no longer in the background. It was as if being in close proximity to her made things different. How, I can't really say. For the two years that she's been back I haven't tried to rekindle what we had; and I think for the most part my feelings for Kelly are the reason. The other part is the "thing" that happened in Milan, the "thing" that changed her. I haven't found out what happened and I'm afraid to ask because I don't want to be hurt. Yet despite all that I think about her everyday, reminiscing about how things were between us. Kelly is smart, she sees with her heart and her heart is telling her that I still love Helen. But I can't say that's what I feel. Do I really still love Helen or is it the romantic musings of a small town boy, swept away in some Fitzgeraldian ideal of love? I really don't know what I feel for Helen; but what I do know is that she is on my mind every single day, which is not fair to Kelly. And now I've hurt Kelly. She'll forgive me; she always does, even though I don't deserve it.

I first met Kelly at a party in Greenwich Village. I was engaged in a rather boring conversation, with a well known author of erotic literature, who wanted to talk about everything but her books, when I noticed an animated young woman holding court with a group of five men. I edged closer to hear what they were discussing.

"That's ridiculous Kelly, you'll never win with that defense," said a rather tall nattily dressed male of about forty.

"You're just saying that Kurt, because you didn't think of it first. You probably would have won the Radnor case, if you did", she said. Though she was by far the smallest person in the group, a mere five-four I would guess, one hundred and ten pounds soaking wet, she towered over the others. It was clear they were no match for her.

"He's not going to do any time. I consider that to be a victory, considering all of the evidence that they had on him."

"*I* would have gotten an acquittal," she said, without once averting his gaze; a gaze that communicated contempt and lust. She was wearing an elegant black silk dinner gown, and stylish black pumps. It was warm and she appeared to be glistening. I was turned on watching her. All of us were, and she knew it.

"Come on Kelly," said another equally well dressed male, "you're good, but not that good, *and this was a federal case after all.*"

"So what? I've won federal cases before."

"Yes you have, but not one with *this much* evidence," one of the men said.

"That's where you and I are different Kurt. You conceded defeat before you even gave your opening. The jury could sense that. I never concede defeat, because I never think that I'm going to lose. I always believe that I will win, at *everything.*" I read her emphasis on the word everything to mean that she could have each and every one of them standing there, chew them up, spit them out, and have them knocking on her door the next day, like pathetic puppy dogs. "Excuse me she said, nature is calling." They all dispersed after she left. I was intrigued. I waited for her to come out of the bathroom. She startled me with what she said.

"If you were any kind of real man, you would have walked over, and taken me away from those panting idiots."

"And if you were any kind of real woman, you would know that a man like me does not have time for parlor games."

"Well done, Mr.?"

"It's Dr., and I'm not concerned with measuring up to your standards, Ms.?" I said with a sly grin. The back and forth was enjoyable.

"Kelly Van Astor." She said it as if I was supposed to know who she was.

"Dr. Alex Marshall," I said.

"You say that with such conviction; I like a man who is confident." She said with a sly smile.

"You like games don't you Ms. Van Astor?"

"Excuse me?"

"I said you like to play games."

"Everyone likes games Dr."

"Some games are more dangerous than others," I said, enjoying the playful banter.

"You're not impressed with me, are you Dr. Marshall?" She said, as she stared at me intensely. She wasn't overly pretty, but her commanding presence and confidence made her the most beautiful woman in the room; I was immediately taken by her.

"How do you mean that, Ms. Van Astor?" I said as I lapsed into lust and imagined her lithe physique astride my waist.

"Why don't you tell me?" She said placing her slender hand in mine.

"I think you know the answer." I said, my six-foot frame peering down at her.

"Yes I do," are you here alone? She asked suddenly.

"Yes."

"I knew it," she said.

"How?"

"I know these things".

"Is that right, and what do you know right now?"

"All I need to," she said.

When I got back to the office I tried Kelly again, but she was still avoiding me; which I can't say I blame her. It was a gorgeous day, and despite the fact I'd messed up I was not going to spend it with a hangdog look, cooped up in the office. On my way out of the door, I ran into one of my favorite grad students, Ashley Winters, a bright young woman, who was destined to do great things one day.

"Dr. Marshall, how's it going, nice tan by the way." She says sprightly, flashing a set of small but perfectly proportioned white teeth that would make any dentist proud.

"Thanks the tan is a bonus from working in the garden."

"Well I like it, makes you look younger."

"This old man thanks you. So, how was your summer?"

"It was nice, but I'm glad to be back, I like the beach and seeing the folks, but after living in New York for the past six years, Malibu can't hang, you know what I mean "Doc?" She asks adjusting her signature ponytail. In the six years that I've known Ashley, I've only seen her without her hair in a ponytail once and that was at a grad school banquet. Though extremely attractive with an athletic build, olive complexion and round hazel eyes, magnified by a pair of beautiful, long eyelashes; Ashley doesn't subscribe to what she calls *the fashion model routine*, preferring jeans and sweat suits. She says the glamour thing is not functional in college.

"Yes I do." I said with a chuckle. So what do you have, one more semester?"

"Yes. I'm going to graduate early."

"Do you have any idea, what you plan on doing?"

"Naturally I'm going to stay in New York, go to Columbia for my doctorate."

"Good choice, I'll write you a recommendation if you like."

"Thanks. Hey Doc?" She asks as I turned to walk away.

"Yes?"

"I heard that you're without a research assistant this year."

"That's true, are you interested?"

"Yes."

"Then you're hired."

"Just like that?"

"Just like that; come by my office tomorrow, around 10, with your schedule."

"Cool, I'll see you then."

I didn't have any plans for the rest of the day. I thought about calling my brother in law, but he was probably out doing some deal. Richard, Carol's husband, is a partner at one of the most prestigious investment firms in the world. His office, which is as big as our whole department or at least it seems that way, is located right in the heart of New York's financial district; Wall Street. On occasion I have gone down to visit Richard, and it was nothing to see someone of immense wealth and importance, either waiting to see him or leaving his office. Richard is only thirty-eight, but he has been a star on Wall Street, since he graduated from Wharton. Figuring that he was busy, I decided to ring him another time. I called my sister instead; perhaps she would like some company.

"Uncle Alex," shouted Rachel and Heather as I headed up their winding black marble walkway, which was magnified by their magnificent landscaping. They live in a humongous colonial situated on five acres about twenty minutes from my house. Imagine one of those homes you see plastered on the cover of one of those magazines that profiles unique estates.

"Hi you guys," where's mommy?"

"She's in the backyard. I'll get her. Come on Rachel, let's go get mommy," said Heather.

"Well hello there little brother,"she said, as she hugged me firmly. My sister has a confident regal air about her that says I will not be ignored. She stands about five feet seven, with short-cropped hair that never seems out of place. She's thin in a model sort of way, but not frail in the least. In addition to her extreme confidence, which she inherits from my dad and late grandfather, what makes her so striking is her sense of style. She's the type of person who always looks like she just stepped out of a fashion magazine.

"Hello yourself, big sis."

"I'm glad you came by, Richard's grilling some steaks, would you like to stay for dinner?"

"Of course, you know I never pass up a free meal." I said distractedly.

Carol has always had the ability to discern what the average person cannot. She knew that I didn't come by just to pay a social call.

"Kids, why don't you go around back and play, Uncle Alex and I are going into the kitchen."

"But mom, we want Uncle Alex to play with us," they pleaded.

"He's staying for dinner, so you will have plenty of time to play with him."

"I promise kids," I said. They both jumped on my lap and Rachel pulled on my shirt.

"Careful you guys, you'll mess up your uncle's clothes." Carol said with a wide grin. I'm very particular about my clothes. I have a weakness for fashion and I confess to spending too much money on clothing, but I figure you only live once. Everyone in Landon knows this about me, so I get ribbed a lot.

We retreated into the kitchen, my favorite room in my sister's house. I love being in there at night, when the moon is full, an ethereal glow permeates through the large rectangular windows, creating a magical presence, eerie, adventurous like Halloween night and trick or treating. Carol put on a pot of water for tea, while I helped myself to a couple of homemade oatmeal cookies; no one bakes them better than my sister.

"So what has Kelly done this time?"

"Why do you assume I'm here about her?"

"Because it's always about her; if you'd only talk to He--." I cut her off midstream.

"Enough about Helen, okay?"

"Okay, but you're crazy if you think things are going to change with Kelly, what's it been, six years now? Is she that good in bed?"

"Excuse me?"

"You heard me. I mean that has to be it, because I don't see what else it could be, you're always complaining about her."

"Not always."

"Uh yeah little brother, *always.*"

"Okay maybe I do bitch about her on occasion, but it's not just about her; there's another situation that I want to talk to you about as well."

"Shoot."

I told her about both situations. Initially she just shook her head. Finally she responded.

"You know, I just don't understand you sometimes. It's amazing that we come from the same womb." I knew that was coming, and I laughed.

"What's so funny," she said, laughing.

"I was just waiting for the womb remark."

"Well you know it's true. Let me get this straight. You don't want to go to the party and you don't want to help the Englishman, but you're probably going to do both anyway?"

"Yes."

"Why?" She asked shaking her head.

"Because I have a hard time saying no."

"That's obvious. All of your life you've been that way. Hey remember the time when Johnny Elgin, talked you into---?"

"Yes Carol, why do you always bring that up? It was a long time ago."

"Because you're still the same, afraid to say no, *except when it comes to Helen*." I cringed. "I know you don't want my advice, but I'm going to give it to you anyway. Tell the Englishman you're too busy, and be firm with Kelly."

"I've already told her no, and I'm going to stick to that. The Englishman sounds intriguing. If it's too much, then I'll stop."

"No you won't. Once you start something, you'll see it to fruition, especially when it comes to the Cyrenaic."

"Those days are over. I tracked the legend for over ten years and I'm not putting myself through it again." I spent a lot of time, money and energy searching for the secret artifact, and all I got was a lot of frequent flyer miles and food poisoning. No thanks.

"Yeah right Indiana Jones." I laughed.

"It's true, besides I have enough on my plate with writing and classes."

"If you say so."

"I do."

"Okay."

"Look I think I know what I'm going to do." I said as I grabbed a handful of cookies.

"Then do it. I don't understand why you make everything such a big deal."

"I don't do that."

"Yes you do, need I give examples?"

"No, but that's never stopped you before," I said. We laughed.

Richard came home around five o'clock, an unusually early day for him. He changed clothes and I helped him with the steaks. I stayed until about eleven and then drove home. I found myself driving past Helen's parent's house. I parked across the street and just sat there. Waves of memories flooded me and for the first time in years I missed Helen.

Jordan Nelson extracted her naked body from underneath the covers, the moonlight filling the room, her body a lithe silhouette dancing on the walls. As she did so she glanced at the body lying next to her, sleeping peacefully like a baby. A thin smile pursed her lips. She stood up and gave her perfectly formed body a once over and then took a second look at her latest conquest, and her nipples hardened. She pinched herself. He was fun, a necessary diversion to satiate her voracious sexual appetite, but she couldn't let him distract her from the biggest prize of all. With that she roused him from her bed and told him it was time to leave. He shifted his body to a position that would cause her to see that his erection thought other wise. "Are you sure you want me to leave," he said with a sly grin as his eyes glanced downward. Jordan's mind flashed to the pleasure he had given her just hours ago and then it flashed to thoughts of the future and what that entailed once she completed the mission. She retrieved his clothes from the chair by her bedroom window, tossed them to him and as she headed towards the bathroom, simply replied, "Lock the door behind you." Jordan smiled. She was ready.

Marseilles, France

For the fifth time in the past two minutes, Pierre opened the dusty, cracked blinds to the window of the abandoned building that was the chosen for the transfer. He turned away from the window and reached down to pick up a leather case. A sharp sensation spiked through his stomach, causing him to step back. Nerves, he surmised. He put the case down and returned to the window. He smiled because what or rather whom he'd been waiting for was walking towards his building. It was late and the remote location of the building, practically ensured that Conrad, his visitor would be safe when he left. Pierre picked up the case again and waited as he heard Conrad's heavy footfalls proceed up the steps. Pierre took a deep breath and then allowed his senses to savor what would be his last moments on earth. He did not have any regrets about the actions he'd chosen to take because he'd chosen a way that was greater and more important than him. He'd chosen the Chamber, and his loyalty and duty to the chamber was the ultimate sacrifice.

Conrad knocked twice on the door and Pierre let him in. Pierre handed him the case and said, "The legacy of the Chamber is now in your hands, guard it with your life. Its ultimate destination is with the gatekeeper, do you understand?"

"I do," Conrad responded. Conrad turned and walked out the door. Pierre turned to his left and picked up a three-foot long sheath. Inside the sheath was a sword with a gold tip. Pierre placed both hands on the sword and raised it above his head, and then swiftly he lowered it, not stopping until he pushed it through his bellybutton. "God bless the gatekeeper," he exclaimed and then he was dead.

Three

Like clockwork, Alistair Pratt rose at precisely 7:02. How this oddity came about he could not recall, but he dare not upset the balance it has given his life. For a man of fifty he was extremely fit, he had the youthful countenance of a man, no older than thirty. He walked over to his expansive closet, to select a suit for the day, not a simple task, considering the fact that he had, at last count, over two hundred. The weather in the States is a might warmer, than it is in London at this time. The temperatures were due to reach ninety degrees. Alistair chose a tan, lightweight summer wool blend. He accented it with an exquisite peach Riley and a tan bow tie. As usual he would be dressed impeccably. He showered and ate a sparse breakfast of grapefruit, apple juice, and a plain croissant.

He watched the news, but as usual he was disappointed in what he saw; stories of despair, of lifeless beings trudging through each day, devoid of pleasure, of happiness. On the roof of his penthouse he watched as the people scurried about, rats trapped in a maze. They are seeking, they want something different and I will give it to them. Poor lost lambs being led to slaughter by the bloodless leeches that seek to control them, not to liberate them as I will. And it would be easy, the brotherhood made sure of it five hundred years ago, he mused. Everything was proceeding according to plan. The stage was set, everyone knew their roles and they were ready, poised to take their places as the arbiters of the new world order. His efficient research team had discovered the identity of the gatekeeper and he'd made sure that everything was in place to take possession of the sacred artifact at the appointed time. Alistair wanted every possible angle covered that's why he concocted the ruse about the research project; he needed to keep Marshall as close as possible. Lydia disapproved, she wanted to simply place surveillance on him and kill him the moment he received the sacred artifact. But clearly she didn't understand the brilliance and resolve of the Chamber. You can't exist for five hundred years without guile and intelligence. She didn't understand the history of the Chamber and the importance of the gatekeeper. The Chamber would take every measure possible to ensure that the gatekeeper received the artifact, even if those measures meant losing their lives. For all Alistair knew, the Chamber may have been on to him and may try to change the process of transfer; they may have Marshall whisked away prior to transfer. Alistair knew that there could be a myriad of diversions the Chamber may employ and vowed to be prepared; the stakes were too high and he wanted nothing left to chance.

This was his moment, his chance to make right where his ancestors failed. Once he and the brotherhood had accomplished their goal, the phrase a "new world order" wouldn't be some trite banal offering bandied about by mindless savants. For too long the world has been governed by the seekers of death; but that was going to change. He stared out the window and tallied all that the brotherhood had accomplished, through various corporations. We control the media conglomerates, military contracts, the oil markets, and the entertainment venues. And now the final piece is about to come to fruition. He salivated at the thought of what the brotherhood was set to accomplish. In one fell swoop, he smiled to himself, *we will have the ancient artifact and the spiritual minds and souls of the entire world and the pious religious leaders, misleaders of the people, the harbingers of death will rot in hell, where they belong!*

I didn't sleep very well alternating between dreams about Helen and Kelly, so when I woke up I seriously considered canceling my nine o'clock class, but that meant talking to Grace and I wasn't in the mood to be peppered with a bunch of questions. Grace is the department's senior administrative assistant, a title she parades as though she were Queen Elizabeth herself. A smallish, but hippy woman, with puffy reddish-gray hair and a penchant for wearing blouses with Peter Pan collars, Grace reminds me of the officious secretary in *Ferris Bueller's Day Off.* She's been at the college for thirty years and pretty much does what she wants, which includes speaking rudely to whomever she chooses; in fact I've heard her chastise the *President* of the college on more than one occasion. He just shrugs it off as Grace being Grace. *Only in a small town.* I got myself together and hustled over to campus. After class I grabbed a cup of coffee from the department lounge and started towards my office when I heard a familiar singsong voice calling my name. It was Grace.

"Dr. Maaaaaarrrrshaaalllll," she said.

"Good morning Grace, is there something you need?" I ask staring at her latest Peter Pan blouse, a mixture of banana yellow and white.

"I need you to sign these forms; you know the ones you promised to sign *two weeks ago.*"

"Oh right, I'm sorry Grace I completely forgot."

"Yeah well, your absent mindedness has put *me* behind," she says adjusting her equally hideous gray, ankle length woolen skirt. Why she insists on wearing wool when it's eighty plus degrees is a mystery to me, so much so that I finally had to ask.

"Grace, aren't you hot in that wool skirt?"

"I certainly am not, what's it to you?"

"Nothing, you just look uncomfortable."

"Well I'm not, now would you please sign these forms?" I did and she snatched them out of my hand, did a military about face and hip waddled to her office, muttering something about inconsiderate professors. As I was walking into my office, Ashley arrived.

"Good morning, Dr. Marshall, I see Grace has been at it again?" Ashley said.

As she was about to answer, Grace popped her puffy hair in the door and said, "It would behoove you to do as I ask Dr. Marshall because one day you're going to need my help." Then she abruptly turned and left, not even bothering to acknowledge Ashley. Typical Grace.

"What was that all about?" Ashley asked.

"Does one ever know when it comes to Grace?"

"Yeah you're right. Here's my schedule, like you asked." I looked it over and placed it on my desk.

"So it looks like you are available for at least three hours each day."

"Yes."

"How does two to five work for you?"

"That's exactly what I was going to propose."

"Great. When would you like to start?"

"How about next Monday?"

"That's fine."

"Great."

"Thanks, Dr. Marshall, see you later."

"Have a good day Ashley."

My meeting with Ashley brought back memories of my days as a student. I was a very good student, but I wasn't ambitious, which infuriated my father. I graduated Summa Cum Laude, but all I cared about was scholarship, which my father said was nothing but laziness. I guess if I were ambitious like the Ashley's and the Carol's of the world my father wouldn't be so hard on me. Even now, with all of my success, he believes that I could have done more. More of what, I always reply. He never has an answer, just mumbles something about being like Carol. I think he's still upset that I didn't become a lawyer. Not surprisingly, he adores Kelly.

At one o'clock I met my best friend, Felix Arroyo for lunch at 'Hollands', which is located in the heart of downtown, a chic bistro, with large smoky windows, adorned with the name *Holland's* spelled out in bold gold lettering; it was an oddity, a contrasting work of modernity, settled in amidst the century old clapboard establishments that have been Landon staples.

"You look tired buddy." He said as we hugged. We met at Columbia University where we were doctoral students. At the time I was in a constant funk because I missed Helen so much. Felix, an outgoing sort, immediately embraced me like a brother, and wasn't having any of my pity parties, his favorite refrain being, "I'm not letting you go out like a punk papi." At first he'd piss me off. I wanted to be miserable, wanted to wallow in self-pity, but Felix wouldn't let me and for that I will be forever grateful. He'd always say, "Man whatever is meant to be, will be." I couldn't help but be upbeat around him and though I still missed Helen, he helped me join the living, and he's been there for me ever since, especially through every Kelly episode.

After graduation he took a position at a prestigious university in the Midwest, where he was going stir crazy. A native of San Juan, Puerto Rico, whose family moved to New York City when he was ten, he had a hard time adjusting to a social life that he claims consisted of country fairs and hog calling contests. As luck would have it, an opening in our department was available, six years ago and the rest as they say is history.

"I just finished working out."

"Dealing with Kelly, I guess you need to find something to work off your frustration," he said laughingly.

"No argument there, my man. So how are you? How was San Juan?"

"San Juan was San Juan, you know how it is."

"Yeah, nice to be home and all, but."

"Exactly; how is Kelly?"

"We broke up again."

He raised his eyebrows in mock disappointment. "What was it this time?"

"She's upset because I won't go to Melinda's party this Saturday."

"Why not?"

"Come on Felix, you know we don't get along."

"Man you need to let that go."

"You're taking her side?"

"I'm just saying you need to do it for Kelly." Felix remarked.

I was about to respond when a familiar face that I hadn't seen in years pleasantly interrupted us; it was Jordan Nelson, a former student of mine, who transferred after her sophomore year. A gangly, insecure child as a freshman, Jordan all five foot six inches of her had blossomed into a beauty. Standing before us in a pair of loose fitting jeans, and a white midriff that exposed a flat midsection, which was highlighted by a small diamond in her belly button, I couldn't believe this was the same young woman who cried in my office on many occasions because she felt like a misfit. I stood up and hugged her.

"Jordan Nelson, it's been a long time, you remember Dr. Arroyo, don't you?"

"Yes I do, how have you been Dr. Arroyo?"

"Fine," Felix said, trying hard not to stare at her breasts.

"What have you been up to?" I asked.

"I've been living in Los Angeles, working as a fashion designer."

"That sounds great. What brings you to Landon, visiting?"

"Actually I've moved back."

"You have, why?" Felix asked.

"I'm going to be working for Helen Adamson."

"How'd that come about?" I asked, my stomach churning from the mention of Helen's name.

"I basically badgered her into hiring me."

"What do you mean?"

"Helen is well-respected in the fashion industry and when I heard she was coming back home to open a boutique, I e-mailed her every day, sent her my work, did everything possible. After a couple of months she agreed to meet me, and she hired me as her assistant."

"That's great Jordan. Would you like to stay and eat with us," I asked as our food arrived?

"No thank you I've got to run. It was nice seeing you, don't be a stranger, come by the boutique and we'll have lunch, I'll *treat*."

"Just so you know I'm notorious for not passing up a free meal."

"I like notorious." She said softly, her hazel eyes flirting playfully. She took a napkin from the table and wrote her number. "Here," she said handing me the napkin, her perfume sensually wafting off her olive skin, as she placed the napkin in my hand. "Do with it as you please." Talk about double entendre!

"It was nice seeing you Jordan," I replied, trying my best to sound unaffected by her flirtation.

"I'll see you soon Dr. Marshall; nice to see you Dr. Arroyo." She turned slowly, not too slowly, but just enough to ensure that I was watching. It's one of those gestures that is hard to describe, but men know what I'm talking about. We watched her leave, her taut athletic frame, swaying rhythmically, the sunlight streaming through accenting her long lines, singsong, *"there she goes so tan and lovely, the Girl from Ipanema goes walking, and when she passes, each time she passes, I go ah!"*

"Damn she's hot and she wants you partner," Felix said with such animation that I think for a moment he forgot he was happily married.

"I know, but she's my *student!*"

"Former student."

"It doesn't matter, besides it takes too much emotional energy to deal with someone that young."

"Yeah, but I bet the sex would be great, not that I'm saying you should mess around on Kelly. I'm just giving a hypothetical." He said.

"Just a what if, huh?" Then he burst out laughing.

"What's so funny?"

"Man you could have a real mess on your hands," he said still laughing.

"What are you talking about?"

"You got Kelly, Helen and Jordan, who's working for Helen. Man you could have your own X-rated soap opera," he said quite pleased with himself.

"You're sick, you know that?" I said throwing a balled up napkin at his head.

I said goodbye to Felix and went home. It was such a nice afternoon that I grabbed a book and headed to the front porch. As I settled down to read, I was under the impression that someone was watching me. Initially I didn't notice anything out of the ordinary, and then I spotted a late model Mercedes parked across the street. In this neighborhood, ordinarily that would not be unusual, but I know all of my neighbors, and I pretty much know who visits them, and this car was not familiar. I was certain that whoever it was, was watching me.

Then the person drove off. Strange I thought. Then I thought about whose house he was parked in front of. Amy Phillips, who was recently divorced, apparently had not wasted any time getting back into the dating scene. It seemed like she was going out with a different guy every night, this could have been one of her many suitors, waiting for her to come home. He probably got tired of waiting, and left.

Timothy Black liked the way the silver S class handled as he drove off, turning left onto picturesque Landon Avenue; like something out of a Norman Rockwell painting, he mused. He reached over to the passenger seat, picked up his cell phone and dialed.

"Hello," answered Alistair Pratt.

"It's a standard alarm system, entry, if necessary, will be a piece of cake." Timothy said.

"Did he see your face?" Alistair Pratt asked.

"No."

"Good."

"Why are we watching him when you've said we won't make a move until he has the artifact in hand?"

"Timothy, are you familiar with the fable of the two frogs?"

"No." Timothy rolled his eyes. *Not another one of these damn fables!*

"Two frogs dwelt in the same pool. The pool being dried up under the summer's heat, they left it, and set out together to seek another home. As they went along they chanced to pass a deep well, amply supplied with water. One of the frogs became excited and said to the other: "Let us descend and make our abode in this well, it will furnish us with food and shelter." The other frog replied with greater caution: "But suppose the water should fail us, how can we get out again from so great a depth?"

"I don't understand," Timothy replied.

"The ending is everything and we must plan all the way to it, taking into account all the possible consequences, obstacles, and twists of fortune that could destroy everything we've worked for. We keep tabs on Marshall because the unpredictable could happen at any moment; he could discover what we're doing, if that occurs we must be prepared to act immediately. Do you understand now?"

"Yes."

"Good. I will see you tonight."

Timothy snapped his phone shut. Once again Alistair had given him something to think about, but it paled in comparison to the information he'd learned when they first met; the thought of it still boggling his mind.

"You've got to be kidding me?" Timothy exclaimed to the finely dressed gentleman with the British accent.

"I am quite serious Mr. Black."

"You're telling me that my ancestor Richard Black founded a secret society and unearthed an ancient artifact that's worth billions of dollars?"

"Yes."

"How come I was never told this story?" Timothy asked.

"I don't know, perhaps your family isn't aware of it."

"Why should I believe you?"

"I haven't any reason to seek you out and make up outlandish tales. It is your history as well as mine."

"Why are you telling me this now?"

"Because I want you to get your share."

"Bullshit. You're here because you need me. Okay mister what do you want?"

After Alistair explained everything, Timothy couldn't speak. What was this man talking about? New world order; new religion; pleasure the guiding principle, the fuel of life. Timothy's head was spinning, but not so much that he was confused as to what he would do.

I read for quite a while, until six-thirty to be exact. I was hungry, so I ordered pizza and turned on the Yankee game. Apparently I didn't make it through the whole game, because when I woke up, the news was on. It was eight o'clock in the morning and I had a nine o'clock class. I showered and rushed off to campus, just in time for "Codes and Conundrums: The True Meanings of Ancient Religious Text."

"Can anyone tell me what Jesus meant in the Parable of the Wedding Feast?"

A sleepy-eyed philosophy major raised his hand. "Jesus was saying that if you're coming to eat with the king you got to have the right clothes." A few students snickered.

"Go back to sleep Laskey," said a curly-haired female in the back row. Everyone laughed.

"Why don't you tell us what he meant Ms. Carmichael?"

"Glad to. In those days it was customary for guests to be given garments to wear to a party, feast or as in this case a wedding banquet and no one dare refuse to wear these garments because to do so would be an insult to the host. What I took this to mean is that the king is a metaphor for Jesus and the rude guest is none other than Satan. So what Jesus basically was saying is that if you act like the rude guest then you're acting like Satan."

"Long-winded as usual Christine," said a young woman in the front row.

"All Jesus was saying is there's only one way to get to heaven; wear my garments, which is a metaphor for the plan of salvation. If you don't, you're going to hell. It's that simple."

"She's right," I said.

"Jesus never meant it to be any other way," Christine smiled.

Maybe it was providence, but for some reason, I can't exactly say what, Christine's comments helped me make the decision to help Pratt. Besides whom was I kidding; the secret of the legend was still a part of me, maybe by helping him with his book I'd find some answers. I called him from my office after class.

"Hello," he answered in his clipped British accent.

"Mr. Pratt, this is Alex Marshall."

"Good morning Dr. Marshall."

"I have decided to accept your offer," I said.

"Wonderful. I was hoping that you would."

"When would you like to get started?"

"Don't you want to know how much you will be paid?"

"I told you, money is not what motivates me."

"Yes I know, but I believe that a man who is handsomely compensated will work that much harder, besides I will not take no for an answer."

"Oh, I never said that I *wouldn't* take the money. I just said that it wasn't a big deal. But since you insist, exactly what are you offering?" I asked.

"One million American dollars."

I was speechless. Did I hear him right? "Did you say one million dollars?"

"I sense hesitancy, is something wrong?"

"One million dollars seems to be an awful lot of money for what you're asking me to do, it just seems highly unusual."

"In my world Dr. Marshall, this is the rule, not the exception, but if you want to decline, I fully understand."

"Let me think it over, and get back to you."

"Take your time Dr. Marshall; I want you to be absolutely sure about this."

"I'll call."

Alistair Pratt hung up the phone. I expected this reaction, he thought, as he poured himself a glass of mineral water. He will agree. A million dollars is a million dollars. Alistair thought about the human mind, how it reacts to money. It diminishes logic, which is exactly what Alistair wanted. Yes, he thought, the good Dr. will take the bait after all he is a product of his culture.

I called my sister, Felix and my parents and asked them if they could come over for dinner the next day. I told them I had something important I needed to discuss. As I drifted off to sleep, later that night, I thought of dad's words. Maybe this was my time to experience the extraordinary.

Genoa, Italy

In a hotel approximately five miles from downtown Genoa, a stocky, honey blond young man, named Conrad was completing preparations for the next phase of his assignment. He was to transfer a leather case to his contact a Brazilian, who he only knew as Victor. Though he knew he had proven his worth he still couldn't believe that he'd been chosen as a link in the chain to the Gatekeeper, that *he* actually had the legacy, the great secret of the Chamber in his possession. He only wished that he would be the one to actually hand it to the Gatekeeper. He walked to the bathroom and stepped inside the shower, letting the powerful jets relax his muscles. Afterwards he toweled off, picked up the leather case and walked a few feet to the open window, where he was greeted by a shower of stars. The night was clear, warm, but crisp, lovers striding hand in hand, street vendors hawking bouquets of roses. Conrad drank it all in, and smiled. He clutched the case to his broad chest. *I will not fail.*

Four

Dinner was at six o'clock. I'm not much of a cook, but I make do. But that's okay because I didn't buy the house for its kitchen. The house is a large white stone three story behemoth, with a wrap around porch and a sun room, that sits on the corner of what can be described as an old fashioned neighborhood, an eclectic mix of colonials, tudors, and Cape Cods, with white picket fences, large trees of different varieties, oak, maple, elm. I love my neighborhood, the hammocks in the front yards and wicker chairs, inhabited by old-timers like Mr. Allen, he of the corn cob pipe and sterling silver flask, "a little brandy is good for the soul", he always tells me; and Lucille Birchfield, of the Plymouth Rock Mayflower Birchfields, she tells anyone who listens.

What I love most about my house is the backyard. It has a running brook, surrounded by a beautiful array of flowers and trees. My backyard provides me with comfort when I'm out of sorts, a feeling that's been with me since the night I drove by Helen's parent's house.

"What's up?" Carol asked as she dipped her feet into the brook.

I told them the whole story. My dad was the first to speak.

"It's your time son."

"Time for what Mr. Marshall," asked Felix's wife, Carmen?

"It's his time to experience the extraordinary."

"What do you mean by extraordinary?"

"Carmen we generally lead ordinary lives, sort of muddling through a set pattern of routines, but at least once; we all have the opportunity to experience the extraordinary."

"Like Andy Warhol's fifteen minutes of fame."

"Not quite, what I'm talking about is much broader."

"What do you mean?" she asked.

"I'm talking about things like someone losing his home to a fire; a loved one sentenced to prison; winning a car in a raffle; trying out for a professional team. I think that we can all agree that any one of the aforementioned could be construed as extraordinary."

"And so this is Alex's extraordinary event?"

"Without question," my dad said his smile wide enough to light the entire village.

"So that settles it dear," my mother said to me, always one to cut right to the chase.

"It's not that simple mom."

"Why isn't it?" Carol asked.

"I think a million dollars is a lot of money to pay just to pick my brain."

"So what, maybe the guy likes to throw away money."

I stared hard at Carol.

"No Alex, I didn't mean it that way. I wasn't saying hiring you would be throwing away money, come on little brother you know what I meant."

"Okay sis, just making sure." I said with a smile. "But what I'm saying is a million dollars seems to be an awful lot for information that no one is interested in. You all saw how poorly my book sold. Why would Pratt think that he'd fare any better? Interest in the subject is nonexistent."

"Granted I'll give you that said Carol, but so what? Help me to understand why *his* willingness to throw away one million dollars has *you* nervous?"

"I really can't say Carol. It just seems odd."

"I agree Alex, it is out of the ordinary, but again I ask, why are you concerned with how he spends his money?"

"Are you saying that I should accept his offer?"

"No, I'm not saying that, I want you to do what you think is best. My concern is why this is causing you so much anxiety? Is it that you think he may not be above board; that he has some kind of sinister motive? Come on Alex that stuff only happens on television."

"And what he's offering is your ordinary *everyday occurrence*?" I said.

"Good point," said Felix.

"Now," said Richard, "tell us why you'd *consider* his proposition?"

"It's a chance to see if I can finally discover the legendary artifact and a million dollars is a million dollars."

"Are you sure you want to put yourself through that again?" Carol asked.

"I can handle it."

"Well that settles it then," my mother said again. It's one of her favorite phrases.

"I guess," I said.

"What is it *now* Alex?" Carol asked.

"It just seems strange that he thinks someone would be interested in the Cyrenaic. I'm probably the last person to write anything about them."

"Alex it's late. Richard and I have to go pick up the children. Look, I think you are putting too much thought into this whole situation; try to relax okay."

"Okay big sis." I hugged her and kissed her on the cheek.

"What are you going to do?" my father asked.

"I'll probably accept. I told him I would let him know by Friday."

"This is your time son," he said.

We all said our goodnights. It was eleven o'clock and I was tired. After they left I debated whether to clean up or leave the mess until the morning. Sleep won out.

Alistair's penthouse was bathed in black-blue darkness, the only visible light coming from seven black ten-inch candles placed behind a long black chalk line, which was drawn on the living room floor. Alistair stood directly behind the center candle. He was dressed in a black silk robe, which had a large letter L embroidered on the tunic's right breast pocket. Standing on the other side of the chalk line also dressed in robes were three men and three women, including Lydia and Timothy; they were the Upper Realm of the brotherhood. Once a week they met at Alistair's penthouse to engage in the ritual of purity; a ceremony dedicated to their leader Arête, who was bestowed the title "The Light of Hellas." But from this night on, as the appointed time came close, the brotherhood would be summoning the spirit of Arête to provide energy for the task that lie before them; the task that would secure the brotherhood as the guiding light of the world.

Alistair picked up the center candle and skimmed the top of the flame with the index finger of his right hand; the others picked up their candles and did the same. Then the seven placed the candles in the center of the floor. Standing, they joined hands and Alistair spoke. "We seek thee oh mighty one, goddess of purity. We seek thee to provide us with the strength to carry out what has been denied us, our rightful place. We seek thee to destroy the infidels, for they stand in our way. We the Light of Hellas are the true and only arbiters of God's word and we cannot let the infidels continue to mislead His people. Give us the power oh mighty one to take back what is rightfully ours and to lead His people as He has destined. To power and truth!"

"To power and truth!" They chanted in unison.

"Now we must purify ourselves," Alistair said as he disrobed. The others disrobed as well and watched as Alistair led one of the women to the center circle. Alistair positioned himself prostrate on his back and the woman straddled him. They began to engage in sexual intercourse. The others picked up their candles and formed a circle around Alistair and the woman. As the intensity increased, the circle became tighter and with each thrust the others would lightly touch the bodies of Alistair and the woman with their candles. The combination of sex and the touching of flesh with the candles signified a burning off of impure spirits. When Alistair and the woman were finished, a new couple entered the circle and the ritual repeated itself until everyone was purified.

It was well past midnight when the ritual had been completed. Alistair sent everyone home and eased his himself into the shower. The hot water felt good on his tired, but satiated muscles. His mind drifted to the enormity of what he and the brotherhood were set to accomplish. As the water trickled down his back anger surged through him because despite the fact that he'd planned everything out perfectly he knew that if his ancestors would have done what needed to be done, it wouldn't have to come to this. *Weakness.* They were weak. But I am strong and I will not make the same mistakes! Alistair increased the intensity of the hot water so that it practically scalded him. The pain a reminder of the lengths he would go to take back what was rightfully his. He stepped out of the shower and walked to his bedroom. He reached inside the dresser drawer adjacent to his bed, pulled out a picture of Alex Marshall and spat on it violently. The gatekeeper, he smirked; then he spat on the picture again. Alistair smiled cruelly as the spittle slid down the picture frame. *Power and truth!*

Five

I woke up earlier than usual Friday morning and saw that as a sign to take Pratt's offer. I never, ever wake up on Friday's before my clock goes off. Why Friday I don't know; I just know it has always been that way. So taking that "extraordinary" event into account I figured it was in the cards for me to help Pratt out. I called him right after my first class.

"Hello," he answered sprightly.

"Good morning Mr. Pratt, it's Alex Marshall."

"Dr. Marshall, so good to hear from you; good news I hope?"

"I guess you could say that; I've decided to accept your offer."

"That is good news."

"When can we get together and discuss procedure?"

"I'm on your schedule."

"How about your place tomorrow morning, say ten o'clock?"

"That suits me just fine."

"I would like to bring my research assistant, if that is okay."

"Fine; the four of us will have a grand time."

"Four?"

"Yes, my assistant, Ms. Sinclair, will be joining us as well."

"The more the merrier, what's your address?"

He gave it to me, a fashionable location on the Upper East Side of Manhattan.

"Good, then I'll see you tomorrow."

"Have a pleasant day, Dr. Marshall."

"Mr. Pratt?" I asked.

"Yes, Dr. Marshall?"

"I'm curious. Why a book on secret societies? There are thousands of publications on secret societies. And even more so, why the Cyrenaic?"

"The aura of secret societies has held my fancy ever since I was a child, as for the Cyrenaic, there religious practices are intriguing."

"Yes, but why do you want to write a book? Forgive my impertinence, but it is highly unlikely that your book will sell."

"I am not interested in money. I have more than I'll ever need. This work will be my legacy and now with your help, my dream will come true."

"I will do what I can."

"Have a good day, Dr. Marshall."

I called Ashley to let her know about my project with Mr. Pratt and to inform her that she would be accompanying me tomorrow. Afterwards I called Kelly again, and she finally picked up. Over the past few days I must have left a zillion messages, apologizing every way I knew how. She was still pissed, but at least she didn't hang up, but when she asked me about the party, I held my ground. I know that seems foolish, particularly after the way I'd screwed up, but I had my reasons for not wanting to go. Kelly listened and then proclaimed that this was really it, we were through. To understand why I'm so pigheaded about this party, you have to know the history between Melinda, Kelly's sister, and I.

When I first met Kelly, the last thing on my mind was marriage and as our relationship progressed into deeper levels of dysfunctunality, I couldn't see why we'd even contemplate something that was sure to end disastrously. I know that seems callous and it probably is, but its how I felt. Kelly has never pressured me about marriage, in fact on several occasions she's told me that she didn't want to get married, because she was afraid that I would leave her and she didn't want to end up alone and abandoned like her dad. "Agreed," I told her. One particular night during a spell when Kelly and I were getting along, we happened to be watching *Sleepless in Seattle*, and I, feeling overly sentimental and romantic, brought up the "M" word. It wasn't a proposal mind you; I was just throwing out the idea. Kelly said she'd think about it.

About two weeks later, Melinda, called me at work and proceeded to blast me for talking to her sister about marriage. She accused me of being insensitive, of toying with her sister's emotions, of being an all around asshole for bringing up marriage when I knew their family's history, and according to her, had no real intentions of marrying Kelly. I thought she was going a bit overboard, but I figured that was the end of it. A year later at a surprise birthday party for their father, Melinda during a discussion about some celebrity who was caught cheating on his wife, launched into a lengthy diatribe about men being bastards, attacking me once again. It was at that point, approximately a year ago, that I made the decision to stay the hell away from her.

"Prompt as usual," said Alistair as he opened the door of his penthouse to let Lydia Sinclair in.

"Preciseness is my business Alistair," she said, dressed smartly in white silk pants, a sleeveless peach blouse, with matching sling backs and hat. "By the look on your face I must surmise that Marshall has accepted the offer."

"Yes he has. I know this must disappoint you, but let us remember that it is the end that is important, not the means."

She ignored his remark the last thing she wanted to hear was that stupid frog fable. "So when do we begin?"

"Tomorrow," Alistair replied, as he poured two glasses of mineral water.

"He will be coming to you I presume?"

"Yes, along with his assistant."

"Assistant?" she asked with a strange tinge of curiosity and anger.

"Yes one of his students; nothing to worry about."

"Is it a female?" Lydia asked.

"He didn't say. Why?"

"Women ask too many questions; questions that they eventually find answers to; am I making myself clear?"

"Yes you are, however I wouldn't worry. They could never figure out our true purpose, I've covered all bases."

"A woman can figure out anything, all she needs is time," Lydia said curtly.

The following morning, the sky enveloped in the kind of white haze associated with the fall, I met Ashley at the Landon train station, a turn of the century depot, whose supporters fought hard to retain as much of the old charm as they possibly could. Located about a mile from the college, it is a beautiful sight in the fall, particularly when the trees in Landon Park, which is directly across the street, become awash in a mixture of red, orange and yellow.

We arrived at precisely ten o'clock and were escorted to Pratt's penthouse by a smartly dressed barrel-chested young man, with a high waist and tree trunks for legs. He didn't say one word to us. It was clear that he was Pratt's security. I guess a man as wealthy as Pratt must need protection.

"Good morning Dr. Marshall and?"

"Ashley Winters," she responded.

"Good morning Ms. Winters." He took Ashley's right hand and planted a kiss. She blushed and stammered out a good morning.

"Forgive me Ms. Winters if I have embarrassed you. In my country, it is customary for a gentleman to greet a lady with a kiss, particularly one as lovely as you. It is a sign of respect for the virtue of womanhood. If I have made you uncomfortable, I apologize."

"There is no need to apologize. In fact it was nice."

"Excellent. As soon as Ms. Sinclair arrives, we can get started. In the meantime is there anything I that can get for either of you?"

"No thank you," I said.

"Water would be fine," said Ashley.

"We will be working in my study; if you like you can familiarize yourselves with its surroundings, while we wait for Ms. Sinclair."

"That sounds fine," I said. The penthouse was enormous, I would say somewhere between six and eight thousand square feet. It was beautifully decorated, with glass and crystal as the dominant theme.

About ten minutes later the doorbell rang.

"Ah, that would be Ms. Sinclair," he said walking towards the door.

"Good morning Alistair," she said. "Have they arrived?"

"Yes."

"The assistant?"

"Female," he replied.

"Damn."

Lydia Sinclair liked to think of herself as an efficient woman, never one to expend energy unless it was absolutely necessary. She had little time for anything that didn't serve a tangible purpose in her life. An attractive woman who kept herself fit through martial arts and horse back riding, she lived alone in a brownstone, not far from Central Park West. She had once been married, but it dissolved within two years and now at forty-two, she'd relegated men to business partners and occasional paramours. She met Alistair through a mutual business acquaintance and her relationship with him has made her a wealthy woman. What made their relationship successful and profitable were the strengths each possessed. For Lydia it was her intuition and it was telling her that Alistair was making a huge mistake allowing Marshall's assistant to be a part of the equation. If it were her decision alone she'd kill the girl, but Alistair wanted her to be patient and let things play itself out. For now, she would agree, but if it became necessary she would do what was *necessary*. The stakes were too large and the prize too valuable for anything less.

"Dr. Marshall, Ms. Winters, let me introduce you to my assistant Ms. Lydia Sinclair," he said as they settled in his study, an expansive room with oversized windows which afforded an awe inspiring view of Manhattan, hand made mahogany furniture, crystal statutes of Egyptian pyramids and obelisks were situated throughout the room, along with original works of Italian and French art, and an immaculate hardwood floor.

"Good morning," she said. I took her to be in her early forties. She was well dressed and her cold blue eyes and steely demeanor gave me the impression that she was someone whose bad side you didn't want to get on.

"Now that everyone is here, we can get started," Pratt exclaimed.

"How do you want to proceed?" I asked.

"Pardon me?" He said.

"Yes, we need to know exactly what you want to know about the Cyrenaic; it will help us to tailor our research."

"Why would more research be necessary Dr. Marshall?" said Ms. Sinclair, her cold blue eyes fixed on the handsome scholar.

"I don't follow," I said.

"You've already written a text on the subject. Couldn't you just recall your notes?"

"Yes, but if it were as simple as that then all Mr. Pratt would have to do is refer to my book."

"So you're talking about conducting new research?"

"Yes. I'm under the impression that Mr. Pratt is looking for more than my book provides. That means we're going to have to conduct an extensive amount of research, which brings me back to my original question, 'how do you want us to proceed?'"

"All of the work I have read on the Cyrenaic focuses mainly on their origins and their beliefs. I am primarily interested in why and how they vanished and whether they planned to reemerge", Alistair said.

"Reemerge? Did I hear you right Mr. Pratt?"

"Yes you did. It is not as farfetched as it seems. Most secret societies left some sort of evidence indicating a plan to reemerge in the distant future. This year is the five hundredth anniversary of their disappearance. It is possible that they may have indicated somewhere that the Chamber would be revived this year."

"Why now? Why not after one hundred years or two hundred and fifty? Why not after one thousand years?" I asked.

"That's what I want to find out," Pratt replied.

"If that's what you want, we'll do our best."

"Excellent."

"Is there anything else we need to know?" I asked.

"No."

"In that case, we'll be leaving now. I'll call you in two weeks to give you an update."

"Oh, I almost forgot. I do have one request," he said.

"Yes?"

"Would you mind if Ms. Sinclair assisted with the research?"

"I have no objections; after all you're footing the bill."

"Excellent and here is your first payment as promised."

"Thank you."

It was one o'clock when we stepped out into the bright New York sun. On the ride back home I was curious to know what Ashley thought of Pratt.

"He seems very passionate about this book, maybe a little too passionate."

"How do you mean?"

"I can't put my finger on it, but I think there is more to this than he's letting on."

"You sound like a character from one of those made for television thrillers."

"I know," she said. "I'll tell you what though, his assistant was weirding me out. Did you check out how she kept staring at us?"

"Yeah I did notice that."

"What do you think that was about?"

"I don't know."

"I don't trust her Alistair," said Lydia Sinclair, as they stood on the terrace of his penthouse.

"Why?"

"She was too quiet and a bit too observant. If we're not careful, she'll figure out everything."

"There is no need to worry, my dear. Everything is going according to plan."

"I'm not worried, I just think that we need to watch her carefully, and if need be we need to think about an alternative plan."

"Come now Lydia."

Alistair turned to stare out of the window. He felt uneasy. Lydia is losing patience, he thought. She could ruin everything. And for the first time, in the history of their relationship, he thought about an alternative plan, for *her*.

Genoa, Italy

The deserted pier was the perfect location to make the transfer, Conrad thought as he ran his fingers along the leather case. The Genoa night was cool, but star filled, the moon's reflection glistening against the inky black waters below. Conrad shook involuntarily, and he felt goose bumps begin to form on his arms, a combination of the chilly night air and nervousness. *This is it.* Momentarily the Brazilian, Victor, would arrive and Conrad's duty to the brotherhood, *to the secret*, would be complete. His sense of anxiety, mixed with his sense of honor heightened when Victor arrived. Introductions not necessary, the two men stood facing one another, arms length apart, poised to fulfill their duties, their destiny, as had the others before them. Conrad spoke first. "It is your duty to take the next leg of the journey, a journey which will not be complete until the sacred artifact reaches the gatekeeper. Are you willing?"

"Yes."

Victor embraced Conrad and then turned away, walking north towards the entrance to the pier.

To Conrad's left, on the deck of the pier was a hunter green suede sheath, he opened the sheath and pulled out a sword with a gold tip. Conrad raised the sword above his head and in one swift motion plunged it through his bellybutton, his screams echoing against the twin blackness of sky and water. He fell backwards as blood poured profusely from his stomach and he was at peace. *Death is always righteous when the cause is just.*

Six

When I returned home from our meeting with Pratt I called Kelly again to apologize. When you mess up, particularly when the offended party is your girlfriend, there is no statute of limitations on apologies.

She picked up on the third ring.

"It's about time you called," she said. "You're still in the doghouse, you know that don't you?"

"Hello to you too, Kelly."

"Don't act like *you're* mad, you're the one who screwed up."

"I know so how long are you going to punish me?"

"I don't know; it depends?"

"On what?" I asked."

"On whether or not you come to the party." Silence.

"You're making a big mistake Alex."

"We've been over this before. Kelly I truly apologize for what I said about your mom. It was insensitive and you have every right to be mad, but your sister"

"You owe me Alex."

"I'm sorry babe, but I can't do it. I know it seems childish, but your sister, she hits a nerve, and I'm not for it, not tonight, not ever."

"That's stupid; what, you're just going to stop speaking to her?"

"Until she apologizes, yeah that would be the plan."

"I can't *believe* you're being such a baby about this."

"It is what it is."

"What do you mean by that?"

"Nothing Kelly, look, I'm not going and that's that."

"That's all you have to say? Our relationship is in fucking crisis mode, and that's all you have to say is *it is what it is?*"

"What more do you want from me? You asked me if I was coming to the party, and I said no; I apologized for what I said; what else is there to talk about?"

"You're an asshole."

"And your point would be?"

"Fuck you Alex."

"That'd be better than what we're doing now."

"Why do you have to be such an asshole," she screamed. She was still royally pissed, but she was softening, just a little.

"I don't know, maybe I should get therapy," I said with a chuckle.

"Cute, don't think I'm not still pissed, because I am."

"I know."

"And don't think you're getting any make up pussy, because we haven't made up yet."

"I'm not thinking anything."

"Yes you are, you friggin liar."

"I mean it Alex, you get nothing tonight."

"Okay."

"That's it?" She asked, disappointed that I wasn't my usual begging self.

"That's what?"

"You're giving up that easy?"

"Tonight, I am."

'Why?"

"I don't know," I lied. I knew exactly why and her name was Helen Adamson. Ever since I'd driven by the house that night I couldn't stop thinking about her, about what we had, about whether I was wrong, about how different she is from Kelly, about how I felt when I was with her, when we were apart, about our first date, about the prom, about the long walks in the moonlight, in the rain, in the snow, in anything and everything. I thought about her, yet I didn't call her, didn't go see her, because despite what I felt; I wasn't sure. I wasn't sure if my emotions were a betrayal, a reaction to nostalgia, a romantic journey down a road closed many years ago; a reaction to my troubles with Kelly. If I turned to Helen, tried to rekindle a long burnt flame, would it be fair to her, to me, to Kelly? But then who's to say Helen wants me back? Who's to say she's still the same? I hadn't reached the point where I was ready to give up on the six years Kelly and I had invested in each other, because despite my thoughts about Helen, believe it or not I was still in love with Kelly. But you know how emotions operate, they confuse you, they maneuver your heart so that you seek refuge in the situation that's least complicated, they blind you so that reality is left out of the equation of choices. Kelly deserved better than emotion, she deserved better than make up sex. She deserved for me to be a man and deal with what I must, and even though Kelly had no idea that she and Helen would be sharing space that my subconscious normally reserved only for her, I still had to make it right, whatever that may be.

"When you figure it out call me. I love you." Kelly said with a trace dismay.

"I love you too, enjoy the party."

Kelly hung up, and for a second stared blankly at the phone. As she disrobed and turned on the water for her shower, she wondered what had gotten into Alex. In their six years together, he always begged for make up sex, always! Now he doesn't want it; but it wasn't just the sex, Kelly pondered; it's what his begging for sex represents; it's *us*; the familiarity that makes what we have a relationship. Not the sex per se, but all the drama, the fussing, the conflicts, the things that define *our* relationship. For some couples it may not be ideal, but it works for us. And now he's breaking the routine, which means something is not right. Maybe I need to change, maybe he's really getting tired of my shit, she thought, as the hot water and the ensuing steam massaged her body.

Kelly turned off the shower and stepped into her bedroom. She turned on the ceiling fan, placed a towel on the bed, a huge, cherry wood structure. The sled like footboard was ornately decorated and boasted two twelve foot spires at the head. The cool of the ceiling fan was heaven to her back, a stark contrast to the heat of anxiety she felt rising in her belly. Am I losing him, she wondered? Is it that bitch Helen? She could feel a familiar emotion welling up inside and she implored herself not to lapse into her old insecurities; not to blame everything in her life on her feelings about her mother; but it was difficult. Tears welled in her eyes as she remembered the day her father told her and her four year-old sister, that mommy would be gone for a while.

"Gone, where's she going daddy, to the store?" Five year-old Kelly asked as she and her sister sat on their father's lap.

"Yes, but she'll be back." Nelson Van Astor said, his sinewy arms holding his daughters closely.

"Is that why you're crying daddy?" Melinda asked.

"I'm not crying; my eyes hurt."

"Why do they hurt?" she asked.

"Sometimes that happens pumpkin, but I'll be okay."

"Daddy what's mommy buying at the store?" Kelly asked.

"Something real nice for you and Melinda," he said, choking back the tears. Melinda reached over into the box of Kleenex on the night table and gave her father one. "Here daddy to fix your eyes", she beamed, her soft hazel eyes giving him comfort. *These two girls will always have me.*

"Thank you pumpkin; hey how about McDonald's for dinner?"

"Yay," they screamed. "Come on Melinda, let's get our shoes." They jumped off the bed and tore down the hallway into their respective rooms. Kelly's mom thought separate rooms would breed selfishness, but Nelson, who shared a bed with three of his five brothers, as a youngster growing up in the poverty-stricken slums on the west side of a city he'd just as soon forget, would have none of it; his girls would not know what it meant to live with one foot in the grave everyday. No sir, he'd tell his wife, *I didn't bust my ass so that these girls would live like I did. Hell, what's the point in owning three successful restaurants, if I can't indulge you and the girls?* He sat on his bed, head in his hands wondering, what went wrong, why she left him for some bastard, who didn't have two nickels to rub together. *It must have been me, to give all this up, to leave us for him!*

Kelly turned over on her stomach, the cool breeze from the fan gently massaging her face; she remembered how she felt, when she was old enough to understand the truth; *my mother's not coming back.* She sat up and retrieved her underwear and gown from the banister outside of her bedroom. As she dressed for her sister's party, she wondered what was going to become of her and Alex. Fully dressed, she slipped on her shoes, a stylish pair of black sling backs, with a three-inch heel, and walked to the entrance of her building. As she walked down the steps, she had no idea, she was being watched from across the street, by a solitary figure, obscured by the dark night and two large birch trees. Kelly slipped into her convertible BMW, let the top down and pulled off. The task complete, the figure walked north towards Madison Avenue, pleased that phase one of the plan proceeded without a hitch.

Monday afternoon rolled around and Ashley was in my office precisely at two.

"Good afternoon Dr. Marshall."

"Hello Ashley how was the rest of your weekend?"

"Nothing spectacular, I did some studying; read some of your book, hung out with friends, and went to the movies with my boyfriend yesterday afternoon. What about you?"

I showed her the boxes of information that I had organized.

"Wow, this is a lot of stuff."

"Yes it is. How much of the book did you read?"

"I stopped at chapter two."

"Good. That's exactly where we're going to begin."

It was about five-thirty when Ashley left. I walked down to Hollands for dinner. I was seated and about five minutes later, in walked Jordan. She ignored the hostess and strolled right over to my table and sat down without being invited. Was she following me, I wondered?

"Good evening Dr. Marshall, where's your sidekick?"

"Probably at home with his family."

"I'm still waiting for my lunch date," She said with a smile. She looked exquisite. She was wearing a yellow silk pantsuit and a pair of gold medium heel sandals. Strands of her long curly hair slightly covered her right eye, giving her a highly sensual appearance.

"I haven't forgotten," I said, slightly disjointed by her presence.

"Are you blushing Dr. Marshall?" she said, pursing her lips."

"No, of course not."

"Yes you are, look?" she pulled a mirror from her handbag.

"It must be the heat," I said.

"I like the heat, very liberating, don't you think?"

"Only if you like it; some people might think otherwise."

"What do you think?" She said.

"I'm noncommittal."

"Come on doc, that's a copout. If I were to guess I'd say you like the heat."

"Why do you say that?"

"Just a feeling."

"So how do you like working for Helen Adamson?" I asked not so much because I wanted to know but so I could hear about Helen.

"It's great, I'm learning so much from her. You should really come by the shop and see what we've got."

"I will, I promise."

As she left I considered what Felix said and for a moment, just an iota, the thought of sleeping with her crossed my mind, as it would most heterosexual males approaching forty. But as quickly as the thought came, it dissipated; the reality of the consequences a deterrent; consequences that I didn't want; losing Kelly; "losing Helen"; having to deal with Jordan; having to face my own immortality, a fact of life when you're intimately involved with someone whose young enough to almost be your daughter. So I let it go, let it make its way into the recesses of my sexual fantasies, the glass to be broken only in case of a hormonal emergency.

It was about seven-thirty when I left the restaurant. As I was walking back to campus to pick up my car, I, again, had the sense that I was being followed. I'm not prone to paranoia, so I was certain that my perceptions were accurate. I glanced behind me periodically but didn't see anyone. I shrugged it off once I made it to campus.

As I drove off, I couldn't help but wonder why someone would be following me. The more I drove the more I convinced myself that I was imagining things. I thought, "Why would anyone be following me?" As I pulled up to my house I noticed the silver Mercedes that I saw the other day, parked in front of

Amy Phillips house. Poor sucker I thought, she is more trouble than she's worth. As I made the turn into my driveway, the Mercedes pulled off.

The next morning I overslept and barely made it to class on time. Afterwards I went to my office and saw that I had a message from Lydia Sinclair, asking me to call her.

"Ms. Sinclair, this is Alex Marshall."

"Dr. Marshall, thank you for getting back to me so promptly."

"No problem. Is there something you wanted to talk to me about?"

"Actually I'd like to get together with you to discuss my role in the research project."

"I thought that was made clear on Saturday. You are to assist Ashley and me."

"That's true; but I want to know exactly what you need me to do. I wouldn't want to duplicate what you're doing."

"Oh, I see. That makes sense. Would you like to come to my office, sometime this week?"

"Actually I would prefer to discuss it over dinner, if that's okay with you?"

"Okay. When?"

"You're an easy man to please Dr. Marshall."

"I never pass up a dinner invitation."

"Are you free this evening, say around seven?"

"Yes, what do you have in mind?" I said.

"Armante's. I'll pick you up at seven."

"See you then."

Alistair looked at his watch; he knew exactly when she would call. Just as he predicted, within seconds his cell phone rang.

"Alistair, it's all arranged."

"Excellent. Things will go accordingly as long as you stick to the plan."

"What do you mean?"

"You know exactly what I'm talking about."

"I have it under control."

"You better."

"Pardon?"

"If you act too soon he'll be of no use to us."

"On the contrary, I'll have him right where we want him. Good night Alistair, I have to get ready."

After I hung up with Ms. Sinclair I called Kelly.

"Hello."

"Kelly it's me Alex, returning your call."

"I know who you are Alex."

"So?"

"*So*, what kind of question is that?"

"Look Kelly I neither have the time nor patience. Why did you call?"

"Okay I'll get to it, and don't worry it has nothing to do with the party, which by the way was very nice."

"Come on already, I have work to do."

"It's funny that you should say work, because this is precisely why I am calling."

"About work; whose work?"

"Yours."

"Mine; what about it?"

"I received a call last night from someone asking me if I had a copy of your book about the Cyrenaic."

"Really, why would someone call you about that?"

"I was hoping you could answer that."

I told her about my latest project.

"That still doesn't explain why this person wanted to know if I had a copy."

"What did you tell him?"

"I didn't say it was a man."

"Okay, well *whoever* it was what did you say?

"Why are you in such a pissy mood?"

"I'm not in a pissy mood, I'm just tired." I was lying. Lately I felt guilty talking to Kelly while I had Helen on my mind. It was like I was cheating on her and she didn't deserve that. So instead of dealing with my guilt, I reacted as most do, with sarcasm and anger.

"Well get some sleep."

"I will. What did you say to the caller?"

"I said I didn't have a copy."

"What was the response?"

"Oh I see; I'm sorry I troubled you. I asked, 'who is this, but the line went dead? I hit star 69 but the number was not listed. What do you make of all of this?"

"I don't know. Did the caller have a British accent?"

"No, why?"

"Nothing."

"Nothing?"

"Yes."

"Whatever Alex; so what are you doing this evening?"

"Why?"

"Just asking."

"I'm going out to dinner with Mr. Pratt's assistant Ms. Sinclair to discuss the book project. She's treating and you know I never turn down a free meal."

"What about afterwards?"

"I'm going home and go to bed."

"I could come over"

"But the other night you said there wouldn't be any make up sex. In fact your exact word were; 'there won't be any makeup pussy' " I said laughingly.

"I've had a change of heart."

"Well maybe this time it should be different." Though the banter was light, images of Helen and I roller-skating at Wollman's Rink in Central Park suddenly flashed into my head.

"Come on Alex, you know you can't resist."

"Is that so?"

"Oh so it is. You always do what I want."

"I didn't go to the party."

"An aberration, nine times out of ten you'd have said yes."

"Maybe."

"What time will you be home?"

"Late."

"Call me when you get in."

"Maybe," I said.

"I'll see you later."

"Goodbye Kelly."

It was two o'clock, time for Ashley and me to resume our work.

"We left off with the birth of Arthur Garrison, who later would be awarded the title Sir. With so many people succumbing to the plague in 1447, it was a miracle that he was born at all. According to my research Sir Arthur's early years were relatively nondescript. By all accounts he was a very bright young man, favoring books over brawn, though he was characterized as quite strong and sturdy of legs and torso. Sir Arthur led a pretty sedate life. He was employed as an educator and he eschewed politics, at least publicly. In 1470, at the age of 23 he was awarded the title of Sir. In 1473, he founded the Chamber of Cyrenaic."

"That's an odd name, where did it come from?"

"The Cyrenaic School of Philosophy, from the Greek city of Cyrene, a Greek colony in Northern Africa."

"That sounds like ancient Greece."

"You're right. The Cyrenaic school of thought flourished from approximately 400 to 300 B.C. and was founded by Aristippus, a philosopher who was a follower of Socrates. He taught philosophy to his daughter Arete, who in turn taught her son Aristippus the Younger and it is believed that he, not his grandfather was the true founder of the school. The Cyrenaic believed that personal experience was the only basis for true knowledge. They believed that man could have an incorrigible knowledge of his own experiences, but not of the objects that caused those experiences."

"You've lost me. What do you mean by incorrigible knowledge of experiences?"

"All it means is that it is impossible for us to be mistaken about what we are personally experiencing, but that we do not possess the ability to understand the causative factors behind those experiences." Ashley looked puzzled. "I'll try it this way. The Cyrenaic believed that man was unable to define an experience but that his only capability was to define how he was affected by the experience. For example if you are moved by the color yellow, they would say I am being yellowed not I see something yellow."

"What are you talking about Dr. Marshall?"

"I know it sounds silly, but the premise isn't as convoluted as it sounds." I said laughingly.

"So what I think you're saying is that the Cyrenaic believed that you couldn't make the statement I see something yellow because man doesn't have the capacity to understand the physical concept of yellow. We can only speak with knowledge about how yellow makes us feel, hence I feel yellowed."

"Correct."

"But I see a flaw in their thinking. How can you know if something makes you feel yellowed unless you have knowledge of the concept of yellow?"

"That's a good point. I think the Cyrenaic would say that there isn't a universal construct of yellow, it's an individual feeling, its perception, and perception is individual. They believed that there couldn't be a universal construct for the external world because our perception of the external world stems from our own individual experiences, which means that we have no criterion outside of ourselves to determine whose experience is right. "

"Interesting, but what does it have to do with Sir Arthur?"

"The Cyrenaic also believed in the value and nature of pleasure. The Cyrenaic start from the Greek ethical construct that the highest good is what we all seek for its own sake, and not for the sake of anything else. This they identify as pleasure. They believed that pleasure is an individual construct and that we should seek pleasure. The Cyrenaic believed in both bodily pleasures, such as sexual gratification, and mental pleasure, delight in one's own intellectual capacities. They exalted bodily pleasure because they believed that it was much more vivid and exact than mental pleasure. The Cyrenaic believed that pleasure was the highest good and that self-control should not be a barometer to attaining it."

"They were anarchists?" I laughed.

"No, nothing like that; they didn't advocate seeking pleasure to the harm and detriment of others."

"This is what Sir Arthur believed?"

"Yes. Sir Arthur was a devout opponent of Christian England. He believed that the religious practices of England were moralistic, judgmental, restrictive, anti-sex and antithetical to the true meaning of God's word. It was his belief that God created man to seek pleasure, to free his soul and mind from the restrictive constructs of false doctrines and organized religion. Being a voracious reader and in search of what he called the 'true religion', he took to studying the Greek philosophy of hedonism and it was there that he discovered Astrippus and the Cyrenaic."

"So the Cyrenaic believed that the bible was distorted?"

"Yes, they believed that the true nature of sex was circumvented by the Protestant Church, in particular the teachings of Christ and the Song of Songs which is in the Old Testament.

"I don't understand."

"The Cyrenaic placed a great deal of emphasis on the text where Christ talks about the notion of asking and receiving and seeking and finding and on Solomon's graphic and pleasurable description of sex. The belief being that if God did not intend for sex to be the highest form of oneness with our fellow man and with him, then he would not have allowed Solomon's words to be recorded in the bible."

"But didn't God place boundaries and guidelines on sexual behavior? How could the Cyrenaic equate God's restrictive teachings with the search for uncontrolled pleasure?"

"Sir Arthur took Christ and Solomon's words to mean that there's no limitation on what man can have, all he has to do is ask. Sir Arthur and his followers believed that neither Christ nor Solomon were restrictive or moralistic or anti-sex, or possessed any of the tenets that man subscribes to him. They believed that the words of Christ and Solomon were distorted by legalistic puritans who established puritanical guidelines in order to de-emphasize man's true relationship with God."

"Which is?"

"An individual relationship with him."

"But Jesus states clearly that our relationship with him is personal."

"That's true, but how many people actually believe what he said."

"What do you mean?"

"It was Sir Arthur's belief that once Jesus ascended to heaven and the Christian church was founded that his doctrine was changed, compartmentalized by the leaders of the church in order to control man's relationship with God. It was then that strict rules and regulations began to surface and man was led down a path of duality. On the one hand we were told that the only way to get to heaven is to profess Christ as our personal savior, but on the other, and this is seen particularly after Paul's Damascus conversion, we are told that if we truly profess Christ as our Lord and Savior, then we will act a certain way. The Chamber of Cyrenaic saw this as a distortion of Christ's teachings. They state that Christ did not impose strict guidelines for serving him, that man's relationship with him was personal, to be dictated between him and God. They believed that the formation of the Christian church was an attempt to sever the relationship between God and man."

Ashley looked surprised and disgusted as she asked her next question. "So are you telling me that they actually believed that Christ's definition of a personal relationship included sexual pleasure outside of marriage?"

"Yes it appears that Sir Arthur, to use the language of your contemporaries was a bit of a freak." She laughed.

"Yeah it does seem that way. I've never heard of anything like that. Were they actually worshipping sex?"

"Yes in a manner of speaking. They viewed sex as a spiritual bond to God, the ultimate act of communication with him."

"How so?"

"The sex rituals they performed were viewed as the true and righteous path to God. They believed that God would not have created sex if he didn't mean for it to be a way to communicate with him."

"I see," she said standing up to stretch her legs, her hazel eyes looking quizzically as if something wasn't quite right."

"What is it?" I asked.

"Mr. Pratt doesn't strike me as stupid, I mean I'm sure he already knows this stuff and I'm sure he knows that your years of searching haven't turned up anything new, yet still he thinks that you can help him. Why?"

"I'm not following you," I said.

"I'm just saying this whole thing doesn't make any sense. I'm telling you Doc, what if he's after something else, not just research for a book."

"Don't you think that you're being a bit melodramatic?"

"Maybe, but I'm telling you something is up, and I think that the more we delve into this, the more we'll discover."

"This is getting good, mystery and intrigue, just like the movies."

"When you finish laughing, can we continue," she said trying hard to contain her own laughter. "Okay it does sound a little crazy, but my intuition is generally right."

"Just what do you think that he is up to? Do you think he's a member of the Illuminati or something?" I asked jokingly.

"Interesting that you should mention the Illuminati, I've been doing a little research on the Illuminati, the Knights Templar, etc."

"Why?"

"A couple of years ago I saw a program on the History Channel talking about the Knights Templar and I've been fascinated ever since."

"And what have you found?" I asked.

"Just a lot of stuff on secret societies, military orders," she said.

"I already know that stuff. What does it have to do with Mr. Pratt?"

"I haven't put that together yet," she said.

"Any more theories before we call it a night?"

"Actually I do. Mr. Pratt is British right?"

"Yes."

"And he's fascinated with secret societies right?"

"Yes."

"And for century's historians, treasure seekers, men of wealth, scholars, and even U.S. presidents have been searching for the so-called sacred artifact right?"

"Yes, what's your point?"

"I'm getting there. Now isn't it possible that the sacred artifact is linked to the Knights Templar?"

"There's no evidence to that effect." I said.

"But is it possible?"

"Of course, anything is possible."

"Well there's your answer." She said.

"Answer, what are you talking about? Then it hit me. "Ashley, you can't be serious?"

"Are you saying that my theory is impossible?"

"Nothing is impossible. But what you're talking about is *highly* improbable," I said.

"Why?"

"Because it just is," I said at a lost for words.

"Dr. Marshall, the lost treasure of the Knights Templar is one of the greatest mysteries in the history of mankind and maybe the sacred artifact is a part of the treasure. I mean there have been thousands of expeditions in search of the treasure, even FDR financed a search; why is it so hard to believe that our Mr. Pratt may be searching for it as well?"

"Because he wouldn't need to be coy about it; he could have just asked me," I said.

"Not if there's more to the story," she said.

"What does that mean?" I asked.

"I don't know, but it's worth trying to figure out."

"Let's not get off track Ashley, Mr. Pratt has hired me to do research for a book. There is no evidence that he's involved in some kind of sinister clandestine scheme to find the lost treasure of the Knights Templar, nor is there evidence that the so called sacred artifact is part of the treasure. And besides even if that were true, it has nothing to do with Sir Arthur Garrison. He wasn't a Templar. In fact it would have been impossible for him to be one because as you well know, Philip the Fair saw to it that they were dissolved in 1307, rather ruthlessly I might add. After that the Templars were no more. Those that he didn't execute either joined another military order or returned to secular life. So even if this were about the treasure, I don't see how the Chamber could be involved."

"I think they are Dr. Marshall. Sir Arthur has a link with them somehow, and that is what Mr. Pratt wants you to find out."

"Let's assume that you're right, which I highly doubt. But let's assume that you are; what do we do next?"

"Conduct business as usual. We can't let on that we suspect something," she said as she paced the floor.

"*We*? Ashley this is all the work of your imagination," I said with a chuckle.

"We shall see," she said.

After she left I sat slumped in my chair, too exhausted to move. I must admit Ashley's theories were intriguing, and possible, but highly unlikely. There has been a recent fascination with the Knights Templar, the Illuminati, etc., thanks to the works of noted authors Dan Brown and Umberto Eco, so it doesn't surprise me that Ashley's overworked imagination could construe such a scheme. I decided not to dismiss her theories, but at the same time I wouldn't encourage them. As far as I was concerned this was nothing but a harmless research project about a mythical legend. It had to be.

Memories of the years I spent tracking down the sacred artifact came back like a tidal wave. The only solace I took from the years of sweat and disappointment is that the quest helped me to deal with the pain of losing Helen. I know that's why I poured so much of myself into it. I heaped the pain of my loss onto my obsession with finding the so-called sacred artifact; obsession and despair, a volatile cocktail that can only lead to ruination. Now I was back at it again, my obsession sure to resurface; like an old athlete who's hung up his sneakers, but then something brings him back and he's determined to relive his past, to find glory again. That was me. I knew I was in it now to the end, no matter where that end took me, even if it meant my life.

Seven

Alistair Pratt summoned his driver to prepare the car for a little trip to Landon, New York.

"What's going on in Landon sir?" asked Henry.

"I have a desire to dine in Westchester this evening Henry."

"Would that be Aramnte's sir?"

"Yes, you're familiar with it?"

"Yes, I've heard of it, but never been."

"Would you like to join me?"

"Sir?"

"I said would you like to join me?"

"No sir. With all due respect, it's not my kind of place, if you know what I mean."

"Yes I understand."

"If you don't mind sir when we get to Westchester I'd like to go visit my sister in New Rochelle."

"No problem Henry."

"Thank you sir."

"I'll be ready to leave in five minutes."

"Yes sir."

Lydia Sinclair arrived at exactly seven o'clock. I was actually looking forward to having dinner with her. She was a welcome break from my normal routine. I stepped into the car and we were off. Armante's was about a five-minute ride from my house.

"Good evening Dr. Marshall."

"Good evening Ms. Sinclair. Since we'll be working together Alex will do. May I address you as Lydia?"

"You may."

"Have you been to Armante's before?" I asked.

"Yes, about three years ago. I thought the food was excellent."

"The food is good. The head chef is from Milan, which explains why her food has such an authentic taste," I said.

"Authentic? You've been to Milan?"

"A couple of times. Yourself?"

"Several, though I prefer Sicily over Italy. Why are you smiling?" She asked.

"Excuse me; I was smiling because I'm impressed."

"Impressed?"

"Yes, most people think Sicily is in Italy. They don't comprehend that Sicily is its own country."

"I have visited and studied Sicily extensively, so I guess you could say I'm an expert."

"Really?" I said.

"Yes. Sicilian culture is both fascinating and misunderstood."

"Misunderstood, how so?"

"The majority of information on Sicily pertains to the so-called Mafia, or Omerta. When in actuality most Sicilians are as involved in criminal activities as you or I," she said with a smile.

"I agree. Here we are," I said as we pulled up to the front door. Armante's is Landon's most upscale restaurant and the food is so good, the atmosphere so soothing, with it's minimalist décor, soft blue and yellow lights, and impeccable service, it's a regular haunt of celebrities and athletes, who are looking to escape the glare and paparazzi of New York City, for a night out of fine dining.

As Alex and Lydia were pondering what to order, Carson Lowery was being shown to his seat. A handsome man, six feet tall, dark wavy hair, with deep set blue eyes, and a sharp angular face, with a hint of a shadow like the models in GQ magazine, Carson smiled at the reaction his looks had on the pretty young woman, who was showing him to his seat.

"Right this way sir, the far corner, just as you requested," the young woman said with a nervous smile.

"Thank you."

"Your waiter will be with you shortly. Thank you for coming to Armante's and do enjoy."

"Here you are young lady." He reached into the right pocket of his dark blue Armani suit and handed the startled young woman a crisp one hundred dollar bill.

"That's not necessary sir."

"I insist. You're in college I would guess."

"Yes I am."

"Then I know that you can use this money."

"Yes sir, I certainly can."

"Then it's all settled." Lowery uttered this last sentence in a manner that conveyed to the young woman that she should be on her way.

"Thank you again sir."

Lowery smiled as the young woman walked away, her hips swaying rhythmically, a show for my benefit, he mused, his vanity oozing like lava from a volcano. Perhaps if business didn't dictate, he smiled. He took note again of where he was sitting. Perfect; they'll never see me from this location; perfect indeed.

"How much longer before we reach Landon, Henry?"

"About another five minutes Mr. Pratt. Is it still okay for me to go and see my sister?"

Alistair did not hear the question. His thoughts were solely on Lydia. Just follow the plan, he repeated.

"So is it okay Mr. Pratt?"

"Is what okay Henry?"

"Is it okay for me to visit my sister in New Rochelle"?

"Of course, didn't I say yes before?"

"Yeah you did, but I'm just making sure."

"Right."

"Here we are sir, Armante's restaurant."

"I will call you when I'm ready."

"Okay sir, enjoy your meal."

"So Alex, what do you think of Alistair?" Lydia asked as they waited for their food.

"He's interesting."

"For as long as I've been working with him I must say I have never seen him this enthused over a project."

"Really? What do you think the reason is?"

"As you can see, Alistair is very wealthy, and like a lot of rich men, he wants to leave a legacy. I think this book is just that."

"Interesting, where are you from Ms. Sinclair?"

"All over. I'm a military brat."

"Are you married?"

"No, divorced."

It was then that she saw Carson Lowery; she had to call Alistair immediately.

"Excuse me Alex; I have to go to the ladies room."

Carson Lowery watched Lydia retreat to the ladies room. He pulled out his cell phone and made a call.

"They're here."

"Did they notice you?" A female voice asked.

"No."

"How can you be so sure?"

"I'm very careful, as always," Lowery said.

"Good".

"I will speak with you in a few days." Carson snapped his phone shut. Though he didn't relish his assignment, Carson would perform at the optimum level, with all that was at stake, he couldn't afford not to.

Havana, Cuba

Janet hated to have to leave Cuba. It had become her second home. But she knew that when she came, her time there would be short-lived. Even though she would not be leaving for a month, she had already begun packing her bags. She wanted to be ready when the time came. She walked over to her window. The rhythms of Havana were in full sway on this humid Saturday evening. Everyone was having a good time. As she thought about what she would be leaving, she felt a wave of sadness. Is it all worth it? She then thought about her purpose in life and her sadness turned to a smile. It's my fate; it can't be any other way.

Lydia called Alistair as soon as the ladies room was empty.

"Hello", Alistair answered.

"Lowery is here," she said, her voice bristling with anger.

"I know."

"You know, how?" *Is he here in the restaurant, checking on me?*

"My dear you know that I leave nothing to chance."

"What you don't trust me?"

"Trust has nothing to do with it."

"Fine, what are we going to do about Lowery?"

"Nothing right now," he said.

"Nothing, are you crazy?"

"Patience my dear, patience; everything in due time," Alistair said.

Lydia returned from the ladies room and asked if we could cut our evening short, said she wasn't feeling well. She dropped me off at home and once I was inside I noticed that my bedroom light was on. I could have sworn that I had turned it off. My first thought was that it was a burglar, even though I didn't see any signs of forced entry. I grabbed a butcher knife from the kitchen and treaded slowly up the stairs. A heightened sense of anxiety coursed through me as I reached my bedroom. Then a familiar scent caught the attention of my nostrils. Kelly. I forgot she still had a key. Sure enough it was her, all decked out in the skimpiest piece of lingerie I have ever seen. I guess she's forgiven me. I didn't ask any questions. I didn't think about Helen.

Eight

When I woke up the next morning, to a beautiful serenade of jaybirds and sunlight streaming through my bedroom windows, Kelly had already left. There was a note on the nightstand that read:

Last night was perfect. Talk to you later.
K.

I woke up feeling nostalgic. Though I wasn't thinking about Helen last night, for some strange reason I now had an impulse to see her. I wanted to smell her, hear her voice. It just goes to show that I have my issues as well. *I mean what kind of person makes love to his girlfriend and then* wakes *up thinking about his ex-girlfriend*? I guess the philosophical question of the day is: *Can man control the random thoughts that pop up out of nowhere, or are his thoughts a byproduct of information he willing exposes himself to?* I don't know the answer to that, but what I do know is that I felt torn between my current love for Kelly and my memories of the love I had with Helen and not having Kelly here would help ease my feelings of emotional infidelity.

I showered, ate a quick bite and headed over to campus, just in time for my class.

After my classes were through for the day I met Felix at Café Landon for a late lunch.

"Afraid you'll run into Jordan," he asked laughing.

"What are you talking about?" I asked.

"Isn't that why we're eating here instead of Hollands?"

"Not at all, I just wanted a change of scenery."

"Yeah right papi. You're scared you might give in."

"I can handle it."

"Well it looks like you're good then."

"She's just flirting, it's nothing," I replied.

"If you say so; how's Kelly?"

"Well you know how it is, up and down, today we're up."

"You're a weak man Alex," he said with a hearty laugh.

"I know, I know."

"What's up with Helen?"

"What do you mean?" I asked as my neck stiffened. It had taken me all morning to shake the sweet memories of Helen out of my head. I really didn't want to start talking about her now.

"Come on bro, you know what I'm talking about. Have you been by to see her or what?"

"Just once, at the opening; remember?"

"That's it! She's been back for *two years*."

"I just haven't had the time." I said unconvincingly, so much so, that I had to laugh at myself. Felix shook his head and gave me that familiar *man you're pathetic* look.

"Whatever man; you know I just don't understand you."

"Not that again Felix."

"I'm serious Alex. Before she came back you hadn't seen her in what, twelve years?"

"So?"

"So I don't understand why you're still tripping over her; she left you and she didn't keep in touch with you, hell she didn't even invite you to her wedding!"

"Felix, I really don't want another lecture."

"I'm just saying Alex, I don't understand why you can't let her go, besides if you were that much in love with her you would have gone out to L.A., but you didn't."

"Like you said, she left me; I wasn't going to chase her."

"Well you've been chasing her in your head for the past twelve years. Let it go Alex. Kelly's a good woman, that's where your focus needs to be."

"Yeah, yeah." I said.

"Yeah, yeah my ass; hey, what's going on with the book project?" I was relieved that he'd changed the subject because he was speaking the truth and I didn't want to deal with it.

"Nothing in particular, just the usual research, though something unusual did happen the other day, Kelly got a call from someone asking her if she had a copy of my book on the Chamber of Cyrenaic."

"That's odd. What'd you think that's all about?"

"I have no clue," I said.

"What are you doing this Friday?"

"Nothing."

"Why don't you come over for dinner, Carmen's frying rock fish?"

"I'll definitely be there."

After lunch I headed back to the office. Ashley was waiting for me when I arrived.

"Have you been thinking about my theory?"

"Ashley, I just don't see it."

"So you're dismissing it?" She asked visibly annoyed.

"I would never dismiss anything you have to say, but until you can show me definitive proof, I think we need to focus on the task at hand," I said.

"Which is?"

"The research we agreed to provide."

"So then what are we discussing today?" She said, still visibly upset.

"Ashley if you don't want to do this my way then you can come back to work for me after I've finished this project."

"I'm sorry Dr. Marshall. I get your point."

"Look Ashley, I'm not saying that you can't explore your theories on your own time. Hell, you may even be right." She smiled. "But while you're here on my time we're going to stick to the task at hand and if you come up with something that's more definitive then I'll listen. Deal?"

"Yes sir," she said.

"Well, as we discovered last time, Sir Arthur eschewed politics. He felt that politics were for idiots and non-thinkers. It was his belief that politicians were corrupt tools for greedy, rich landowners."

"Wasn't he afraid of being killed?"

"Apparently the ruling parties in London dismissed him as a harmless zealot, so there was never any thought to killing him."

"What about the townspeople? What did they think of him?"

"Most of them thought he was a lunatic."

"You said that he was a man ahead of his time. What did you mean?"

"Sir Arthur's theories, views fusing religion and sex were a shock to staid and moralistic England. During his day, this was not a topic for discussion, especially in mixed company, at least not publicly. Sir Arthur held discussions like these everyday and it is believed that from these discussions came his followers."

"But if it were known who the members were, how were they a secret society?"

"Good question. First of all no one knew for sure who the members really were. It was believed that they were comprised of the people who attended his discussion groups because after he formed his core group public discussions abruptly ceased. When questioned as to why these discussions were no longer public, it is rumored that the phrase 'the blanket covers the body, but not the head,' was the response."

"What the heck does that mean?"

"There have been many theories postulated. The general consensus is that it refers to the notion of the tree in the forest."

"Now *you're* confusing me. I mean I know the concept of the tree in the forest, but what does that have to do with what we're talking about?"

"Many people believe that just because one doesn't see or hear a tree fall in the forest, doesn't mean that it didn't fall. The phrase 'the blanket covers the body, but not the head' means that just because you don't see the body doesn't mean that the head is not still thinking and talking. Does that make sense?"

"Yeah, I guess, though that analogy is a bit of a stretch."

After hours of reading and discussing research material we quit for the evening.

Parked across the street from campus Timothy waited patiently for Alex to leave his office. He had his schedule memorized. Marshall was so predictable. Timothy's major concern was how to get into his office, without being seen. Alistair wanted the job done tonight.

As I left my office I once again had the feeling that I was being watched.

Jordan sat in her car and watched Alex as he left the campus. As she followed him to his house she thought about making her move, but decided to wait. She told herself to be patient, but patience was not one of her strong suits. She thought it was stupid to wait until "the appointed time", but as with every part of the mission, she did as she was told. Because If she moved too soon, did things on her own, she could jeopardize years of planning, an act that would have dire consequences for more than just herself.

Though I had a hearty lunch, I was famished. I hadn't taken anything out, so that meant pizza. I checked my messages. Kelly called, asking me if I wanted to come to the city for dinner. I wanted to see her, but I didn't feel like taking the trip to Manhattan. I called her back and suggested that she come to Landon. She said she would be over in a couple of hours.

The campus was slowly thinning out. Timothy was impressed with how beautiful it looked at night. He watched the students leaving evening classes, watched the parking lot empty and then looked at the security schedule. Campus police made rounds every two hours, hitting Alex's building at quarter past the hour. Plenty of time, Timothy reasoned, to accomplish the task at hand.

Kelly arrived around eight-thirty.
"You're right on time the pizza just arrived."
"I know. As I was pulling up I saw the delivery guy driving off."

"Where are we going with this Kelly?" I asked her abruptly. As much as I loved her, and even though things were going well, I was tired of the back and forth. Either we were going to make a commitment to permanently change the tenor of our relationship or we needed to leave each other alone.

"Going with what?"

"You know what I'm talking about?"

"Where would you like it to go Alex?"

"We can't keep going back and forth like this."

"What do you suggest that we do?"

"Maybe we should go to counseling, see a preacher."

"Why, we're not married?" She said.

"True, but since it is quite obvious that we're not serious about breaking up, then we need to do something to make things better."

"But if we're still together, then why do we need to fix it? For some reason we both seem to enjoy the nature of our relationship, so why should we meddle with it?"

"I don't enjoy this at all."

"Sure you do." She said.

"No, I don't."

"Yes you do. If you didn't then you would have left a long time ago."

"I just want a normal relationship."

"Normal? What exactly does that mean?" She said angrily. I was taken aback by her sudden change in disposition. I wondered what nerve I had struck *this time*.

"Don't put me on the witness stand. You know what I mean by normal."

"No, I don't."

"Yes you do," I said.

"And how would I know that Alex? I didn't exactly have it modeled for me when I was child, or did you forget that my mother left us, no of course you didn't forget, *did you?*"

92

"Kelly I'm sorry about the other day. I was angry and it slipped out"

"Nothing just slips out Alex. Look let's just drop it before we both say something we'll regret; let's just eat and watch the movie I brought, *alright?*"

"All right."

"Good."

"Why are you suddenly being so conciliatory?" I asked.

"There's no pleasing you Alex Marshall. Here I am trying to make an effort not to start a fight and you want to know why. Let's just enjoy the moment."

"You're right, I've just never seen you be so accommodating."

"Well if you keep talking, it won't last. Now shut up and eat."

The campus police officer had made his rounds and now Timothy was free to enter the building. Alex's office was on the third floor, directly across from the elevator. This was not necessarily a good thing because if someone were to come to the third floor, they would easily see that something was amiss in Marshall's office. But Alistair had made sure that no one would be reentering the building that evening, with the exception of the campus police officer. Timothy marveled at Alistair's ability to cover every nuance. Somehow Alistair was able to account for the whereabouts of each person who would have reason to enter the building. He told Timothy that tonight had to be the night, because it was the only night for the next few weeks, in which the building would be completely empty. Breaking into the office would be easy. The building was an old one, and the locks on the doors were your standard key variety, a piece of cake for a professional like himself. As he expected, he entered without any problem.

He surveyed the office. After examining it twice, he knew exactly where to put the bug. He checked his watch and smiled. The whole process had taken him precisely eight minutes, just as he planned.

Kelly and I were having a nice evening. The movie she rented was very good and the pizza was even better. I was looking forward to what the rest of the night promised. It occurred to me that if Kelly and I could have great sex when we were angry at one another; imagine how much better it would be when we were actually enjoying each other's company. Kelly wanted some ice cream, so I went to the supermarket, which was about five minutes away, and as luck would have it I ran into Helen.

"So stranger why haven't you been back to the shop? It's been two years since the opening." Even at that time of night Helen looked great.

"I've been busy, but I plan to get around to it," I said calmly, my demeanor belying the butterflies twirling around in my stomach.

"Well don't be a stranger; I mean I hope I'll see you again before the reunion."

"Reunion?"

"Yes Alex, our twenty-year high school reunion, on November eighth."

"You know Helen I completely forgot." It felt good to say her name.

"You will be there won't you?"

"Wouldn't miss it for the world," I said. She looked at her watch.

"Am I keeping you from something?" She laughed.

"TCM is having an Audrey Hepburn marathon." I smiled. Helen knows every line to every Audrey Hepburn movie.

"You still like Audrey huh?"

"She's timeless." She lingered as if she were going to say something else, maybe about us, but thought better of it.

"Well I don't want to keep you. It was nice seeing you. *It was nice seeing you? The first love of my life and all I say is it was nice seeing you?*

"You too Alex, I hope to see you at the shop."

"I'll come by, I promise."

As I watched her walk to her car, I was faced with a dilemma; do I tell Kelly I saw Helen? The right thing to do would be to fess up, but Kelly would turn it into some sordid clandestine affair, accuse me of setting it up. Sometimes doing the right thing isn't the best thing, and at that time it clearly wouldn't have been the best thing. Of course the consequences of lying could come back to haunt me, but it's a chance I was willing to take. In hindsight I knew the real reason that I didn't want to mention my chance encounter to Kelly was because I was still conflicted about Helen. Seeing her, talking to her, *saying her name*, clouded everything, and I knew I wouldn't, couldn't be devoid of emotion if I told her. My feelings for Helen would have shone through like a magic marker under a neon light.

When I got back I noticed that Kelly wasn't in the entertainment room. I figured that she was in the bathroom. I called her name, but she didn't answer. Her car was still here, so I didn't know what was going on. Then I thought about the previous night, and I figured that she was upstairs waiting for me. I called her name again, but she didn't answer. I approached the bedroom and when I looked in, there she was, sound asleep. I placed the covers over her and just sat and stared. It was a beautiful moment. The streetlights cascaded through the open blinds, highlighting her exquisite features. As I watched her it occurred to me that this was the first time that Kelly and I had spent the night together and didn't have sex. As much as I enjoy sex with her, this moment really touched me. I took off my shoes, lay down beside her and put my arms around her and just held her, and it felt good. First Helen, now this, damn *now I was really confused!*

Nine

Carson Lowry glanced at his watch for what seemed like the hundredth time. What's taking her so long? Why hasn't she called? This wasn't like her, he thought. She's always punctual. He shuddered. Something had to have happened to her. Just as the endless stream of possibilities floated through his head, the phone rang.

"Hello," he answered slightly perturbed.

"It's me," said the woman.

"It's about time you called. Why are you late?"

"Business," she said.

"Business, what other business could be more important than *this?*"

"You heard me. Don't worry I have my end under control. Have I ever failed to do my job?" she asked him.

"There's a first time for everything."

"I noticed you the moment you walked in Armante's the other night. Chances are they did as well."

"You were *there*? I thought that you were in". He stopped midstream. *How does she do it?* He wondered. "I don't think they saw me."

"Just be more careful, there's too much at stake."

"Yes ma'am."

I woke up to the smell of bacon and eggs, Kelly was cooking breakfast something she rarely did.

"To what do we owe this occasion?" I said as I took a seat.

"What do you mean?"

"Kelly, you hardly ever cook, and now you're acting like Emeril?"

"I thought it would be nice to have breakfast."

"Oh, I'm not complaining. This is actually very nice."

"I'm sorry for falling asleep on you."

"That's okay. I enjoyed watching you sleep. You looked so angelic."

"That's nice of you to say."

"It's true."

"I don't know how much more of this I can take," she said.

"What do you mean?"

"Us being nice to each other, it's not natural", she said laughingly.

"Yes it is strange."

"How's the book project going?"

"Slowly, but we'll get there. Speaking of, have you received any more calls?"

"No, should I?"

"I don't think so."

"You don't think so. Is there something you're not telling me?"

"No. I just wonder if Ashley's right."

"What does she think?"

"She thinks that Pratt is not all that he seems."

"What does she mean by that?"

I told her Ashley's theory.

"Interesting," Kelly replied. "Do you think it could be true?"

"Anything is possible, but I don't place much stock in it. I think it's just the product of an overworked imagination."

"I wouldn't be so cavalier if I were you."

"Why? Surely you don't think there's anything to what she said?"

"Nothing is impossible my dear."

After Kelly left I thought about what she said. Perhaps there was something to Ashley's theory but I wasn't going too waste any energy thinking about it, after all we were only conducting research for a book. How dangerous could that be?"

Over the next couple of weeks Kelly and I spent a lot of time together and we didn't argue. Perhaps our relationship was finally turning a different corner. I didn't understand why, but I did all I could to help keep the peace. I wish I could say that the Garrison project was as successful. Ashley and I were having a hard time finding any new information, particularly on Sir Arthur's behavioral theories, and Ms. Sinclair was striking out as well. We met with Mr. Pratt to give him an update, and he encouraged us to keep on plugging. He said he had faith that what he was looking for would one day fall into my lap. One particularly evening in early October I was on campus working rather late, when I heard a knock on the door. I assumed it was Officer Harrelson making his rounds. His knocking struck me as odd, because he knew that I had been staying late.

"It's just me Glenn, Alex Marshall." No answer.

"Glenn, are you out there?" I opened the door, but no one was there. I shrugged it off and went back to work. About fifteen minutes later, I heard knocking again. I opened the door, and again no one was there, but this time an envelope was left on the floor. It wasn't addressed to anyone, but I assumed that it was meant for me. I opened it and inside was a note that read:

I'm coming Dr. Marshall you will be my gatekeeper.

My first inclination was that it was Kelly being mysterious. But that thought immediately dissipated when I remembered that she was in Los Angeles at a legal conference. Now I was perplexed. As I was sitting at my desk trying to figure it out the phone rang.

"Hello."

"Did you receive the envelope?"

"Who is this?"

"Did you read the note?"

"Yes. Who is this and what is this all about?"

"You must be prepared; 'I' will soon be yours."

"What?" Click, the caller had hung up. The voice was muffled, so I couldn't tell if it was a man or woman. I couldn't dial star 69 because the lines at the college don't allow you to do so. I sat in my office for another hour trying to figure out what was going on. I decided that I would take the envelope to police headquarters the next day and see if they could lift any prints off of it. I left the building and as I walked to my car I was certain that whoever left the note was watching me.

Jordan waited for Dr. Marshall to leave the parking lot. She didn't want to take the chance of being seen, so she took another route to his neighborhood. She wanted to make her move, but remembered that she must be patient. If she did anything outside of the parameters of the plan, she would mess everything up. She didn't want that to happen. She watched from a safe distance, but she did not see him pull up. She waited and as she was about to leave, she saw a light come on. He must have parked in the front. Why would he do that, she thought? She decided that it wasn't important and drove off.

Adolescence wasn't kind to Jordan Nelson, the middle child of a prominent Seattle Washington family. A gangly young woman, who didn't know how to manage her height, she cried herself to sleep every night, egged on by her younger sister, a beautiful young girl, whose self-absorption was eagerly encouraged by her parents. Jordan exacted revenge in the classroom, exhibiting a measured cruelness that was hidden by the unwritten adolescent rule: *ugly girls can't afford to be mean.* When it came time to choose a college, Jordan, who was bombarded with scholarships from every top school in the country, chose tiny Landon College. She hoped that she could become someone new, but she was miserable, and but for the kindness of her Introduction to Religion Professor, Dr. Alex Marshall, she may have committed suicide. It was Alex Marshall who listened to her problems, who made her feel like she was someone important, who shared his own painful stories of adolescent ridicule. Yet despite his kindness, she still didn't like Landon and she transferred after her sophomore year. Now years later, she was back in Landon, a transformed woman involved in stakes whose payoff meant true freedom. This time the outcome of her time in Landon would be different, *very different.*

Havana, Cuba

Hector Rodriguez couldn't sleep. It was an extremely humid night, even for Havana, and he could not get comfortable. He peeked over at his wife. She was dead to the world. That woman could sleep through anything he mused. He walked to the kitchen and poured himself a glass of water; then he checked on his two children. They were sound asleep as well. Hector decided to go for a walk. He left his wife a note saying that he couldn't sleep and that he had gone for a walk, though he was certain that he would be back before she awakened. The streets in his Havana neighborhood were empty. He thought about how just a few hours earlier, the block was alive, and now it was as if that world was an illusion. As he was walking he noticed someone running. He didn't pay it any mind; probably some kid who was out past curfew trying to sneak back home. After being out for about a half an hour Hector returned home. The next morning he was watching the news when he saw a report about an apparent suicide. What sparked his interest was that it happened down the street from where he lived. The cause of death was a gold tipped sword plunged straight through the bellybutton. The time of death was around four am. Hector remembered that he was out at that time and that's when he saw the figure running. He started to call the police, but thought better of it. If they say it's a suicide, then that's what it is.

Janet found the package exactly where Victor said it would be. She looked around to see if it was okay to leave. It was imperative that no one saw her. Confident that she was the only person out on the streets of Havana at four in the morning, she took off running, unbeknownst to her a gentleman with a bout of insomnia watched her with startled curiosity.

I didn't sleep well that night. I was up trying to figure out what that strange note meant. The next day, during a break between classes I drove over to the Landon Police Department. I had called Matt Gladden the police chief to let him know I was coming. He and my parents are good friends, so I knew that he would see me right away.

"Alex, come on in," boomed the chief. Matt Gladden was a bear of a man, broad shouldered, with a thick neck and forearms the size of tree trunks. When he was younger he competed in body building exhibitions, but age and inactivity has softened him somewhat, particularly around the belly, of which he was fond of patting every time he laughed.

"Thanks Chief. How's the family?"

"Connie and the girls are fine. Jennifer is getting married next week and Cynthia is expecting her third child."

"Congratulations."

"Thanks. Now, let's take a look at that envelope."

"I didn't use gloves, so my prints are all over the envelope. Will that wipe out the chances of finding other prints?" I asked.

"No, if there are prints on there other than yours, we'll be able to lift them."

"How long will this process take?"

"About fifteen minutes, can you wait for the results?"

"Yes. What do you make of this Chief?"

"I don't know. The note doesn't appear to be threatening, so I wouldn't say that you are in any physical danger."

"Physical danger, that thought hadn't even crossed my mind."

"I'm sorry to alarm you; I was just pointing out the obvious. Maybe it's from a girlfriend or a secret admirer."

"It's not from my girlfriend. She's in Los Angeles, besides it's not her style."

"Maybe it's a secret admirer."

"Perhaps," I said. *Helen?*

Fifteen minutes later the results came back.

"Sorry Alex, but the only prints that we found were yours. Whoever left this note was wearing gloves. Look, keep an eye out for anything else that is out of the ordinary and if you see or hear anything, give me a call."

"Thanks for your help Chief." I was somewhat disappointed that it wasn't Helen, or at least it didn't appear to be.

"No problem."

Carson Lowery was perturbed. He had followed Alex and was not pleased that he had gone to see the police. The last thing they needed was for the police to become involved. This was not good. He had to let her know.

"Hello," he said.

"What is it? I thought we were not to contact each other again until next week?"

"We have a situation," he said.

"Well what is it?"

"Marshall just came from the police station."

"So?" She said.

"So?"

"Yes, what's the big deal?"

"What's the big deal, are you serious? He has to know something; why else would he go to the police?"

"Get a hold of yourself. There are a million different reasons why he may have gone to see the police, and I assure you that *our situation* is not one of them. He doesn't have a clue. When he does we will know," she said.

"What makes you so sure that his visit was not about *this*?"

"Because if it were, Pratt would be in play as well and right now he isn't so calm down."

"I'm still concerned. Perhaps I should find out why he was there", Carson said anxiously.

"You will do no such thing. If you start inquiring into police matters, you'll mess up everything. Just keep still and let things play out as we planned."

"Okay," he answered skeptically.

"Have I ever steered you wrong?"

"Never."

"Then trust me on this one."

"Yeah, okay."

"Oh and one more thing."

"Yes?"

"Make sure it's a real emergency before you interrupt another one of my massages."

"Right."

I left the police station without any answers. Why would someone make the effort to ensure that finger prints were not left on the envelope? Of course the simple answer is whoever it was didn't want to be identified; but why; and what did that cryptic message mean; *"The gatekeeper?"*

That Friday I had everyone over for dinner; collectively I figured we could decode the mysterious note.

"I'm inclined to agree with Matt. I think it's a secret admirer," said my father.

"I don't think it's that. I think that somehow it has to do with this Cyrenaic business," my sister remarked.

"You can't be serious?" I said.

"Yes I am."

"But all we're doing is compiling research for a book. On a topic I might add that no one cares about."

"Your sister may be right, maybe it was Mr. Pratt that sent you the note," said Ashley.

"Why would he do that dear?" asked my mother.

"Because maybe he thought that it would pique Dr. Marshall's interest and spur him on to work even harder. Or maybe he isn't what he claims to be."

"Ashley, not that again," I said.

"Ignore him Ashley," said Carol. "What do you mean?"
Ashley told them her theory.

"Maybe she's right Alex," said Felix.

"Look, I respect Ashley's opinion, but I just can't see it. It's just a *book*."

"Well then how do you explain the note?" said Carol

"I can't, but I don't see what it has to do with our research."

"Alex, I think I may have the answer," Felix said.

"What is it?"

"The note may be from the girl at the restaurant, the one who was coming on to you."

"Jordan?" I replied.

"*Who's Jordan*?" Carol asked.

I told them about Jordan and our last encounter.

"This could only happen to *you* Alex," said my sister.

"I completely forgot about her."

"I know Jordan, freshman year we were roommates," said Ashley. "She's kind of hyper, possessive."

"What do you mean?" I asked.

"Well she used to call her boyfriend every night, and if he wasn't there she would leave these messages accusing him of sleeping around and telling him that she better not catch him, because if she did he would have hell to pay. I thought she was harmless though."

"Why'd you think that?" Carol asked.

"Because her boyfriend was miles away and she was already insecure. You know how girls can get when they're away from their high school boyfriends. I just thought that she was all talk. After we came back from winter break, she stopped making the phone calls. I asked her about him and she said that he was no longer in the picture, and that was that."

"Did she go out with any other guys?"

"Yeah, but she was relatively cool with them. I mean I didn't see her acting crazy or accusing them of anything."

"Do you think it was her?" I asked.

"No, I doubt it. The Jordan I knew wasn't subtle. I mean even though she kept to herself and was unhappy, she was anything but shy. It was kind of weird because she slinked around campus not saying much to anyone, but in the dorm she was always complaining about the other girls at floor meetings. So if it were Jordan you would know, but who knows, maybe she's changed."

"It might be her Alex," said Felix.

"Richard you've been awfully quiet, what do you think?" I asked.

"I don't think it's the girl and I don't think it's a secret admirer. I think Ashley is right. It has something to do with the research you're doing."

"So what do you suggest that I do?"

"Perhaps it's time you did a little research on Mr. Alistair Pratt."

Ten

Alistair Pratt was born in London, in 1950. He is the great-grandson of the legendary oil baron Jeremiah Pratt. It was rumored that Jeremiah used unsavory means to corner the oil market in the United States. Alistair, an only child became sole heir to his grandfather's fortune, when his parents were murdered, execution style seven years ago. The police surmise that they were executed because they were cooperating with prosecutors in relation to activities involving organized crime, though there are some people in London who believe that Alistair was responsible, despite the fact he was never considered a suspect by the police.

He attended Harvard University and the Wharton School of Business, and lives in both London and New York. Prior to his inheritance, he had already made billions, the majority stemming from real estate and various investments. He is a generous philanthropist. He is considered to be a private man, who avoids the limelight. He is married and has two children, though predictably, they are rarely seen. He admits to having very few interests outside of his work and his children, with the exception of his interest in secret societies. In a rare interview he discussed his fascination with the concept of secret societies, and how one day he had planned to write a book on them. He went on to say that he was particularly curious about the

Cyrenaic. When asked why he was so interested in such an obscure Order, he replied that it was because of how they mysteriously vanished without a trace.

That was it. So far I didn't see a smoking gun. Nothing stood out that would give me the impression that he wasn't who he said he was. Besides what could I possibly have that would cause him to misrepresent himself? I told Ashley as much when she came to the office.

"I did some research on our Mr. Pratt and he seems harmless." I told her what I had discovered.

"I'm still convinced he sent the note."

"But for what reason? You haven't given me a plausible explanation. All you keep saying is that he's not what he seems to be. I could argue that none of us are what we seem to be."

"What do you mean?"

"What I mean is that we all wear masks."

"Masks?"

"Yes. Life requires us to be different things to different people. We're actors in a series of vignettes that make up our lives. In order to convey the appropriate message, it is important that we wear the proper mask. One could say that we are practicing the art of illusion. We want people to see what's not really there."

"That sounds like an oxymoron."

"On the surface it does, but think about it, everyday we play roles, some we like and some we don't. Think about all of times you've acted in a way in which you felt it wasn't the real you."

"I've done that quite a few times." She said.

"We all have. We do it everyday. When we play roles we want people to think this is whom we really are. That's what I mean by wanting people to see what's not really there. We know inherently that the role we're playing at the time is not really who we think we are, but we have to be convincing."

"If that's true then how can a person really know himself?"

"That's a good question. I don't know Ashley I guess that's for each one of us to figure out. Some of us are so consumed by the different roles that we play that we think those roles define who we really are."

"But isn't that the case?"

"What do you mean?" I said.

"Maybe our real selves are nothing but a composite of the roles that we play. Maybe there is nothing wrong with wearing masks. Or better yet, maybe we don't have a choice."

"You're right."

"All that being said how does this relate to Mr. Pratt?"

"I should be asking you that."

"Why?" she said.

"Let's say I agree that Pratt isn't all that he seems to be, in the context of the note, what does that mean? Maybe he does have another reason for soliciting my services that still does not explain why he would leave the note."

"That's what we're going to find out."

"You're convinced it was him?"

"As sure as my name is Ashley Elizabeth Winters."

That evening I picked Kelly up from the airport. Our relationship had been going well so I was happy to see her. I had an elaborate evening planned at my house, but she said that she needed to go home to check her mail and her messages. When we reached her street, we immediately noticed that something wasn't right. There were police cars everywhere, and people milling about shaking their heads. As we got closer we saw that the police had cordoned off the entrance to the brownstone next to Kelly's. One of the officers's recognized her and he allowed us to slip under the yellow police tape.

"What's going on Patrick?" said Kelly.

"Hello counselor. We've got an apparent suicide. Do you live in this building?"

"Next door; excuse me, Alex this is Detective Patrick Morris. Patrick this is Dr. Alex Marshall."

"Hey, how you doing?" He asked as he extended his hand.

"Fine," I said.

"Did you know the dead girl?" Patrick asked Kelly.

"No, I didn't even know the building was occupied. How'd she do it?"

"The strangest thing I've ever seen and I have been a cop for twenty years." He stopped talking and let the last part of his sentence linger for effect.

"What do you mean?"

"She took herself out with a gold tipped sword, straight through the belly button."

"A gold tipped sword, through the belly button?" I repeated.

"Yeah doc," Detective Morris said, still amazed at what he'd seen.

"Can I get into my building?" Kelly asked the detective.

"Yeah go ahead."

"Do you want me to come with you?" I asked her.

"No, I'll be fine. I'll be right out."

"So?" I asked the detective, "You're pretty sure it was a suicide?"

"Yeah, from all accounts it looks as though she did it herself."

"That's a relief. I mean it's a relief that there's not a murderer running around." I paused.

"It's okay Doc, I know what you meant. I feel the same way; I've got a wife and two teenagers."

"You ready Alex?" Kelly asked when she returned.

"Yes. Nice meeting you Patrick, despite the circumstances."

"Yeah you too; take it easy counselor, see you in court."

Michael didn't like New York City. And a few hours ago when he signed the lease for the brownstone he took solace in the fact that he would only be there until nightfall. He was told that Janet would be coming to him with the package. Plans had changed because of concern that *they* may have figured out what was going on. Once she delivered the package he had to leave immediately. He was instructed not to speak to her, nor was he to see her. He was to secure the package and leave. He knew that once the package was in his hands, his days were numbered, but he didn't care. To be chosen for duty was an honor that had no peer.

Even though she knew this was the end, Janet was amazingly calm. Initially she thought that she would have a hard time finding the brownstone. She had only been to New York City once, and that was when she was nine. But she knew that she had to find it, if she didn't the ramifications would be disastrous. She knew that he was waiting. Janet reached the brownstone and placed the package in the place in which she was instructed. She waited until she heard him come and go and then she calmly plunged the gold tipped sword right through her belly button.

"What do you make of that bizarre suicide?" Kelly asked as we drove down the Henry Hudson Parkway.

"I don't know; sounds like she was performing some type of ritual, she must have belonged to a cult."

"Sounds like it. It's just weird; I hope that it really was a suicide and not some crazy person running around."

"Your friend seemed pretty sure that it was."

"Patrick's been a cop for a long time, if he says it was suicide, then more than likely he's right."

"Just the same, perhaps you should stay at my house for a while."

"I was going to do that anyway."

"Yes that is our pattern. You'll stay until we start to work on each other's nerves."

"Alex, don't mess things up. I'm really making an effort not to be such a bitch, but I can revert back," she said with a slight smile.

"Don't remind me." We both laughed.

The fact that Kelly and I were getting along so well, should have made it easier to complete the Pratt project, but finding new information was a lot more difficult than I anticipated. I'd hoped that modern technology would make my search this time around a lot easier than it was ten years ago. Ashley and I scoured the Internet in hopes of finding anything related to the group's mysterious disappearance and Sir Arthur's writings, but we were coming up empty.

"We have to be doing something wrong?" I said.

"Like what?" she said.

"There has to be a record of Sir Arthur's writings, somewhere. We're not putting in the right queries."

"What about the libraries in London?" She asked.

"Called them, and they don't have any record of anything written by Sir Arthur Garrison."

"That could just mean that he never had his work published."

"If that's the case, then it will be virtually impossible to find anything he's written." I said.

"Maybe not," Ashley said, a glimmer of hope reflecting from her hazel eyes.

"What do you mean?"

"I'm thinking that if we track his family history, maybe we might find a living relative who has some knowledge of his work."

"That's over five hundred years of family history. That's a lot of story telling to be passed down," I said with a chuckle.

"Yeah I know. It's a long shot, but at least it's something."

"You're right, anything is better than what we have right now."

It took us a few days, but we were able to locate a blood relative, something I hadn't been able to do during all of my years of research for the book. I thought it was strange that it was so easy to find it now, but I shrugged it off. His name was Archibald Garrison and he lived in Seville, Spain. He was thirty-seven years old, married with three children and a banker for one of Seville's most prestigious financial firms. He seemed eager to talk with us about his legendary cousin.

"Thank you Mr. Garrison for speaking with us."

"My pleasure, so what do you want to know about my ancient cousin?"

"Well, as I explained to you in my e-mail, I am assisting a client with a research project on secret societies and the Chamber of Cyrenaic is included in the project. The book I wrote on the Cyrenaic is limited and my assistant and I are having a hard time filling in the rest of the story. I was hoping you could provide some additional information."

"But I'm five hundred years removed."

"Yes I know. I was hoping the story was passed down through the generations."

"My father and grandfather on several occasions would tell my sisters and me about him, but they seemed guarded when they would talk about him, as if they had something to hide."

"Something to hide; what do you mean?"

"I really don't know. I just got the feeling that there was stuff that they didn't want us to know. I never pressed them, because I wasn't all that interested." I could feel a surge of excitement welling inside my stomach. It was like I had never left my own personal journey.

"So they never talked about how the group mysteriously disappeared."

"Not really. What I mean is that they alluded to it, but they didn't or wouldn't say how or why?"

"Wouldn't, I take it you think that they knew?"

"I'm certain. I mean this was a long time ago, but I can recall my grandfather fidgeting nervously when my older sister would ask for details."

"Why do you think that was?"

"I don't know."

"Did they ever talk about Sir Arthur's writings?"

"No."

"Never?"

"Not that I recall."

"Thank you for your help Mr. Garrison. If there is anything that you can think of please give me a call. Do you think that your sisters would speak with me?"

"I'm sure they would, though they probably won't be able to tell you anymore than I could. I'll ring them up and let them know that you'll be calling."

"Thanks and goodbye."

Archibald Garrison didn't like lying, but he couldn't tell Dr. Marshall what he knew, if that really was Alex Marshall. He felt as though he were already a dead man. If the caller was Marshall, then chances are the conversation was bugged. If it wasn't Marshall then, he shuddered to think about the rest. Though he didn't divulge what he knew, he was still worried. He knew that the Cyrenaic and the Light of Hellas both had their reasons for keeping the information from Marshall until the appointed time. He knew they would kill him if they thought he would talk. Archibald thought about his wife and three girls, and he knew he had to call the woman; it was his only hope.

Carson Lowery was sound asleep, when his cell phone rang.

"Hello," he said groggily. It was her.

"Archibald has been contacted by Marshall," said the woman.

"Oh shit."

"That's right. I'm sure that Pratt knows. You've got to get to Seville right away. You have to get there before he does."

"Did you call the pilot?"

"A driver should be there for you in less than an hour."

"Do you think Pratt's already left?"

"No, but don't worry about that, I'll stall him."

But Carson was worried, *very worried*.

Alistair Pratt arose to the harsh ringing of the telephone. Who on earth, he thought, could be ringing me at this ungodly hour?

"Hello?"

"Am I speaking to Sir Alistair Pratt?"

"Who is this?"

"I have something you want Mr. Pratt."

"What? Who is this?"

"I have what you want."

"What are you talking about?"

"Come on Mr. Pratt, don't patronize me?"

"Who and what do you want?"

"I know what you're after. Does the legend of the artifact sound familiar?"

"What artifact?"

"You're making me angry Mr. Pratt. This isn't a fucking game. Keep it up and your wife and children are dead."

"You're bluffing."

"Are you sure about that? Does the name Heinz mean anything to you?"

He knew she wasn't bluffing. "What do you want?"

"Meet me at the main entrance to the South Street Seaport in an hour, and come alone. If I spot anyone with you, I will give the order to execute your wife and children. It would be a shame to blow up your villa in France, where your wife has just settled down with the children for breakfast. Tell her green is very becoming on her." The caller hung up. Alistair shuddered. Whenever he was away from his family, he would always ask his wife what she was wearing and that morning she was wearing a hunter green dress.

The seaport was deserted when Alistair arrived. What the hell was going on? He waited for an hour and still no one. As he approached his car, he saw a white piece of paper on the windshield. His first thought was that he had gotten a parking ticket, but that didn't make sense because meter maids aren't on duty at four in the morning. He cursed when he saw what it was. In exquisite handwriting were the words: **See you in Seville**.

Eleven

Alistair Pratt tried to remain calm as he drove back to his penthouse. He couldn't believe what had happened, but he had no choice. When she mentioned what his wife was wearing and the name Heinz, he had to take her seriously. Alfred Heinz was a former business associate of Alistair, who was found dead in his Long Island home. The cause of death was ruled a suicide, but Alistair knew that wasn't the case. Heinz had agreed to cooperate with federal authorities in matters that were indirectly tied to the heads of several major corporations, all of which conducted business with the Pratt Corporation. Alistair wasn't indicted, but several important players in the world of finance were. Two days before the trial was to begin, Heinz turned up dead of a prescription overdose. Alistair knew that it wasn't a suicide and he knew that they had hired *her* to do it. How, he wondered did she know about *this* business, and more importantly, who hired her. Whatever the case, he knew he had to get to Seville immediately, and he had to contact Lydia. This latest development was a matter that required her unique talents.

Lydia was not answering her phone, a matter that greatly perturbed and concerned Alistair. It wasn't like her to not answer her phone. Where could she be? At that moment the unthinkable dawned on him. Then he thought better of it, not Lydia, impossible.

Lydia felt the humming of her cell phone. It's got to be Alistair. She chose not to answer it. She had other business to take care of; he would have to wait.

Carson Lowery's first order of business, when he reached Seville was to contact Archibald Garrison. He knew that time was of the essence and if he didn't get to Archibald first, he was a dead man. He was relieved when Archibald picked up on the third ring, as was arranged.

"Thank God it's you," replied Archibald.

"Have you seen anyone lurking about?"

"No, but it's just a matter of time before they kill me."

"Did you say anything to Marshall?"

"No."

"Then you have nothing to worry about."

"I should have never agreed to speak to him. They're going to kill me; their afraid I'm going to tell him the secret." Archibald was sweating profusely.

"The Cyrenaic wouldn't kill you, you're a Garrison."

"It doesn't matter, they will stop at nothing to protect the secret, to keep it until the appointed time; the same goes for the Light of Hellas."

"We will protect you as we have always done."

"My family, are they safe?"

"Yes, they are."

"Okay, thank you." Archibald hung up.

Archibald never knew what hit him. The assassin's gun, fitted with a state of the art scope and silencer, fired one shot, hitting him square in the middle of his forehead. The assassin coolly packed away his tools and called the number as instructed.

"It's done," said the assassin.

"Do you know where the sisters are?"

"Yes," said the assassin.

"Good."

Carson Lowery knew something was amiss when he arrived at the remote location, twenty miles south of Seville, a wooded area, populated with large birch trees and wild flowers. The building, an old abandoned villa, was devoid of the usual cadre of armed guards. Carson pulled out his gun and circled the building, but he didn't see anything. Slowly he opened the front door, where he found nothing amiss. He ran upstairs and searched each room; still nothing. Though it was unlikely, he wondered if Archibald had left, but where would he go? His fears were confirmed when he discovered Archibald's body lying face down in the cellar. He dreaded having to call her, but decided not right now. He had to get to the sisters before they suffered the same fate.

For two days I tried to reach Archibald Garrison to see if his sisters had given the okay for me to contact them. I was just about to call him again when Ashley called.

"Hi Ashley, what's up?"

"Archibald Garrison is dead."

"Dead, what happened?"

"According to the news reports, he was murdered."

"How?"

"He was shot." Pause. "Dr. Marshall, are you still there?"

"Yes, I'm still here. I was thinking about how I was just talking to him a couple of days ago, and now he's dead. Do the police have any idea why he was murdered?"

"Right now they don't have a motive."

"You think that it has to do with the book, don't you?"

"Yes I do. Are you convinced now?"

"I still think it's a bit farfetched, but my ears have opened a little wider."

"So what do we do now?"

"I think I need to pay a visit to Alistair Pratt."

"No, you don't want to do that."

"Why not?"

"We don't want to tip our hand. If he thinks that we know what's going on, we could be the next targets. In order to find out what he's really up to, we have to conduct business as usual. In the meantime let's get in touch with Archibald's sisters."

"That's if they're not already dead too," I said.

"Did you just say what I thought you said?"

"Look Ashley I may still think all of this is a bit farfetched, but I'm not a fool. If he had Archibald killed, then it goes without saying that he'd kill the sisters as well."

"Archibald was our only way of contacting the sisters, now how are we going to get to them?" she said.

"Have you ever been to Seville?"

As luck, or the extraordinary Gods would have it we were able to catch a flight that night to Seville. I've been to Seville several times and yet each time I come, it's like it's the first time. The largest city in southern Spain, according to legend it was founded by Hercules and its origins are linked with the Tartessian civilization. It was called Hispalis under the Romans and Isbiliya under the Moors.

Seville lies on the banks of the Guadalquivir and is one of the largest historical centers in Europe. It has the Mohammedan minaret of La Giralda, the cathedral, and the Alcazar Palace.

Part of its treasures include Casa de Pilatos, the Town Hall, Archive of the Indies, the Fine Arts Museum, plus a host of convents, parish churches and palaces.

Seville was the home of famous and infamous figures of history, the legendary "Don Juan" started from here to conquer the hearts of women all across Europe. Prosper Merimee's "Carmen" was a worker in Seville's old tobacco factory, which now serves as Seville University.

While all of that is impressive, for me Seville is a seductive, sun-drenched city replete with orange blossoms, it seems as if orange trees are on every corner; flamenco dancers, guitar players and the mouth watering aroma of Spanish cooking, on every terrace and on every patio birds sing and geraniums bloom.

My reverie was broken by our driver's pronouncement that we had arrived at our hotel.

"Ashley, wake up."

"What?"

"Wake up, we're at the hotel."

"Wow, this is beautiful."

We were staying at the Hotel Alfonso XIII. Named for the king who commissioned its construction in 1928, Hotel Alfonso XIII was originally built to house heads of state and high-ranking guests of the 1929 Great Ibero-American Exhibition. The hotel is a Mudejar-Revival palace. The property encircles an enormous central pation, and is the showcase of marble floors, wood paneled ceilings, Moorish lamps, ceramic hand-painted tiles, and antique furnishings. The hotel occupies a premier address among the arches and arabesques of Seville's historic center, and is right across from the Seville Cathedral and next door to the old tobacco factory.

Carson Lowery sat at the bar and watched Alex and Ashley as they entered the lobby. He finished his drink and then placed a call on his cell phone.

"Hello," she said.

"It's me, they've arrived," Carson replied.

"Try not to let them get killed."

"Drop it. It wasn't my fault that I didn't get to Archibald in time, besides there's nothing that can be done about it now."

"Yeah well." She started to continue, but decided to let it go. He was right. It wasn't his fault and there wasn't anything that could be done to bring him back. She was actually angrier with herself. "You're right."

"Are the sisters still safe?" He asked.

"Yes."

"Marshall and the girl don't have a clue on how to find them, are we going to give them some assistance?" He asked

"Yes."

"What about Pratt, he'll know."

"Don't worry I can handle him."

Where is Lydia, Alistair wondered as he was ushered to his private suite at the Hotel Alfonso XIII? Is it possible that she's dead? He dismissed that thought, confident that she would turn up. He had more immediate concerns. Marshall and the girl were in Seville and he knew that they were here to find the sisters. The incident at the seaport had thrown him off balance, but not for long and he knew just what he had to do.

After getting settled, Ashley and I met in the hotel lobby and headed out to eat and formulate some sort of plan of

action. The task of finding the sisters of Archibald Garrison was going to be a difficult one. For some reason none of the local newspapers made mention of his family members. It was Ashley's belief that this was done intentionally to protect them from befalling the same fate. However Archibald Garrison was well known in Seville and it seemed inconceivable that whoever killed him would not know the identities of his remaining family members. Be that as it may, we didn't have any idea of their names or where they lived and for all we knew they may be dead already.

We dined at Meson Don Raimundo. It's located near the cathedral on Argote de Monina. The food is excellent and because Seville, at night can be a bit raucous, it's a perfect place to engage in conversation.

"This place is nice Dr. Marshall; I see why you like to come here." *My first time was with Helen during the summer before our last year of college.*

"It's one of my favorites. So, do you have any ideas on how we can locate Archibald's family members?"

"I think that we're going to have to talk to the locals."

"What makes you think that they'd give two American's information?"

"Money, it's the universal language," she said.

"I thought about that, but how do we know that they'll be truthful? They may take the money and give us false information."

"True, but that's a chance that we're going to have to take. We're also going to need to get a couple of guns."

"Guns?" I said, taken aback.

"Yes. Think about it, we're in Seville poking around about information concerning a man who was murdered. This man may have been murdered because of information concerning the group of people that we are researching. The man who may have been responsible for this murder has hired you to help him write a book, which as you know, I believe is a cover. Now here we are snooping around Seville trying to get answers. I think that if we're going to play detectives then we are going to have to protect ourselves."

"I can't refute your logic, but where are we going to get the guns?"

"Leave that to me," she said.

I let out a heavy sigh.

"What's wrong?" She asked.

"A couple of weeks ago, my only connection with guns and murder, was in the magical world of fiction novels, and besides how do you know so much about guns?"

"My dad used to take me to the range. It's the tomboy in me; I like that kind of stuff."

"Guns, we're talking about real guns Ashley."

"We can always go home. You can give Mr. Pratt his money back and drop the whole thing." *Fat chance; like the siren who seduces her prey, I was sucked in.*

"For some reason, I don't think that's an option."

"You always have options Dr. Marshall?"

"That's what scares me."

"I don't follow."

"If I return the money and tell him I'm through, the only option I see for us is death."

"Death, now whose being melodramatic, as you said, there could be a number of reasons why Archibald Garrison was murdered?"

"Yeah, but you know there's only one reason, don't you?"

"Yes."

"Well now so do I, so let's get to work," I said.

After paying out several large sums of money, and going through several "brokers," we were able to buy two Glock automatics, "top notch killing machines," said the guy who sold them to us. Now that we had ample protection, our next order of business was trying to find out information on Archibald's sisters.

Carson Lowery watched the gun transaction and prayed that they didn't do anything foolish enough to get themselves killed.

Because we spent the majority of the evening searching for guns I suggested that we dispense with business until the morning, and spend the remainder of our evening sampling Seville's nightlife. The rest of our trip would be inundated with work, so I wanted Ashley to have at least one night of fun. Our first stop was Seville's famous tablaos de Flamenco, where we were treated to a spectacular display of Flamenco dancing. We then made our way to Betis and Alfalfa streets, for some dancing. It was about three o'clock in the morning when we began our short walk back to the hotel. Though the streets were still relatively crowded, Ashley felt certain that we were being followed.

"Someone's following us," she said.

"How do you know?"

"There's a guy who's wearing a white baseball cap, who's been watching us ever since we left that last club."

"How do you know he's following us? He could be going in the same direction."

"That's possible, but I'm certain he's keeping an eye on us."

"We're armed; let's go see what he wants," I said.

"Easy Rambo; if he is following us, he's not going to admit it. I have another plan. I am going to keep walking and I want you to reverse your direction and then run to the other side of the street. It's so crowded that there is a great possibility that he won't see you but if I'm correct he will continue to follow you."

"Why?" I asked.

"If he is connected to this Garrison business then he's going to make sure that he maintains eye contact with *you*, not me, you follow me?"

"Yes. Okay, once you double back and cross the street, then what?"

"I want you to lead him down an alley?"

"An alley, won't he get suspicious, won't he think that he's being set up?"

"Set up, by you and me, the professor and his sidekick? I don't think so."

"But won't he find it strange that I've decided to walk down an alley?"

"Probably not; my guess is that if he is connected to Pratt, then he knows that you've been to Seville before, and may figure that you're taking a shortcut back to the hotel."

"Okay, but how would Pratt have knowledge that I've been to Seville before and won't our man in the baseball cap find it strange that you're no longer with me?"

"If Pratt is behind the murder of Archibald Garrison, and after the lost treasure of the Knights Templar, then I don't think it's beyond the realm of possibility that he has researched your life and our man in the cap may think that I decided to hang out a while longer. With all due respect, we're wasting time with all of this talk."

"Alright."

"Act like you're kissing me," Ashley said.

"What?"

"Act like you're kissing me. I want him to think that we are parting amicably and that you are going on back to the hotel."

"Okay."

"I'll see you in a few minutes."

I did as Ashley instructed and sure enough our man took the bait. I was beginning to sweat, but I felt somewhat comforted by the knowledge that I had a gun. I did my best to maintain a steady, but normal walking pace, as not to arouse any undue suspicion. I had no idea what Ashley was going to do once she came up behind him, but I felt secure in the fact that she would be there. The alley that I chose was deserted and it was a logical detour to take. From this vantage point the hotel loomed in the background. The moment was too surreal. The night was warm and humid; the moon full and there was a real possibility that we could be killed at any moment.

"Hey? Put your hands up slowly and don't try to run." It was Ashley and she had her gun pointed at the man's back. "Dr. Marshall check to see if he has a gun."

"Senorita what's this all about?"

"Why don't you tell us, you're the one following us?"

"Senorita, I was not following you."

"Yes you were. Look you better start talking or I'll shoot it off." She pointed the gun right between his legs.

"Okay Senorita, I do not want any trouble. I was asked to deliver this envelope to Dr. Marshall." The stranger said; his forehead beading with sweat.

"Then why didn't you just do that?" I asked.

"I was waiting for the right time to give it to you." The man was shifting nervously, his eyes darting back and forth between Ashley and myself.

"Right time, what does that mean?"

"I had to wait until we were someplace where we couldn't be seen; fortunately you chose to walk down the alley."

"And what if I hadn't come down the alley, then what?" I asked.

"I don't know Senor." The man was sweating profusely. "Please Senor I mean you and the senorita no harm, I am only a messenger."

"Who sent you?" I asked.

"That I do not know Senor, I am just a messenger. Here is the envelope, can I go now?"

"Wait."

I opened the envelope. The message was brief.

I can help you. I will send someone for you tomorrow evening. He will be dressed in a gray and black tuxedo and he has a scar on the right side of his forehead. If you want to know more, I implore you to come.

"Who is this from?" I asked the man again.

Senor, I am telling you, I don't know. I'm just a messenger, please can I go now?"

"Yes you can go." He took off running.

Carson Lowery watched the whole incident with concern and slight amusement. He didn't know what the note said, but he was certain that Marshall was getting closer to the truth. He called her immediately.

"Marshall's been contacted," Carson said.

"Which means that he's one step closer"?

"What do you want me to do?"

"Make sure he stays alive," she said.

"What about the girl?"

"Her too, she's of value to Marshall."

The double knock, followed by three single knocks, spaced out in five second intervals assured Alistair that the visitor was not an enemy. He let Timothy in.

"Marshall was contacted," Timothy said.

"Contacted, by whom?"

"I don't know. A local followed him and the girl as they were walking towards the hotel."

"How do you know he was following them?"

"Come now Alistair, this is what I do."

"Alright, get on with it". Timothy told Alistair what he saw.

"Damn"

"What is it?"

"This is not going the way I planned."

"What's more important, the plan, or the end results?"

"That's not the point."

"*It is* the point Alistair and you better not forget it, too much has been invested. Marshall and the girl have proved to be a little 'less predictable' than we thought. So we improvise, isn't that what you're always telling me?"

"Have you heard from Lydia?" Alistair asked suddenly.

"What?"

"Have you heard from Lydia?"

"No."

"I think we may have a problem."

"You don't think?" Timothy said.

"Yes I do."

"I'll take care of it."

"No not now."

"Not now?"

"No, wait until Marshall has the package."

"Are you sure you want to wait?"

"Yes."

Lydia's plane arrived in Seville the next morning at a little past eight o'clock. She knew that Alistair would have questions and rightly so. She also knew that her life was probably in danger. She smiled to herself. He will have answers soon enough. She made a call.

"I'm here," she said.

"Good," answered the female on the other end.

"Where's Marshall?"

"He and the girl have not left the hotel. Don't worry I won't let them out of my sight."

"Have you spoken to Alistair?"

"Not yet, but I will."

"I've got to go; Marshall and the girl are leaving the hotel."

"Ashley are you sure this is a good idea?" I asked as we exited the hotel and headed south.

"Look, we need to find out what Pratt is up to. I'm sure he knows that you received an envelope last night. In fact I wouldn't be surprised if it was him who sent it to you."

"But why, the note said that we would get our answers? If he already knows the answers then why would he send me a note asking me to meet him?"

"Since when did any of this make any sense?"

"Good point. Still I don't think it was him that sent the note, though I do think that he would have us followed."

"Yeah and the moment we find the information he wants he's going to kill us." She said.

"Maybe we should go to the police." I said.

"And tell them what? We don't have any evidence that Pratt had Garrison killed, nor do we have any facts to support that he wants us killed, it's all conjecture."

"So where are we going now?" I asked.

"Nowhere in particular, a little wild goose chase," Ashley said with a smile. *She was actually enjoying this.*

"What about tonight? How are we going to elude them?"

"I have a plan."

"Are you sure you're just a graduate assistant?" I couched the question in a humorous tone, but I was beginning to wonder.

"Well of course I'm not just a graduate assistant, what a silly question."

"What are you talking about?"

"Like you said, we all wear masks and we all play different roles. Being your graduate assistant is just one of them. What did you think I meant?"

"Nothing, forget it."

Twelve

"What do you mean forget it?" She asked.

"It's nothing."

"Are you feeling okay?" She asked.

"Yes I'm fine."

"Well something's on your mind and I think you should tell me, especially since it concerns me."

"It strikes me as odd that none of this stuff seems to faze you. It's as if you've done this before," I said.

"So, you're wondering if I'm who I say I am."

"The thought has crossed my mind."

"And?"

"I don't know."

"I have a confession," she said twirling her ponytail.

"Yes," I said almost afraid to hear it.

"I have done this before," she said.

"What?"

"I said I've done this many times before."

"What? How many?" I was staring at her, totally confused.

"Hundreds."

"Hundreds?" I said. She started laughing uncontrollably.

"What's so funny?" I asked, slightly perturbed. "You've just admitted to me that you're not who you say you are and that you've been involved in this kind of stuff hundreds of times, and you find that funny?"

"I am who I say I am that hasn't changed."

"Wait a minute. If you've done this before then the student persona is just a cover, correct?"

"No. I am a student and a graduate assistant."

"Then what's all of this 'hundreds' stuff?"

"When I said I've done this hundreds of times, I meant in my imagination. Do you remember your remarks about my obsession with spy novels?"

"Yes," I said relieved, but a little pissed. We're here in Seville eluding murderers and she's making *riddles*?

"Well in my mind I've lived what we're going through hundreds of times. That's why I was able to figure out what to do."

"But this is real Ashley not *fun and games!* We're talking real guns and real murders."

"Then thank God for my imagination, because without it we'd probably be dead." She said, slightly annoyed that I was angry.

"Why didn't you say so?" I asked, my anger subsiding rapidly.

"Just having a little fun, I'm sorry."

"I guess it's your time too."

"My time?"

"My father has a theory that everyone, at least one time, will experience an extraordinary event. I know this is my time and I believe it's yours as well."

"But if I've lived this in my mind, then are these set of circumstances really extraordinary for me?"

"Good question. I guess that would depend on if the extraordinary has to be physically experienced. You'll have to ask my father."

"We're being followed," she said suddenly.

"Yes I know."

"You're learning Dr. Marshall; I'll make a sleuth out of you yet."

"What do you want to do?" I asked.

"Continue what we're doing."

What we were doing was walking in a veritable maze, in hopes of tiring and confusing our pursuers. We toured the Seville Cathedral, which is the third largest in the world. From there we visited Reales Alcazares and Arabian style palace, whose original construction date is said to begin in 884. Next was the Moorish Alcazar palace. Our next stop was the Museo Provincial de Bellas Artes de Sevilla, a restored convent, which dates back to 1612. It houses some of Spain's most important art collections. From there, in succession, we led our pursuers to the Torre del Oro, the 'tower of gold', then the Museum of Navigation; the Palace of San Telmo, the Plaza de Toros de la Real Maestranza, Seville's most famous bullring; Santa Cruz, one of Seville's most fascinating and enchanting sections. It is said that every street corner has a romantic legend attached to it. With the fragrance of jasmine pervading the air and its abundance of winding gateways and courtyards, it's easy to see why. After about three hours we headed back towards the hotel, via Maria Luisa Park. I noticed him immediately, so did Ashley.

"It's the man from the alley and he's gesturing to us."

He was standing by one of the pavilions. I clutched my gun, just to reassure myself that it was still there.

"Let's make him come to us," said Ashley.

We gestured for him to come to us and he did.

"What do you want?" Ashley asked coldly.

"Senorita I am your friend. I am on your side, I do not bring trouble."

"What do you want?" she asked again.

"I was sent to arrange your transportation for tonight's meeting."

"You're lying," I said. "Instructions for transportation were included in the envelope you gave me last night. Why are you really here?"

"To warn you Senor."

"About what?"

"To be careful, no one is who they seem. You and the lovely senorita must be very careful."

"Why?" I asked, then he slumped forward, as if he were having a heart attack; but it wasn't a heart attack, blood was oozing from his back; he'd been shot. Immediately we took off running, heading north out of the park and bracing for the next round of shots, but none came. I glanced back several times, but I didn't see anyone. We didn't stop running until we'd made it back to the hotel.

"They weren't trying to kill us," Ashley said once we'd made it back into my room. I looked out of the window, gun in my hand, but I didn't see anyone out of the ordinary; just tourists with umbrellas to protect themselves from the baking sun.

"I know, if they wanted to they could have done so easily," I said retreating from the window and slumping down on the bed. I was soaking wet and my adrenaline was pumping at maximum volume.

"So what was that all about?" Ashley asked as she threw me a towel she'd gotten from the bathroom.

"I don't know, but I hope we get some answers tonight." I said.

"You still want to go?"

"We have to."

"I assumed that you wanted to head back home."

The thought occurred to me, but I couldn't leave now, despite the danger. I was on the verge of discovering *something*. Maybe it was the lost treasure, maybe it was the ancient artifact of the Cyrenaic or maybe it was the Holy Grail. Whatever it was I wanted to know and I was determined to find out. We just had to stay alive.

"After what we've been through, there's no way we're leaving here empty handed. One way or the other we're going to solve this mystery."

Timothy Black had watched the whole bizarre scene unfold in the park and after following Alex and Ashley back to the hotel he immediately went to Alistair's room.

"Alistair the man who delivered the envelope to Marshall was killed this afternoon."

"How?"

"He was talking to Marshall and the girl in Maria Luisa Park, when he was hit by a sniper."

"You know what that means?"

"Yes I do."

"What about Marshall and the girl?"

"They're okay. The shooter obviously was not after them."

"Where did Marshall and the girl go today?"

"To a bunch of tourist haunts."

"Where are they now?"

"In the hotel."

"Continue to keep an eye on them." Alistair paced the floor after Timothy left. He took a glass from the bar and clutched it so hard that it broke causing his hands to be covered with blood. He ran his index finger across his mouth, smearing blood over his thin lips. This has to be the work of the Cyrenaic he mused, who else could it be? They're trying to get me to act impulsively, to crack, but I will not be deterred, *we, the Light of Hellas will not be deterred*. He was in the bathroom cleaning his wound when his phone rang; it was Lydia.

"Where the hell have you been?" He replied angrily.

"Now, now, is that any way to speak to a lady?"

"Where have you been?"

"I had some private business that needed to be addressed."

"Why didn't you let me know?"

"My personal business does not concern you." She replied.

"Don't be coy, you know what I meant, why didn't you tell me that you had business to take care of. You know damn well that I could care less about the details of your personal life."

"My mistake, call it poor judgment."

"Are you finished with this personal business? Are you ready to get back to work?"

"Of course."

"When can you get here?" He asked.

"Where, to your room?"

"Yes, but you would have to come to Seville first," Alistair replied sarcastically.

"I'm already here."

"Already here, so your personal business was here *in Seville*?"

"Yes."

"That's quite a coincidence."

"Why do you say that?"

"It just so happens that Marshall and the girl are here as well."

"I didn't know that," she said

"I don't believe you."

"And I don't care what you believe. I came here to deal with a family matter."

"You have family in Seville? I didn't know that."

"And why should you, we're not lovers, we're not even friends. I provide a service and you pay me."

"You make it sound so impersonal my dear."

"But isn't it?"

"I suppose it is. Anyway, when can you get over here?"

"In less than a minute, I'm on the floor above you."

Lydia smiled to herself. The ability to deceive has been a skill that has been quite useful throughout her life, but she knew that one day it would catch up to her. She just hoped that today was not that day.

Kelly was worried. What the hell had Alex gotten himself into? She was tempted to cancel her appointments and catch the first available flight to Seville, but Alex assured her he would be fine. She took a long shower to calm her nerves and retreated to bed, though she knew she wouldn't be able to sleep. She turned off her night-light, when she heard a loud crash that sounded like it came from the kitchen. She grabbed the gun that she kept under her bed and slowly treaded towards the kitchen. She reached the kitchen and flicked on the light. Her sink was littered with broken glass, courtesy of a huge rock with a sheet of paper tied to it. The letters had been cut out of a magazine and read: **You have what I want and if I don't get it, you will die.**

Though visibly shaken she managed to check behind her house, but the culprit was long gone; after regaining her composure she called her friend Detective Patrick Morris and told him what happened, he was there in less than ten minutes.

"Are you okay?" He asked.

"Besides a broken window and a death threat, I'm fine," she said weakly.

"Do you have any idea what this is all about?"

She told him what was going on with Alex.

"It's possible, but the note seems too personal. Aren't you defending Carlo "the Splinter" Rizzoli?"

"Yeah, but it's got nothing to do with that"

"Why are you so sure?"

"Trust me; my guy would rather do a hundred years than snitch. He's an old-school gangster."

"Can you think of anyone who may have a grudge, a victim of someone you got off, old disgruntled boyfriend?"

"No."

"Old girlfriends of Alex?"

Kelly started to say something about Helen, but then dismissed the idea. She'd do her *own* investigation of Helen Adamson.

"No, I think this is related to Alex's project."

"Is there anywhere I or one my guys can take you?"

"I'm going to my dad's house."

"Where does he live?"

"In Riverdale."

"Is he coming to get you?"

"I didn't tell him yet. I'm okay Patrick I can drive myself."

"The hell you will. I'll have one of my guys' drive you and another will follow in your car."

"I'm okay Patrick."

"No, you're not okay. You're shaking like a leaf. Besides you could still be in danger."

"Okay. Let me take a few minutes to get some things."

Tonight Michael would transfer the package. He wasn't privy to the details, but he did know that he was one of the last guardians. Soon the package would be with the gatekeeper. He didn't understand why it was necessary to resort to such elaborate methods, when they all knew who the gatekeeper was. Why not just give it to him directly? Of course he did not verbalize his thoughts, because it was not his place to question why. He placed the package in the appointed location. He said a brief prayer, removed the sword from its sheath and completed his duties.

Ricardo found the package right where he was told it would be. He was sure that he was chosen because of his ability to remain calm under immense pressure. He was the last vestige before the transfer to the gatekeeper. Unlike the others, the package would be in his care a great deal longer. He knew that the longer he had it, the greater the likelihood the Light of Hellas would find him, but he was not worried he recited the prayer of the brotherhood: *Lord, who may dwell in your sanctuary? Who may live on your holy hill? He whose walk is blameless and who does what is righteous, who speaks the truth from his heart and has no slander on his tongue, who despises a vile man. He who does these things will never be shaken.*

Thirteen

Nightfall descended upon Seville. My nerves were on edge, a combination of fear and excitement.

"Dr. Marshall, are you ready?" Ashley asked.

"I'll be right there." I made sure my gun was secured and then stepped outside.

"Come on we have to hurry."

"What's the rush; we've got another twenty minutes."

"I know, but we have to stick to the plan, or have you forgotten?"

"No I haven't, I'm just wired up."

"Well clam down and let's go over it again. Remember we're going to walk outside and linger for about five minutes," she said.

"I still don't understand how this is going to work."

"It will, trust me."

After five minutes we were back inside.

"Now we go to your room right?" I was a ball of nervous energy.

"Yes, our guest will be expecting us." Two minutes later there was a faint knock on the door. I opened it and in walked phase two of Ashley's plan, Carmen and Oliver Rodriguez. For Five Thousand dollars the Rodriguez' agreed to put on our clothes and act as though they were us. They were to get in a limousine and the driver was to create a diversion while we snuck off to the appointed location.

"Do you think Pratt will buy it?"

"Yes. It's dark and all they'll be able to make out is the clothing."

"What about the sunglasses? Won't that look a little conspicuous at night?"

"They'll think that we're trying to disguise ourselves."

Carmen and Oliver exited as planned and they were immediately followed. Approximately fifteen minutes later a man fitting the description in the note pulled up. We were blindfolded and instructed not to ask any questions. Everything, we were told, would be made clear.

The driver was worth the two thousand we paid him. He took his pursuers on a meandering, agonizing ride through the Seville countryside until he pulled onto a cobblestone roadway, about one hundred meters long, stopping in front of a baroque styled palace. He stepped out and opened the car door for Carmen and Oliver. Alistair, Timothy and Lydia followed suit, but at a distance, just in case they were being set up for an ambush. Carmen and Oliver then walked to the entrance of the palace and opened the door, leaving it slightly ajar.

"Something's not right said Lydia. I don't think it's them."

"Of course it's them."

"Then why would they leave the door open? I think we're being set up."

"There's only one way to find out," Timothy whispered. They pushed the door open a little further and walked in. It was dark, drafty and huge, probably once the home of a king, Timothy surmised. With guns drawn they walked with their backs to the stonewalls searching for Marshall and the girl.

After a few minutes, Timothy had the eerie feeling that Lydia was right. Within seconds his suspicions were confirmed.

"You are trespassing." It was Oliver, and he was holding a sawed off shotgun. "Drop your guns, all of them. Now turn around slowly." Pratt didn't recognize the voice as belonging to Alex.

"Who are you?" Pratt asked.

"That's what I should be asking you Senor."

"Where are Marshall and the girl?" Alistair asked angrily.

"Senor, I know of no Marshall and I suggest that you vacate my home before I lose my patience."

"Let's get the hell out of here," Alistair said angrily.

Carson Lowery watched Pratt storm out of the palace; he waited until Pratt left and then he went in. After a few seconds he too stormed out. He smiled at their ingenuity, but his smile quickly faded. She was going to be pissed when she found out that he had lost them.

We finally came to a stop. Someone opened the door and we were led along what appeared to be a stone pathway. The air smelled like orange trees and lavender. Our blindfolds were removed once we were inside. It appeared as if we were in a castle. We were led to a brightly colored room that was consumed with windows. The modern furniture seemed out of place. A long table closest to the entry way was filled with food. We were told to help ourselves.

After what seemed like an hour we were led to another room and it was in stark contrast to where we had previously been. It was practically pitch black, with the only semblance of illumination coming from two tiki torches that were located at the entrance. My nostrils burned from the pungent aroma of incense and my shirt was drenched in sweat, not from fear, but from the fact that there were no windows and it was unbearably hot. Yet the thought of leaving was out of the question. We were informed that we could not leave until given permission to do so, and if we tried to the six figures dressed in black, would not hesitate to shoot. I needed water, but I dare not speak. We were told that we were not to speak until we were addressed. As we sat there, still and completely silent, I was filled with absolute horror and remorse. Not only had I let my curiosity endanger my life, but I had dragged Ashley into a situation that seemed as though the end result would be death. *Our deaths.* After what seemed like an eternity, we were given water and allowed to go to the bathroom. We were blindfolded and brought back into the room and told to remain silent. About an hour later a voice from the front of the room addressed us.

"Welcome, Dr. Marshall, Ms. Winters. I am sorry for your discomfort, but it was my way of testing your resolve," said the female voice. We didn't respond. We waited until given permission to do so. "You may speak now," she continued.

"Who the hell are you and what the hell is going on?" I said my voice a combination of fear and anger.

"Dr. Marshall calm down, I had to test your resolve."

"Test *our resolve*, what do you mean by that?" I asked.

"I needed to see if either one of you would crack."

"What?" Ashley interjected, her anger matching mine.

"It's a matter of life and death." The woman said.

"What are you talking about? Do you mean us?"

"In a manner of speaking."

"Look," I said, "I've never done well with riddles so can you get to the fucking point!"

"Patience, Dr. Marshall, you must exhibit patience. All will be revealed as it should." I thought I was going to explode.

"Is this another test?" Ashley asked suddenly. *Test? What was Ashley talking about?*

"Isn't all of life a test Ms. Winters?"

"I suppose one could look at it that way."

I was getting angrier by the second, but I realized that if there was going to be any information forthcoming it would be done on her terms.

"Wouldn't that depend on how you define test?" I asked as calmly as possible.

"I don't know," said the mysterious woman, "you tell me?"

"You have determined that this is a test for us, because you have assumed that we have never encountered circumstances like these before."

"Am I correct in my assumptions?" She asked.

"I don't know, you tell me?" I said.

"Touché," said the woman.

"That doesn't answer my question?"

"Yes you are correct."

"Am I also correct in assuming that whatever it is that you may or may not tell us, is of such vital importance, that it could spell peril and doom if the wrong person got a hold of it?"

"Why would you think that?"

"Why else would you put us through this?" I asked.

"Through what?"

"Through this cloak and dagger shit. Look, cut the spy games and tell us what the hell is going on." *So much for remaining calm, I muttered to myself.*

"I'm afraid I can't do that, but soon you'll know everything you need to."

"*Gee thanks,* Ashley don't let me forget to send this nice woman a thank you card. Oh but that would be impossible, *since I don't know your fucking name!*"

"You didn't ask me my name." The woman said.

I'm in the goddamn Twilight Zone, I muttered silently. "Are you kidding me?"

"All you had to do was ask."

"Okay, what's your name?"

"It's Louisa Garrison." For a moment I didn't say anything. My brain was transmitting signals to my mouth, but nothing came out.

"Louisa Garrison, as in Archibald's sister?"

"Yes."

Carson dreaded making the call, but she had to know.

"I lost them," he said.

"It's okay, everything will be fine."

Carson was incredulous. He stared at the receiver. "Do I have the right connection?"

"Everything's under control just get back to the hotel."

"You know where they are?"

"Just get back to the hotel."

Alistair was fuming as they drove back to the hotel. How could this be happening he wondered? How could I have underestimated Marshall?

"So what's our next move Alistair?" Lydia asked.

"We'll have to wait until he's contacted."

"But that may be too late."

"Not if I can help it."

"Where is the package now?" Lydia asked.

"With the one who is to transfer it to Marshall."

Lydia frowned. "I still don't understand why we haven't intercepted it already." Why do we have to wait until the *appointed* time? Alistair slammed his right fist into the back of the seat in front of him.

"Because it is the will of God, don't either of you understand? He has revealed to me that the brotherhood will take its rightful place at the appointed time. He has told me that we must wait until the day we are commanded to destroy the infidels. If we were to act outside of his will, all would be lost. An epic battle between good and evil will take place on that day and then and only then will we take back what is rightfully ours. So we must wait. If we act before the appointed time, we will be cursed forever."

Fourteen

Ashley and I were given a change of clothes and more water. The air conditioner was humming at full blast, dissipating the stifling heat. A million thoughts ran through my head as I tried to process what I'd just been told. *This woman was Louisa Garrison?*

"If you really are Louisa Garrison, how was Pratt able to get to your brother, but not you and your sister? And where are Archibald's wife and children?" I asked her.

"Archibald's wife and children have been safely transported to a location in the United States. As for my sister and I, let's just say we're more resourceful than my brother and that he wouldn't listen to us."

"Yes, but how were you able to get your brother's wife out of the country so quickly."

"She hasn't been in Seville for almost two months."

"So you knew Pratt was going to come after you?"

"Yes."

"Then why didn't all of you leave Seville?"

"We couldn't?"

"Why not?"

"Patience Dr. Marshall, in due time I will explain everything." *I swear if she said that one more time!*

"No, you won't be explaining anything." It was as if everything was happening in slow motion. The speaker was one of the men dressed in black.

"What the hell is this?" cried Louisa.

"Just what I said; *you* won't be explaining anything to anyone." The other men who flanked the speaker did not move.

"What are you waiting for?" yelled Louisa, "shoot him." The men didn't flinch. Then it registered to her that she had been betrayed.

"Who are you and what do you want?" she shouted.

"We're here for Marshall and the girl."

"Who are you?" I asked, trembling with fear. I was certain that this time we were going to be killed.

"Friends, Dr. Marshall." I wasn't reassured by his pronouncement of friendship.

"And why should we believe that?"

"Because we're the only ones who can keep you and Ms. Winters alive," the man said calmly.

"I don't believe you," said Ashley.

"That's understandable Ms. Winters, but you have to trust us, we're your only hope."

"Hope for what?" I asked.

"We can tell you what you want to know," the man said.

"Bullshit. That's what Ms. Garrison said."

"That's not Louisa Garrison," the man said.

"If that isn't Louisa Garrison, then who is it?" I asked.

"She's the sister of your benefactor."

"Benefactor?" I said.

"Yeah, her name is Alexandria Pratt."

"Alexandria Pratt!" I exclaimed.

"Let's go, I will explain in the car." He motioned to one of the other men to take us outside.

"Aren't you coming?" I asked, not sure why it mattered.

He ignored me and calmly motioned again that we be taken outside. In an instant the quiet stillness of the Sevillian countryside was interrupted with the sounds of gunshots. He had killed her.

"Where are you taking us?" I asked.

"We're not going to harm you."

"Let me get this straight. You and your men pose as security for this woman who claims she is Louisa Garrison, yet you say is Alexandria Pratt. You then tell us that we're coming with you, but before we leave, you kill her, and you tell us that we're not going to be harmed. By my count, in the relatively short period of time that we've been here two people have been murdered so why should we believe what you say? For all we know, that may have really been Louisa Garrison and you're working for Pratt."

"I understand your trepidation."

"Trepidation?" I responded, "It's a hell of a lot more than trepidation."

"Patience, Dr. Marshall, soon you will know everything."

"Where are you taking us?" I asked again.

"Somewhere safe."

"You said that you were here to help us and that you were friends."

"Yes I did."

"Then that means that we are free to go, right?"

"I'm afraid I can't do that."

"Just what I thought. And I guess that if we try to flee, you will kill us just like you did Louisa?"

He didn't answer.

"Well?"

"Let it go Dr. Marshall, I think his silence speaks very clearly." Ashley said.

We were taken to the airport, given two tickets back to New York and told that we would be contacted.

"Contacted?" I asked.

"You must trust me."

"Trust you?"

"Dr. Marshall, I assure you everything you need to solve this mystery will be provided to you."

"Why should I believe you?"

"Trust me."

"Trust you? You've got to be kidding?"

"Your anger is quite understandable, but when you calm down, you will see things much more clearly."

"Much more clearly? How can I see things much more clearly, when I don't know what's going on? All I know is that since I agreed to do this project, two people have been murdered, we've been followed kidnapped, and no one is who they say they are."

"Dr. Marshall, I understand your anger, but rest assured you will be protected. Soon this will be over and your life will return to normal."

"Somehow I doubt that."

"Everything will work out Dr. Marshall, its destiny," said the man.

"Destiny?"

"Yes". Said the man. "You are the gatekeeper."

"The gatekeeper of what?" I asked. I turned and he was gone.

We didn't say much during the plane ride home. Ashley fell asleep, about twenty minutes after we took off. I thought about what he said and he was right; I did want to know what this mystery was all about, despite the fact that people were being murdered. We had endured too much to turn back now.

Fifteen

"Holy Father," asked Cardinal Augustine as he and Pope Mark Peter took their regular evening stroll in the Courtyard of St. Damaso, "Do you really think this conference is going to amount to anything?"

Pope Mark Peter didn't answer right away because he understood the Cardinal's skepticism. The Council for Religious Unity, a two-year-old organization founded by Pope Mark Peter, is set to hold its first conference and its theme is "Religious Reconciliation". The Council, which is comprised of the world's great religions has been criticized as nothing but a grandstanding ploy by the Pope, a charge that hurt Mark Peter deeply. The idea for the council was borne out of the tragic events of September 11, in particular the vilification of Islam. Pope Mark Peter spent many days anguishing over the cruelty that his Muslims received and he decided that the only way the world could truly heal after such a devastating event would be to work towards unity amongst the different religions. After months of telephone calls, e-mails and meetings, the Council was assembled and in November the first conference would be held in Landon, New York.

"Yes I do Augustine. God has said so."

"But with so many different ideologies, how can there be common ground?"

"God is the equalizer my friend."

"This Landon, is it safe? Why aren't we meeting in Rome?"

"We must be seen as impartial, to hold the conference in Rome would be seen as a power play. The little hamlet we have chosen is nondescript, neutral."

"But what about the terrorist aren't we setting ourselves up for an attack?"

"God will protect us Father Augustine. He has ordained this historic gathering, he will not let harm come our way."

"With all due respect your holiness I think we're courting disaster."

"Have faith Father, November eighth will be a great day for all God's children, you will see. The air is getting brisk, let's go in."

Sixteen

Despite the danger that I was certain we faced, it felt good to be back home, and that buoyed my confidence; though I no longer had a gun because we had to leave the guns in a garbage can in Seville. I could see the headlines: *Professor and assistant arrested for trying to smuggle guns on plane to New York!*

My first inclination was to call Helen, but I didn't, and I didn't call Kelly either, despite the fact that I knew she'd been worrying the whole time we were in Seville. I know it was insensitive of me not to call her right away, but all I could think about was Helen. When I finally did call Kelly, she was pissed, and rightly so.

"It's about time you called!" She yelled, but despite her anger I could detect a sense of relief.

"I'm sorry. I was so tired from the flight that all I could think about was sleep." *I lied.*

"Sleep! Shit Alex it would have taken all of two seconds to call and say you were home. Are you telling me *you were too tired to do that!'*

'Babe I'm sorry."

"You've already said that. Look Alex I don't know what the fuck is going on with you, but I don't like it."

"For Christ's sake Kelly I was tired and I didn't call; I'm calling you now, so why are you making such a big deal out of this?"

"You know you're such an asshole." Then the line went dead. I knew I had messed up again, and I knew it was because my heart was divided. There was a part of me that wasn't concerned at all about Kelly's feelings; that part belonged to Helen, or rather the memory of her. It was that part which caused me to put my foot in my mouth once again. I called Kelly back and begged her to forgive me and she did, even though I didn't deserve it.

That evening I went to her father's house to pick her up for dinner at my parents. Kelly's dad lived alone and I suspect in loneliness, in a sprawling three-story mansion in Riverdale, an upscale section of the North Bronx. Kelly says he's never really gotten over her mother leaving him and though he puts up a good front, she suspects his business is all that really keeps him going..

"Alex, it's been a long time." He said as we walked into the living room and sat down.

"It's nice to see you Mr. Van Astor."

"Kelly's upstairs; she'll be right down." Mr. Van Astor shifted his body so that he was sitting directly in front of me, which made me nervous because I got the feeling that he thought Kelly's predicament was my fault. I decided to head him off before he had a chance to strike first.

"Mr. Van Astor, I'm sorry for getting Kelly involved in this mess."

"No need to apologize that is as long as you fix it."

"I intend to do just that."

"Well, then everything is alright." He motioned me to come closer to him, and then he whispered, "I like you Alex. I know that she can be difficult, so I empathize with you, but, if anything happens to her, and it's remotely related to you, I will kill you. Do you understand?"

"Yes sir I do."

"Good."

"What are you two talking about?" Kelly asked as she entered the room.

"Your father emphatically warned me that if anything happened to you he would kill me."

"Daddy!"

"Just apprising the good doctor of the possibilities; I've got to get to the restaurant. I'll see you in the morning, good night Alex."

"Good night sir."

"Don't pay my father any mind."

"I think he was *serious.*"

"Well nothing is going to happen to me, so it doesn't matter, right?"

"Right."

"So what's our next move?"

"Our?"

"Yes, you don't think I'm going to sit back and not help do you?"

"No, I guess not."

"What's wrong?"

"Kelly, this is serious. Three people have been murdered, someone has threatened you by throwing a rock through your window, and I have no idea what to do or why the hell I'm being called the gatekeeper?"

"We'll figure it out," Kelly said.

"How? Ashley and I have poured over materials, gone to Seville and we still don't have a clue."

"The three of us will figure it out. Now let's forget about that for tonight, you know what I mean?"

"Kelly, there's no way we're screwing in *your dad's* house."

"I know. After we leave your parent's, we're going to the Plaza."

"Unbelievable, it sounds like a plot from a Robert Ludlum novel." My mother said as I recounted Ashley and my adventures in Seville.

"Yeah mom it does, except the bullets in Seville were real."

"So what are you going to do?" Carol asked as she glanced warily at Kelly, for what seemed like the millionth time. Kelly simply smiled, which I know angered my sister. It's not that Carol has anything against Kelly; she just thinks that Helen would be better for me.

"We've got to figure out what Alexandria Pratt was trying to tell us before we were abducted."

"Alex, didn't the note you received say *I'm coming Dr. Marshall will you be my gatekeeper?*" asked Felix

"Yes."

"So then, maybe all you need to do is wait for whatever it is to come."

"But who knows when that will be." Ashley said.

"Maybe we do." I responded.

"What do you mean?"

"I get the nagging feeling that there is something that we've missed, and I think it's very simple."

"Why do you say that?" asked Richard.

"The wild goose chase that we were sent on was calculated and was done to bring us to this point. In fact I believe that whoever orchestrated it, wanted us to realize that we would not get the answers in Seville. They want us to figure it out here and they know that we can. In fact it's imperative that we do."

"Why?"

"That I haven't figured out yet, but I will."

"Maybe it's some secret plot to take over the world," said Carol sarcastically.

"That wasn't necessary Carol," said my dad.

"Well all of this sounds crazy."

"And maybe crazy will keep us all alive," he said.

"You were awfully quiet this evening, are you okay? Was it Carol and her staring?" I asked Kelly on the drive to the Plaza. She laughed slightly.

"I'm fine, just thinking about stuff."

"Stuff, you mean as in us, that kind of stuff?"

"Yeah, I'm weary and I'm tired Alex. All of my life I've been angry because of what my mom did. I have literally hated her and I have vowed never, ever to speak to her again. I haven't told you, but she's been calling the office on a regular basis, but I haven't taken any of her calls. Then there was the last fight that you and I had. I had convinced myself that I was through with you, but then I realized that you, my sister and my father are the only true constants in my life. I'm thirty-four years old and I'm tired of fighting. Am I making sense?"

"Yes."

"I know that a lot of our problems stem from my anger towards my mother. Most of the time I really wasn't mad at you, I was mad at her. I know that I will not be at peace and I won't be able to make it work with you until I'm able to forgive her; you know what I mean?"

"Yes."

"I know I've got shit with me, but I'm trying and you've got to help me."

"I will, I promise."

"That's not what I mean."

"I don't understand."

"When I said you've got to help me, what I meant was that you've got to let me know what's going on in your head. You've been acting weird lately and I don't know why. Are you seeing someone else?"

"No, of course not."

"Are you thinking about Helen?'

"Damn Kelly, why do you always have to put her in things? I told you it's been over between us for a long time."

"Well *something's* going on with you."

"It's nothing Kelly, just stress from this Pratt business, that's all."

"Bullshit Alex."

"It's just stress, honest." *Honest?* I glanced at Kelly as she looked out the window and I knew that I didn't deserve her. Despite her issues, her heart was totally committed to me and I was too much of a coward to tell her that I was torn. But if I confessed then I could lose her, and I didn't want that. I wondered if something was really wrong with me. Or was it simply a case of never falling out of love with Helen? I wanted to stop the car and scream because out of nowhere I felt an outbreak of sensory overload coming; everything going on in my life leapt into my head at the same time; Kelly, Helen, Pratt, murder, gatekeeper, Jordan, my classes, all of it was coming down on me like an avalanche and I couldn't stop it.

I met Ashley in my office the next morning around nine. It was Saturday, which meant that we would probably be the only ones in the department. After hours of reading and rereading our research and rethinking and re-discussing various points we were no closer to discovery. We were tired and weary when we heard a knock on the door.

"Who is it?"

"It's Felix."

"Felix, what are you doing here?"

"I figured you two might need some help." Then he took a piece of paper from my desk and wrote: "And I think that we should use my office."

"Why?" I mouthed.

On the same piece of paper he wrote: *I'm no expert at this, but with everything that's happened it's possible that Pratt has bugged your office.* We nodded in agreement and left.

The sudden interruption in speech could only mean one thing, Timothy Black mused. *They think there's a bug in the office.* He immediately called Alistair.

"Alex, last night you said that we were missing something, what were you thinking?" Felix asked.

"I think it has to do with a specific date."

"And you think the answer lies amongst all of this research?" asked Felix.

I was about to answer when my cell phone rang. It was a number I didn't recognize.

"Hello."

"Go to your office and look in the right hand corner of the middle drawer on the left side of your desk." The caller was a woman.

"What? Who is this?"

The caller hung up. A myriad of thoughts ran through my head; who was the caller; what the hell was she doing in my office; how'd she get in without being detected; what had she left in my office? I did as instructed and I found a single sheet of paper and on it were a string of words, which didn't make sense. It appeared to be some sort of riddle. *Fucking great!* I cursed silently.

The typeset was old English text and read:

𝔙irtue is now expected only because man rewards enlightenment. 𝔒ne answers, correctly, truthfully via obligation.

"What does it say?" Felix and Ashley asked in unison. I showed them the paper.

"What is this supposed to mean?" Ashley exclaimed.

"My sentiments exactly." I sighed. "It doesn't make sense; *Virtue is now expected only because man rewards enlightenment. One answers, correctly, truthfully via obligation.* What the hell is that supposed to mean?" I said futilely.

"It's some kind of code." Felix said stating the obvious.

"No shit Sherlock." I answered in exasperation.

"No, you're in deep shit Sherlock, if you don't figure out what this means."

Ashley started to say something, but she didn't and I think it's because she thought there was going to be tension between Felix and I, but it wasn't. Sarcasm has a healthy place in the equation of our relationship, it's a product of our personalities and neither one of us take the other's remarks personally, but I could see how Ashley would think otherwise, so I eased any discomfort she might feel.

"Everything's fine Ashley, Felix and I are always like this."

"No problem." She replied. "I guess it's going to be a long night trying to solve this riddle; I'll order pizza."

"You two will have to work on it, I can't stay." I said.

"Can't stay? What's more important than this?" Felix asked quizzically.

"I promised Kelly we'd go out and if I cancel, well let's just say I'll be going from the doghouse to the shithouse, excuse my language Ashley." She laughed.

"But I'm sure she'd understand." Ashley replied.

"Kelly?" Felix, hissed as he said the words, "not in a million years; go on papi, Ashley and I will take a stab at it."

"Thanks guys."

I didn't have much to say on the ride into the city; my mind was consumed with a multitude of thoughts, in particular the cryptic riddle that was left in my office.

"Are you thinking about the riddle, you know you could have stayed, I'd have understood?" Kelly said as we headed south on the West Side Highway, on our way to meet my sister and Richard for dinner and a movie. I wanted badly to stay and work on the riddle, but the riddle and the Cyrenaic were only a cog in my life and despite the fact that it was an important cog; I didn't have the luxury of putting the other cogs on hold. As much as I wanted to believe Kelly, the fact remains that if I would have chosen the riddle over her, she'd been hurt, and I owe it to her not to allow that to happen. On the ride to her father's house and on the way to meet Carol and Richard I found myself wondering what choice I would have made had it been Helen and we'd been having problems. As much I'd like to think that Helen would have been okay with my staying, I know that's a falsehood borne out of romanticism, an idealistic picture of a woman who has been gone for years.

"Yes I am thinking about the riddle, but I was also thinking about what you said the other night."

"So you're going to finally tell me what's going on?"

"There's nothing going on Kelly. I was talking about what you said about making changes in your personality."

"I wouldn't say it's a change in my personality."

"No?"

"No. It's more a change in how I want my relationships to be. My personality is fine per se."

"But doesn't your personality determine how you interact with others?"

"Yes it does, but I don't think it's necessary to overhaul it. I think it's more a process of fine-tuning it. For example, I think there are aspects of my personality that have been detrimental in my personal relationships, but are absolutely necessary for my line of work."

"I can see that."

"But that same manner that I use in the courtroom has not helped me in my personal life."

"It's helped to keep the wolves away."

"That's true, but it hasn't helped *our* relationship." I didn't respond immediately. "What's wrong?" she said.

"Nothing's wrong, it's just difficult to fathom that just a few weeks ago we were at each other's throats and now things are so different. It's as if things changed overnight."

"So?"

"So, that's not how it's supposed to happen. People just don't change they grow into change. It's a process that takes time. Things have happened so fast for us that I'm afraid it's too good to be true."

"Alex, sometimes things are what they are."

"What do you mean?"

"There isn't a generic formula that prescribes how change will occur. Everyone is different. I woke up and decided that I was tired of the way my life was going. When a person is fed up with something they simply stop doing whatever that thing is. There isn't anything mystical about change and it doesn't happen the same way for all people. I knew what I needed to change. It wasn't necessary for me to go through a long drawn out process of analysis. I have known for years why I've acted the way that I have, but I never felt secure enough to step out of my comfort zone. But then I made the decision that I was fed up. I looked at my life, didn't like the path that I was treading and decided to get off. It's that simple. Now does that mean that it won't be a struggle? Of course not! You and I will argue again and we will disagree, but now instead of running I'm going to stay and deal with whatever it is. That's what's changed. I was tired of running. Because you see, I wasn't running from you, I was running from the memories of my mother."

"And she doesn't haunt you anymore?"

"No."

"I love you," I said. And I'm still in love with Helen I wanted to say, to purge my soul, but of course I didn't.

Richard and Carol were already waiting for us at Armante's. We were seated and I was actually looking forward to the evening, riddle and all, of which I was about to fill them in on, when I saw him. I closed my eyes and then reopened them just to make sure that it wasn't a mirage. It wasn't. It was the man we saw murdered in Seville and he was headed towards the men's room. I must have been a sight, because Kelly asked me if I was all right.

"Alex what is it, you look as if you've seen a ghost."

"I just need to go to the bathroom."

"Richard go with him," said Carol.

"It's okay Richard; I think I'm coming down with something. I'll be fine." I rushed off to the men's room.

He was standing there as if he were waiting for me.

"You, what are you doing here? I thought you were dead? I saw you get shot."

"You saw what we wanted you to see Dr. Marshall."

"But you went down right in front of us, and I saw the blood in the back of your head."

"An act."

"Why?"

"In time you will know all."

"How did you know that I was here?"

He chuckled. "Come now Dr. Marshall, do you think that we would leave *this* up to chance?"

"Leave what up to chance?"

"I want you and the young lady to meet me at this address tomorrow afternoon, and please come alone."

"Why should we trust you?"

"I'm on your side."

"I don't believe you, but we'll be there."

"Wise choice and rest assure you will not be harmed."

"Rest assured, are you kidding me?"

"I will see you tomorrow."

He smiled and walked out, completely ignoring Richard.

"I said I was all right." I snapped at Richard, as I splashed my face with water, for what reason I'm not sure.

"I know," said Richard, "but when you didn't come out right away. Are you sure you're okay?"

"Yes."

"Who was that guy?"

"What guy?"

"The one who just left, I know that you were talking to him."

"No I wasn't."

"Alex, this is me you're talking to."

"I know, but the less you know the better. I don't want to get you involved."

"Somehow I'm sure that's no longer a reality," He said as he held the door open for me, ushering me out with a languid wave of his left hand.

Kelly and I rode back to my house in silence; she was pissed that I was still going to meet with the "dead man". Despite her anger she agreed to stay overnight. When we reached the front of the house, I noticed a manila folder on the steps and on the outside of the folder was a picture of a gold tipped sword, and underneath the picture were the initials: L.S.

Seventeen

I picked up the folder and looked inside, but it was blank. I ran to the edge of the walkway and looked up and down my street, but I didn't see anyone, though it wasn't as if I expected to. Kelly and I walked around the back of the house, but we didn't find anyone or anything. We returned to the front of the house where I cautiously inserted the key in the lock.

"Alex, I don't think that we should go in," Kelly said as I turned the key.

"There's no one in here."

"How can you be so sure?"

"Because the alarm is still set and I think whoever left this package is a friend not a foe."

"They could have disabled your alarm and then reset it."

"I doubt it."

"*You doubt it?* Aren't these the same people who've already murdered two people?"

"That's Pratt; whoever left this folder can't be working with Pratt."

"Can't be? You don't know who is who, so really I don't think you're in a position to say who can and can't be doing anything."

"Okay, okay, I get your point. Just stay with me."

We tiptoed through the house nervously checking every room, and to our relief we didn't encounter any surprises; nor did anything appear to have been touched.

Lydia watched them from across the street. She wanted to make sure they saw the folder. It was only a matter of time, she thought.

Kelly and I retreated to the living room. "Didn't your detective friend say that the woman next door to you killed herself with a gold tipped sword?"

"Yeah he did, what are you thinking?"

"I'm not sure, but here's this picture of the same type of sword with this note attached; this has got to be related to the Pratt project."

"You think?"

"Ha, ha, very funny, smart ass. It's got to be related, but how?"

"I don't know. I remember you saying that you thought the girl probably belonged to some cult," she said.

"I don't see the connection with the Cyrenaic."

"It may not be that farfetched."

"What do you mean?" I asked.

"I'm no expert, but wouldn't you say that secret societies are really nothing but cults in disguise."

"I guess there are similarities but how does that help me?"

"That my dear is for you to find out."

"And how do you propose I do that?"

"Find out who L.S. is."

"That's easy, who else could it be but Lydia Sinclair; but why would she help me when she's working for Pratt?" I was talking to the air. Kelly had fallen asleep, a tired, ten decibel snoring kind of sleep. I slowly moved her head from my lap, turned off the lights in the living room and walked outside to my backyard. The air was still, unseasonably humid for an October evening. I couldn't believe what was happening. For years I'd searched for the mysteries of the Cyrenaic; for the ancient artifact and I'd painfully come up empty and yet now clues were falling into my lap. Why? I wondered. I read the riddle again, and again, and again and looked at the picture, again and again. My back felt funny, stiff and I thought it was part of my dream, a wonderful dream filled with birds and bacon and eggs, but I wasn't dreaming. It was morning; I'd fallen asleep in a patio chair; that's why my back was stiff. The birds and the sweet aroma of Kelly's cooking had woken me up.

Later that morning I called Felix and Ashley and asked them to come to the house. Kelly wanted to stay and help, but with her mafia trial beginning in less than a week she had work to do.

"He's not dead!" Ashley exclaimed when I told them about my encounter at Armante's.

"No and he wants you and I to meet him this afternoon in the city."

"Did he say why?"

"No, just that he's on our side."

"There's nothing we can do about that now, so let's get cracking on the riddle." Felix interjected.

"There's something else that happened last night," I replied.

"What?" He asked. I showed them the package that was on my doorstep.

"L.S., it's got to be Lydia Sinclair. But why would she help us, it doesn't make sense?" Ashley asked, as she tightened her ponytail holder.

"Who says she's helping?" I countered, trying to stretch out my lower back.

"You okay?" Felix asked.

"Okay? Oh, my back. Yeah, I fell asleep on the deck while trying to decipher the riddle."

"Why else would she do it?" Ashley said.

"Maybe it's a set up of some kind." I replied, though I was just as much in the dark as she was.

"What about tonight, do you think that's a set up as well?"

"I don't know what to think."

"What's first the riddle or the folder from L.S.?" Felix asked.

We chose the folder.

"Do you think Lydia's folder is connected to the woman who killed herself with a sword in New York City?" Ashley asked.

"It's possible, but there's nothing to indicate that the Cyrenaic were sword worshippers." I said.

"But what if there were similar suicides." Felix chimed in.

"Even if there has been more, I still don't see the connection?" I said.

"I've got a feeling that the two are connected Alex. Suicides with gold-tipped swords are not the normal method for offing oneself." We all chuckled.

"Okay, but how are we going to find out if there have been others?" I asked.

"Maybe we'll get lucky and find something in one of the news stories." Ashley interjected.

We left the job of researching news articles to Felix. It was one o'clock and Ashley and I were supposed to meet the "dead" man from Seville at a mid-town Manhattan restaurant at three. We gave Felix the address and told him to call the police if he didn't hear from us by a specified time. We took the train. Ashley thought that we should drive, but I figured that if we had to make a quick exit, it would be easier to elude our pursuers by cab and train.

The "dead" man chose a nondescript steak joint on 54th Street. It was relatively crowded, which was a comfort, though I reminded myself that we were in the driver's seat, so the likelihood of him trying anything was remote. He was not alone. With him was the man that "rescued" us from Alexandria Pratt.

"You were wise to come Dr. Marshall," said the "dead" man.

"What do you want with us?" asked Ashley.

"Relax Ms. Winters we are not here to harm you. If we wanted to kill you, you would have been dead by now."

"Relax? I don't need to rehash what we've been through, do I? Maybe this is normal stuff for you, but I'm just a fucking student, so don't tell me to relax."

"Look", I asked, "why did you ask us to come here?"

"To give you this." He handed me a sheet of paper with a list of cities.

"What is this?"

"*This* is the key to the mystery."

"This list here?"

"Yes."

"You people, whoever you are, are crazy," I said.

"You're a smart man Dr. Marshall. Let your emotions dissipate and then look at the list, you'll figure it out." They stood up to leave.

"*This,*" I said "is the reason why you had us meet you?"

"Yes."

"So if we figure out the meaning of the list then we will understand *everything*?"

"Just about."

"Just about, what does that mean?"

"We must go now," he said, "I will be in touch."

"Who are you?" I asked.

"One of the last."

"One of the last what?" They left, and we sat there staring blankly at each other.

"So," Felix asked when we returned to my house some hours later.

"So what?" I replied.

"What happened, what did you find out?" I tossed the sheet of paper at him, but it flew aimlessly though the air; symbolic of how I was feeling at the moment.

"It's a list of cities, what does it mean?"

"He wouldn't tell us; all he said was that it was the key to the mystery."

"Well let's get to work." Felix said.

"Not here. I think we'd be safer at Kelly's father's house."

Now armed with the list, the three of us piled into my car and headed down to Riverdale to Kelly's father's house. Why I thought it would be safer there was beyond my comprehension. I guess the determining factor was Mr. Van Astor himself. His pronouncement that he would kill me if anything happened to Kelly; left a lasting and frightening impression. So I figured anyone who could casually whisper that he could kill, without blinking seemed like a safe bet to me.

The list contained the names of eight cities. There did not appear to be any order or rhyme or reason to the choices, just eight random cities.

"This list doesn't make any sense," Ashley said.

"Read them again," I asked her.

"They are London, Caracas, Montreal, Genoa, Havana, Seville, New York City, and Landon."

"What do these cities have in common?" I asked.

"I can't see a link," said Felix.

"Come on guys, there has to be something that we're missing."

"Alex we've examined every possible connector, from geography to political affiliations, and we've come up with nothing."

"I know, but there's something and it's right under our noses."

"Dinner's served," said Mr. Van Astor. He had prepared a scrumptious meal of lamb with mint sauce, garlic mashed potatoes, and spinach sautéed in a white wine sauce; it was just what we needed.

"I've been listening to you guys and the reason why you're having a hard time is because your process of deduction is all wrong."

"What do you mean Mr. Van Astor?" asked Ashley.

"Please, call me Nicholas. What I mean is that you all are working backwards."

"Backwards?"

"Instead of looking for the simplest and most logical connection, you're looking for the most complex. That's the wrong approach? What you should be doing is starting from the premise that the answer you're looking for is the one that is the simplest."

"But wouldn't that be too easy?" I asked.

"No. Look, in the restaurant business I have always operated from the notion that the customers want the basics, in America, that means meat and potatoes. As long as my customers know that the staples are there, then they may be willing to branch out and try something different, something a little more complex to the palette. Do you see what I'm getting at? Human beings operate from the simple to the complex, not the other way around."

"So how will that work for us?" I asked.

"What you have to do is look at the overall nature of this thing and ask yourselves how does the list relate? Then you need to take into account when you received the list and how it relates to anything else that you've received."

We spent hours formulating lists and searching the Internet, but coming up with nothing. I suggested we try to decipher the riddle and come back to the list.

"I don't think this is meant to be a literal interpretation." Felix said after reading it aloud.

"I agree," Ashley said. "I mean it doesn't make any sense, not as a whole statement '*Virtue is now expected only because man rewards enlightenment. One answers, correctly, truthfully via obligation.*'" The second sentence standing alone is clear in its meaning."

"That's true. The second sentence is talking about how one tells the truth only because he feels obligated to do so. While it makes sense, I don't see the link; and that first sentence, I don't know what that means." I said.

"That's because you can't look at its literal meaning," Felix said tossing his hands in the air in mock exasperation.

"Enlighten us Felix," I said as I walked to the kitchen to put on a pot of coffee.

"Riddles are never meant to be interpreted literally, that's why they're called riddles. I know I'm stating the obvious, but many people are tripped up by this fact."

"But what about what Kelly's dad said, that we need to look at this from the simplest position?" Ashley asked.

"What do you mean?" Felix asked.

"Maybe this riddle is supposed to read in the literal, maybe it's that simple." She said.

"I don't see it in this case." Felix said.

"Then what is it?" I asked.

We spent the next few hours examining the riddle from every possible angle, referencing everything from Dan Brown novels to Ellery Queen mysteries, when the answer suddenly came to me. It wasn't an epiphany; it came to me as I recalled something one of my students said in class.

"Dr. Marshall, I think the Bible is full of hidden codes and meanings, I don't think it's as straightforward as you suggest, isn't that why this course is called 'Codes and Conundrums' " Christine Carmichael offered with her addictive one hundred watt volt smile.

"You have a point Christine, but to suggest that there are cryptic clues in the scriptures, I just don't see it. The closest example I see could be Jesus and the parables, but as you all know, he explains the meaning behind each one, so exactly what are you talking about?"

"The Bible is one big ancient riddle full of hidden codes."

"How Christine, for God's sakes, how?" Ryan Laskey, my favorite sleepy-eyed philosophy major shouted in mock frustration; everyone laughed.

"Laskey be quiet." Christine offered in retort.

"Mr. Laskey's point is well taken Christine. You've yet to show us how."

"It's pretty complex and I've yet to work it out, but I believe that if you take the first letters of each sentence that Jesus uttered, it will spell out phrases that would give us deeper insight into Jesus' message." The entire class buzzed with curiosity and disbelief.

"That's interesting Christine. What have you come up with so far?"

"Like I said I'm still working on it and when I do you'll be the first to know."

"I can't wait." Laskey replied, to more laughter.

I ran into Mr. Van Astor's study, which was adjacent to the living room, where we were situated, suddenly and without a word and I'm sure Felix and Ashley had thought I'd gone mad. I returned with sheets and sheets of copy paper.

"What's this for?" Felix asked, looking me over to see if I'd bumped my head or something.

"I know what we need to do to figure out the riddle." I said excitedly.

"What Dr. Marshall?" Ashley asked. I told them about Christine Carmichael.

For the rest of the night, amidst coffee, mountain dew and chocolate donuts we worked out thousands of word variations, when I solved it.

"I've got it." I said exhaustedly. On probably paper number six hundred I wrote:

Now Only Virtue Is Expected Man Because Rewards Enlightenment.

One Correctly Truthfully Answers Via Obligation.

"This doesn't make any sense papi." Felix said.

"Perhaps if I do this it will." I replied with a half smile.

<u>N</u>ow <u>O</u>nly <u>V</u>irtue <u>I</u>s <u>E</u>xpected <u>M</u>an <u>B</u>ecause <u>R</u>ewards <u>E</u>nlightenment.

<u>O</u>ne <u>C</u>orrectly <u>T</u>ruthfully <u>A</u>nswers <u>V</u>ia <u>O</u>bligation.

"The underlined letters spell Noviembre Octavo; Spanish for November Eighth," Felix said. "So, what does it mean?"

"I think it's the day I'm supposed to receive the information."

"But if that's true, why didn't the person who left the riddle, just say so, what was the point in being so mysterious?" Felix asked, the combination of lack of sleep and too much caffeine adding a noticeable edge to his voice.

"It makes sense," Ashley interjected. "From the start everything about this whole thing has been mysterious."

"Ashley's right. Now we know, or think we know when the information is supposed to be transferred to me, the big question is what's in it?" Ashley had a gleam in her eye.

"It's not the lost treasure of the Templar Knights." I said.

"We don't know that for sure." Ashley said smiling.

"She's right Alex."

"Are you crazy too Felix?" I said with a chuckle. "Look, Ashley may be right, but I think we need to press on just in case she's wrong."

"Okay, but I think I'm right," Ashley smiled.

"While you two are debating the lost treasure, we need to get back to the list."

The sun was beaming through Mr. Van Astor's living room window when we figured out the meaning of the list, or rather Ashley had. Felix and I had fallen asleep, the product of advanced age. Though we were both only thirty-eight, we were no match for Ashley's twenty something youthfulness. She pressed on while we slept. It was the combination of the sun and Ashley's excited exclamation "I've got it" that woke both of us. I had that nasty need to brush my teeth taste in my mouth and I needed a shower, so I was anxious to hear what she had to say.

"What?" we both asked groggily.

"I've linked the eight cities."

"How?" I asked padding to the kitchen to pour myself a glass of apple juice, in an attempt to extricate the unpleasant taste from my mouth.

"In each of these cities I bet there was a suicide like the one that happened next door to Ms. Van Astor, and I'm sure they're linked to the information you're supposed to receive on November 8."

"How ?" I asked.

"I bet if we look up when these suicides took place each one occurred on either the eighth of that particular month or on a date that allowed for some sort of combination that resulted in the number eight."

"Okay, but that still doesn't explain how the suicides are connected to what Alex is supposed to receive on the eighth, and even if they are connected how would Sir Arthur have made provisions to leave the information to *Alex?*"

"That's easy. I believe that Sir Arthur was the last one to live and that he left instructions for this information to be passed down, but not to be revealed until 500 years later." Ashley said.

"That sounds good, but it begs a lot of questions," I interjected.

"Such as?"

"Sir Arthur purportedly wrote this information 500 years ago, even if the papers were stored away, they would be nothing but dust by now. Secondly, what happened to the bodies of the other members in the brotherhood?"

"As for the bodies, he either burned them or buried them in a remote area."

"But how could he have buried all of those bodies without anyone knowing?"

"Then he must have burned them." She added matter-of-factly, as if she were discussing picking a movie.

"What about the papers?"

"Since he left instructions for the papers to be passed down he probably also instructed that each caretaker re-transcribe them so that they would always be fresh."

"That explains that," said Felix, "but what about the suicides? How are they related to the information?"

"We've got eight cities on the list with Landon being the last, right?" I said.

"Yes," Felix replied.

"As far as we know there hasn't been a suicide in Landon yet, right?"

"Right."

"Okay, so what we suspect so far is that there have been seven of these suicides in seven of the cities on the list. Landon is the last city. On November 8th we believe I am supposed to receive some valuable information, right?"

"Okay, go on."

"Now from all accounts this information is extremely valuable, so much so, that our friend Alistair Pratt created a ruse about a book project, so that he could solicit my services. During the course of this project at least two people have been murdered."

"Alex we know all of this, what are you getting at?"

"I'm almost there. Sir Arthur knew that this information was so powerful that he wanted to make sure that every precaution was taken to get it to the person designated to receive it."

"But Dr. Marshall, he was alive five hundred years ago, unless he is Jesus himself, there is no way he could have predicted that you would be born, so how can you say that he was making those precautions for you?" Ashley said, adjusting and readjusting her ponytail.

"I don't know, and I don't know if it really matters, what does matter is it's supposed to come to me."

"Okay, but are you saying that for five hundred years it lie dormant?"

"Yes, only to be transferred to the next caretaker for the purpose of re-transcribing."

"Doesn't it seem highly illogical that someone in that chain didn't take the information and use it for his own purposes?" Felix said.

"Not if the caretakers were devout followers of the order."

"You mean you think the Cyrenaic are still active?"

"Yes and I think this is the moment they've been waiting for."

In a matter of minutes we were able to get the dates for each suicide and they were all somehow correlated to the number eight.

"What do you make of all of these gold tipped suicides?" Ashley asked.

"Maybe Sir Arthur wanted to take extra careful precautions, so as soon as the information is passed to the next person, the prior holder kills himself. Like a deadly relay game."

"Why would someone be willing to take his life for a five hundred year old order?"

"Devout belief and obedience," I said with a half smile.

"So what we're saying is that the person that is supposed to deliver the information to you is going to kill himself, right in front of you?"

"That's not going to happen," I said.

"How are you going to stop it?"

"I don't know, but I will."

"Guys, we still don't know what's in the information," reminded Felix.

"I think I know who does," said Ashley.

"Who?" Felix asked her.

"L.S."

"Lydia Sinclair?"

"She works for Pratt; she only knows what he tells her." I interjected.

"That's what she wants you to think." Ashley said.

"How can you be so sure?"

"Just call it gender familiarity."

"What?" I asked.

"No disrespect Dr. Marshall, but you wouldn't get it in a million years," Ashley replied. I called Lydia and asked her to meet me later that evening at Armante's.

Alistair was anxious, and he didn't like the feeling. Lydia had phoned him about an hour ago telling him that Marshall wanted to meet with her. He couldn't fathom why. He knew that Marshall had figured out the book project was a ruse, so he wouldn't want to meet with Lydia to compare research. His anxiety merely confirmed his concerns about Lydia and reaffirmed what he needed to do once this was all over.

I don't know why I decided to meet with Lydia. Sure it was probably her that left the folder on my steps, but so what? She worked for Pratt, why on earth would she be truthful?

"Good evening Alex."

"Good evening Lydia."

"It seems so long ago that we were here, when in actuality it has only been a couple of weeks."

"A lot can happen in two weeks", I said.

"Yes it can. Why did you want to see me?" she asked.

"I want to know why you left the folder."

"I want to help you Alex."

"So you admit to leaving the folder?"

"I admit to wanting to help you," she said.

"Why do you want to help me?"

"Because you need it."

"And your boss approves?"

"My boss wants me to help."

"Your boss wants to help? He tried to kill Ashley and me."

"Did he really?"

"Are you serious?"

"Think about it, *when* has he attempted to take either you or the girl's life?"

"I know what I know." I said.

"And what else do you *know?*"

"Archibald Garrison, I *know* he had him murdered and I *know* that he sent that threatening note to my girlfriend."

"You *know*? What proof do you have?"

"My intuition is proof enough."

"Alex, you've been around enough lawyers to know that won't hold up in court."

"Don't patronize me."

"I'm not, I am just pointing out the facts."

"I'm convinced that you know what's going on, all of it."

"I'm flattered, but I only know as much as Alistair tells me; as far as I know I am here to help him write a book."

"Lydia cut the bullshit; we both know that's not why he hired me."

"That's what I was told."

"So that's how you want to play this?"

"Play what?" Lydia felt guilty but she couldn't tell him what she knew, not yet. She took solace in the fact that soon he would know and *understand* everything.

"You're wasting my time." I said goodbye and headed home, frustrated, angry and a bit scared. November eighth was looming around the corner and I had no idea what was to transpire on that day, if anything at all; which is all supposition, because I couldn't say for certain that I'd really solved the meaning of the riddle. On the drive home I found that I was thinking of Helen and Kelly, interchangeably; it was like being caught between Scylla and Charbodis, the proverbial rock and a hard place. Why Scylla and Charbodis came to mind at that moment I couldn't fathom. I also couldn't fathom why it suddenly dawned on me that my life has always revolved females. My sister protected me; my mother sanctioned anything I did; my sister introduced me to Helen; Helen was the first love of my life and she replaced the lustful attraction I had for pert breasted Taylor Wallace; Helen, or lack of Helen, was the reason I initially chased the myth of the Cyrenaic's years ago; Kelly, is well Kelly, and yet I can't extricate myself from her presence; Helen is back in the picture, literally and figuratively; then there's Lydia Sinclair, Ashley and now Jordan Nelson; women everywhere. I pulled in front of my house, turned off the ignition and sat, just sat, in complete silence, contemplating, what someone in my situation should be contemplating and not figuring out a damn thing.

Lydia left the restaurant shortly after Alex and walked across the street to her car. She immediately called Alistair.

"What did he want?" asked Alistair.

"He wanted to know why you're trying to kill him."

"What?"

"Don't worry I diffused it."

"Anything else?"

"He wanted to know what's *really* going on."

"What did you say?"

"I told him that as far as I knew you want research for your book."

"I know he didn't believe you, did he?"

"No, but he let it go."

"Anything else?"

"No."

Alistair was not pleased with Lydia's behavior, but he dismissed her as something that would be dealt with later. He learned as a young man that no one, absolutely no one could be trusted. When he was twelve his father, recited to him a Sufi proverb concerning trust: *Pick up a bee from kindness, and learn the limitations of kindness.* Alistair has governed his life on the basis of that simple proverb. The bee brings the sweetness of honey, but her sting is deadly, therefore you must approach her with all defenses intact, otherwise you will die. He was too smart to let himself be stung by Lydia; too smart to let her or anyone stand in the way of his destiny.

The wheels were in motion and everything was on course for the eighth. His sources had confirmed that the Council for Religious Unity would indeed be meeting in Landon on the eighth. He chuckled at the arrogance of these men, the so-called spiritual fathers of mankind. How, he mused could they really think that in a world consumed with deceit, lies, hypocrisy, back room deals, of which the church, the mosque and the synagogue were not immune, that their plans wouldn't be betrayed for a few shillings? Fools; are they that pious that they believe there was only one Judas Iscariot. Oh well, Alistair mused, as he peered out of his window and watched the trees as they swayed in Central Park, their arrogance, only makes my task that much easier. He paused for a moment to think about all that would be achieved. *To power and truth!*

Eighteen

My annoying clock radio blared signaling that it was time to get up; I was back at my house. Kelly's dad said we could stay with him for as long as we liked and as much as I felt safe there, I knew I needed to be at home. November eighth was tomorrow and I needed to be home because I was certain the information would be delivered there. I glanced over at Kelly's angelic figure and asked God to keep her safe. I showered and dressed, then woke Kelly, who refused to let me stay in the house by myself. I walked down the hall and knocked on the guest room door. 'I'm already up said Ashley'. She also refused to let me stay in the house by myself. I told you it all comes back to women.

November eighth was also the day of my high school reunion. At one point I actually looked forward to attending, but now I didn't want to. When I asked Kelly to go I hadn't been pining away for Helen like I am now. Now with Helen certain to be there, and Kelly excited about going, I was courting disaster.

"If I go to the reunion I may miss delivery of the information." I said, though I knew a few hours at the reunion wouldn't make a difference. The real reason I didn't want to go is I didn't want Kelly and Helen in the same place together. It wasn't Kelly I was worried about; it was myself; I was afraid my conflicting feelings, would cause me to do something stupid.

As I watched Kelly cooking breakfast I wondered what the hell was wrong with me? Why was I still fantasizing about Helen, when she hadn't shown the slightest interest in rekindling our relationship?

"Alex, don't worry about the information; whoever wants you to have it will make sure you get it; if it's as important as you seem to think, then going to your reunion will not be a deterrent." She said as she flipped a pancake.

"Yeah Dr. Marshall the reunion will be a good thing for you." Ashley added much to my dismay.

"How can you two think about partying at a time like this?"

"Dr. Marshall, everything is going to be fine," said Ashley.

"How can you be so nonchalant?" I asked her.

"Because I'm not worried about tomorrow, everything will work out, that's why you should go to the reunion."

"Is there something you're not telling me?"

"Not at all, I just happen to believe that good always defeats evil. It's ordained by God."

"I didn't know you were a believer."

"I haven't been going to church like I should and I've been doing some other stuff that I shouldn't, but I know the story, and I believe it, I just need to practice it."

"If you believe then why are you putting that gun in your book bag?" I asked with a chuckle.

"God didn't say we shouldn't be prepared."

"But David fought Goliath with a slingshot," said Kelly

"Yeah well there weren't any guns back then." We roared with laughter.

We finished breakfast and headed out of the house on our way to campus.

❖ ❖ ❖

The Landon Inn is a quaint little hotel, located in the heart of downtown. Ricardo was impressed with Landon. I could live here, he thought. He checked in, making small talk with the attractive attendant. The lobby was empty and she was the only one at the desk.

"Are you a musician?" the woman asked him.

"A musician?"

"Yes, that looks like a musician's case you have in your hand."

"Oh that. Yes I play the saxophone, perhaps I can serenade you." The woman blushed.

"You will be in room 317. Is there anything else that *I* can do for you, Mr. Ricardo?"

"No, not know. Why don't you ring me tomorrow when your shift is over and I'll play something for you?"

"Why not tonight?"

"I have an important meeting tomorrow morning and I need to be rested, if you know what I mean?"

"Yes I do."

"So I will see you tomorrow?"

"You can count on it."

Ricardo placed his luggage and the elongated case on the bed. He lamented the fact that he would not get a chance to serenade the beautiful attendant, but duty called. He was the last link to the gatekeeper, and he had to stay focused.

The woman exited the plane and was taken aback by the warm November sun. She never remembered New York being this warm, this time of year. She cleared customs and was whisked to a waiting limousine. She dialed the number.

"I'm here."

"Everything's arranged," said Carson Lowery.

Jordan let the shower massage her body, toweled off and then slid effortlessly into a lime green pantsuit. She reached under her bed for her shoes and felt the cold steel of her .44 Magnum, and she recalled the weasel that sold it to her. It was three years ago at a remote roadside gun haberdashery twenty miles north of San Diego.

"That's a big gun for such a little girl," said the store's proprietor, a pot bellied, sweat drenched character with green beady little eyes, which traversed from Jordan's breasts to her ass.

"And I guess now you're going to tell me that you have just the right sized gun," she said menacingly. The tone of her voice and the look on her faced scared the hell out of him. The man had read about evil, had heard about it, but had never seen it that is until she walked into his shop.

"Miss I apologize, I was just having a little fun. That will be one hundred and fifty dollars."

Jordan threw the money at him and walked out.

I should have killed him she thought as she retrieved the gun and placed it in her bag. *"And what good would that have done,"* asked the voice? Shut up will you, just shut up! Jordan replied.

What are you going to do with that gun Jordan? Shut up, she told the voice, snapping herself back to the present. She glanced at herself in the mirror and snatched her keys off the counter. I'm entitled to what's mine. *Yours?* The voice asked her. But Jordan ignored the voice because tomorrow all questions would be answered for *everyone*.

This was the first time Kelly had attended one of Alex's classes and she found the back and forth to be amusing. Though she thought Alex was smart, she didn't believe it took a great deal of intelligence to brainwash impressionable young minds. Now convincing a jury to let a person off who is obviously guilty, that took intelligence. But as she watched what took place she realized that what he did was not as easy as she thought. As they walked to Felix's office she told him so.

"Dr. Marshall I have a new found respect for what you do."

"Do you now?"

"Yes."

"Now you see it's not just a matter of standing up there and running off at the mouth. It takes a certain amount of skill and charisma, which your boyfriend obviously possesses."

"My boyfriend, I thought we were talking about you," she said.

"Good morning Dr. Marshall, Ms. Winters," said Grace Waters, eyeing the three of us suspiciously, particularly Kelly. "Why are you going into Dr. Arroyo's office?"

"Hello Mrs. Waters," said Ashley.

"Good morning Grace. My computer has crashed and I left my lap top at home, so Felix has graciously allowed me to use his office."

"Oh I see." I expected her to move on, but she stood there with this perturbed look on her face. "Where are your manners Dr. Marshall?" She was waiting for me to introduce Kelly. I thought I had.

"I'm sorry Grace; this is my girlfriend Kelly Van Astor."

"I've seen you before. You're the lawyer that's representing that Mafia boss, aren't you?"

"Yes ma'am."

"If you ask me they all should fry, the lawyers included, no offense to you Ms. Van Astor, just how I feel, that's all."

"No offense taken Ms. Waters."

"It's *Mrs.* Waters; I've been married to Walter for 47 years."

"Forgive me."

"Yeah well."

"Is she always that way?" Kelly asked after Grace was out of earshot.

"This was one of her nicer days," said Ashley.

"Okay."

"What are you looking for Dr. Marshall?" asked Ashley.

"I'm checking the local news to see if there were any suicides."

"Find anything?"

"No."

"And you probably won't, because it's not the eighth. Dr. Marshall you've got to relax."

"Yeah Alex, Ashley's right." Kelly said.

"You're both right." I said.

"How long will you be using Dr. Arroyo's office?" Grace asked, popping her head into the office.

"Not that it's any of your business Grace, but my computer should be ready by Monday morning."

"You don't have to be so rude."

"And you don't have to be such a goddamn busy body Grace!" After I said it, it seemed as everything stopped. The silence was so deafening that you could here a pin drop in China. I didn't really mean what I said. It was my nerves talking. Grace just stood there, shell-shocked as if she'd just been slapped in the face by a close relative. I knew I'd fucked up and I wasn't sure how to repair it.

"Grace I'm sorry, I'm truly sorry." What happened next confirmed that this was indeed my time to experience the extraordinary. Grace walked over to me, stood on a chair so that we could be eye level. I braced myself for a well-deserved smack in the face. Kelly and Ashley stood their frozen, conflicted on what to do; let her smack the hell out of me, or stop her. The smack never came. Grace reached out with both hands, seized my face, and planted a big juicy kiss on my lips. I was shocked, relieved and repulsed at the same time. Kelly and

Ashley stood there mouths agape. Then Grace stepped down, smiled and said, "It's about time you showed some backbone Marshall, backbone is good for the sex life, you ought to make old Mafia gal real happy now. Keep it up Dr. Marshall." Then she shuffled her wide hips out the door before I had a chance to say anything.

"What was?" Kelly started to say.

"It's called small town living," I said, shaking my head in utter disbelief, as I closed Felix's door.

Though I was reluctant to leave Ashley alone, she insisted that it was okay; she was going to the salon to get her hair done for the reunion. I made Ashley promise to come with us to the reunion because I didn't think it would be safe for her to be alone. Kelly said she'd never be seen without an appointment; Ashley laughed and reminded her we were in Landon. Kelly and I went to my house where I planned to wile away the nervous hours grading papers. I had to do something to keep my mind off of tomorrow. Kelly retreated to the study to work on her mafia trial. I sat on the floor in the living room, papers sprawled all over the place, but I was kidding myself; there was no way I could grade papers. I needed to do something, but I didn't know what. I felt like a child on Christmas Eve, anxiously awaiting the first crack of morning. I read and reread the riddle, as if doing so would give me some sort of clue as to what would happen tomorrow. I knew nothing would come of it, but I had to do something that was connected to the mystery. When I realized that my efforts were nothing but a slow journey to insanity I peeked in on Kelly to see if she wanted to get something to eat.

"Where are you going?" She asked, peering up at me from mounds of note pads, casebooks and legal briefs. She looked delicious in my boxer shorts and Yankee t-shirt.

"To get some takeout from Holland's, I won't be long." Then it dawned on me that I shouldn't leave her alone. "On second thought you better come with me."

"Alex please, you're going overboard with this Garrison stuff! I'm perfectly safe here, besides I have the gun, and the police are less than five minutes away. Go on to Holland's and bring me back a double cheeseburger with everything and some fries."

"Kelly I really think you should come." As she was about to answer the doorbell rung; it was Ashley.

"Wow Ashley your hair is beautiful." Kelly said. "Ashley's here Alex so now you can go."

"Go where?" Ashley asked.

"To Hollands to get some takeout, he didn't want to leave me alone, scared the big bad boogeyman Mr. Pratt would hurt me."

"It's not funny Kelly."

"Relax Dr. Marshall, we'll be fine, we have guns remember?"

"Do you want anything?"

"A burger and fries," Ashley replied, staring in the mirror at her new look, an up style, with a wisp of hair hanging over her right eye. It really did look nice, a welcome change from her trademark ponytail.

I was at Hollands in a manner of minutes and once I stepped inside I thanked the heavens for Kelly's refusal to come with me, because sitting at a table directly across from the takeout section were Helen and Jordan. I only had a split second to act before they saw me. If I left I could tell Kelly that Hollands was crowded and I didn't want to wait. I hesitated too long; Jordan was calling my name. Though I heard her I was concentrating on Helen the whole time. My God she was beautiful. She was wearing a pair of loose fitting jeans, a black fall mock neck sweater adorned with an elegant string of pearls. Her skin seemed to be glowing and she was wearing the same perfume that she'd worn in those long ago days of bliss and romance that was the hallmark of our existence. Jordan, what can I say, she looked so hot that I had to force myself not to stare. She stood up to invite me over to their table and she had on a lime green silk pantsuit with matching high heel sandals, an outfit that would have normally called for a jacket in November, but with the extended Indian summer it wasn't necessary.

"Dr. Marshall, I guess the only way we'll get to see you is at Hollands. You still have not come by the shop."

"I've been busy. Hello Helen how have you been?"

"Good Alex. You look well."

"You two know each other?" Jordan asked with a mischievous smile.

"Yes we were in high school together." Helen replied with a wistful look in her eyes. "But that was a long time ago wasn't it Alex?"

"Yes, twenty years to be exact. Are you still going to the reunion tomorrow night?"

"Wouldn't miss it for the world, maybe you'll save me a dance."

"When they play 'Thriller' you'll be the first person I seek."

"If you say so," Helen said with a sly smile.

"What do you mean?" I asked. I knew what she was talking about and I have to say a rush went through me. She was talking about clearing it with Kelly and the way she said it intimated a hint of jealousy, which meant that she still cared.

"Nothing, nothing at all." Helen and I laughed. It felt good to do something, anything in unison with her.

"Excuse me," interjected Jordan.

"I'm sorry Jordan," Helen started to say, but she stopped when Jordan's cell phone rang.

"Excuse me, but I've got to go." Jordan said stuffing her phone back into her purse.

"Is everything okay?" Helen asked.

"Everything's cool, man business, you know how men can be, they're like little babies?"

"Yes I know exactly what you mean. I'll see you tomorrow?"

"First thing. Good seeing you again Dr. Marshall."

"So now that leaves you and me, huh Alex?"

"Actually I've got to leave myself, my order's ready." I retrieved our food from the counter.

"That's a lot of food for one person," Helen remarked staring at the three bags.

"It's for Kelly and Ashley Winters, my graduate assistant." I said.

"Alex, you freak, I didn't know you had it in you." Helen said with a devilish smile.

"What? It's not like that, Ashley is helping me with a project."

"The Garrison project?"

"How did you know about that?" Carol must have told her.

"Come on Alex, you know your sister fills me in on every detail of your life. I know all about your near death experience in Seville. Boy, your life is really interesting these days."

"What else do you know about my life?"

"Your food's getting cold; I think you better get home."

"No, you brought it up, what else do you know?" I asked.

"I know about the troubles between you and Kelly. After what Carol's told me I don't understand why you stay with her."

"I guess I should just leave her like you did me?"

"Alex that was different."

"How? You've never explained to me why you broke it off, just some generic bullshit about us becoming different people."

"It's complicated Alex, and I don't think we need to get into it. It's too late."

"It's not late, it's only nine o'clock."

"No, I'm talking about it's too late for us, for this. I know seeing me has dredged up old memories, memories that you've romanticized, but the bottom line is you're with Kelly; you've been with her for the past six years and no matter what you say, you're not going to leave her. You may physically walk out on her, but she'll always have a place in your mind and in your heart."

"Like you do?" I wanted to grab her face, just like Grace did mine, and smother her with my lips, but I didn't. She sensed what I felt as well.

"You see what I'm talking about?"

"What?" I asked.

"You want to kiss me, don't you?"

"What I want and what's prudent; are two different things."

"*What's prudent*? Alex are you serious? You've got to make a choice, either her or me, but I can't share you."

"Are you saying you still love me?"

"Hey doc, you want me to keep that warm for you, because it looks like you're going to be here for a while." It was Jimmy who works behind the takeout counter.

"Yeah Jimmy thanks."

"My answer shouldn't matter." Helen said.

"Why do you say that?" I asked.

"Because whether or not I still love you shouldn't have anything to do with how *you* feel about me."

"So what do you want me to do?"

"I can't answer that?" She said.

"Well can you answer why you changed after you came back from Milan? Can you tell me what really happened while you were there?"

"It's the past and it doesn't matter. What matters is you and what you're going to do. I have to go, I'll see you tomorrow night at the reunion."

Jimmy watched her walk out and he handed me back my food. "Women," he said with a shrug.

"Jimmy my man you don't know the half of it." I said as I headed towards the door.

"Keep your chin up doc, it'll pass, just send her some roses, always works for me." If it were only that easy; now I had a dilemma. Do I tell Kelly that I ran into Helen? It seemed as though I had played this same tape a few weeks ago, the only difference is that then it was the grocery store. I wondered what the hell was wrong with me. Did other men have these issues? The fact that she wouldn't tell me what happened in Milan bothered the hell out of me. How could I trust her again? And what about Kelly? Helen was right about my feelings for Kelly, but at the same time, I knew it was just a matter of time before Kelly and I had another blow up. And what about myself, was it right to subject Helen to my faults, my idiosyncrasies, my issues? The Alex that I am now is not the same person she knew years ago; I've changed, and some of it isn't good. My dysfunctional relationship with Kelly has added a bitter edge that wasn't present before, would it be fair to subject Helen to that? I thought about this on the way home. I thought about how familiar Kelly and I are with each other, that despite our problems, we have a bond, an understanding, a love that I never had with Helen, a love I'm not sure I could ever have with Helen. I was conflicted because Helen was my first love, and for most people that first love always has a place reserved in the heart's closet; I wasn't any different. So here I was on November 7, the day before what could possibly be the biggest event in my life, an event that has involved intrigue, mystery, ancient artifacts, murder, and possibly the threat of more murder, and I was conflicted about my love life. But as my father said that's why these events are extraordinary, they occur within the normal course of life, I just wish for once my father wasn't right.

Nineteen

Pope Mark Peter didn't like riding in helicopters, and tonight was not any different. He wanted to drive from the airport, but his security force convinced him that the ride to Landon would be quicker and safer by copter; so uneasily, he acquiesced. His copter would be the first to arrive followed by six other roaring birds; in intervals of thirty minutes. Their destination was the old Landon Armory, a military fortress that had been vacant for years after the Air Force closed it down due to budgetary constraints. As the bird began its descent, the Pope flashed a sardonic smile. The armory had been chosen as the clandestine site for the Council for Religious Unity's groundbreaking conference, a conference that is steeped in irony. While its goal is to unite all of the world's religions, the Pope knew that because of September 11, Council leaders had to meet in secrecy for fear of reprisal by their respective enemies and by fanatical followers who would see the conference as a sell-out. The Pope's copter touched down and he breathed a sigh of relief. The seventy-three year old pontiff was accompanied by his right hand Cardinal Augustine, long rumored to be Mark Peter's successor. Though the two have divergent views about the direction of the Catholic Church they have been friends for a long time and it is rumored at the Vatican that

Cardinal Augustine is the only person that is privy to the Pope's innermost thoughts.

The door opened to the helicopter and two men dressed in dark suits, with gold and blue ties, and automatic weapons in their hands, jumped out. The men seemed uncomfortable in their clothing and for good reason. They were used to wearing tunics of gold and blue that billowed, matching pantaloons and spats, black flat shoes that looked like ballet slippers, and black berets, the traditional uniforms of the Swiss Guards, the Vatican's super elite security force. The men did a check of the area, and then they helped the Pope and Cardinal Augustine disembark. Within hours, all of the world's major religious leaders had landed safely at the Armory and sequestered into their quarters.

The Air Force would have never imagined that the building, now occupied by the most important spiritual leaders of the modern world, would be transformed. Except for the outside, the building no longer resembled a military compound. It had the look and feel of a five star resort, replete with spas, restaurants, rooms of worship and suites that would make the Plaza look like a motel. It was agreed by the Council that this would be their new home, where they would meet every year for a week's worth of events, workshops, culminating with the conference, where strategies would be discussed. Because the area around the Armory has been labeled off limits for years, the leaders were assured that there would not be any security breaches.

Tired from his journey, each leader went to his respective suite, to sleep and rest. Pope Mark Peter felt restless. Something was nagging at him, a sense that something wasn't quite right, but he couldn't put his finger on it. After an hour or so, he shrugged it off as nerves and retired to his suite, where he fell asleep instantly. Little did he know that the foreboding feeling that scratched the pit of his belly was accurate, the magnitude manifested by the actions and planning of one Alistair Pratt and the Light of Hellas.

Twenty

When I arrived home I felt that overwhelming sense of guilt one has when he's about to lie or in my case conceal the truth. But fortunately I didn't have to address the issue of Helen at all because when I reached my door, there was an envelope taped to my door and in black ink the word Cryonic was written. I opened it and it contained another riddle. In the same font as the last riddle it read:

On morrows night,

Hold Ann S. within the cover of silver and white,

The swirl of this mystery will flush to light,

Two stories above, where the air is sweet,

Lies one more riddle that you must complete.

Who is Ann S. was the first thought that came to mind? Was she someone I went to school with, who'll be at the reunion, I wondered? And if so, how was she mixed up in this? I opened the door to find Ashley completely captivated by "Breakfast at Tiffany's", which was weird considering I'd just seen Helen, a devout Audrey Hepburn fanatic. Kelly was still hard at work in the study and both of them seemed oblivious to my presence. "I'm back," I shouted. No one moved. "I said I'm back, with the food."

"I heard you Alex. Can you bring mine in the study." Kelly replied.

"You can bring my food in here Dr. Marshall," Ashley seconded.

"What am I the butler?" I quipped. "I want you to come to the kitchen I've got something to show you." When they came I showed them the envelope and the riddle.

"What do you think it means?" Kelly asked in between bites of her burger.

"I'm not sure, but I don't think Ann S. is a real person. What I do know is that according to the riddle I can find the final riddle tomorrow night. The question is where?"

"Within the cover of silver and white, maybe the author is talking about the stars and the moon, which means that the riddle will be located somewhere outside." Ashley offered.

"I thought so too at first, but then there's the line 'two stories above where the air is sweet', that indicates to me a building." I said.

"Maybe the riddle is a reconfiguration of words like the first one." Kelly offered.

"Let's see if you're right." We spent the next three hours putting together several word combinations, phrases, but none of it made any sense.

"Wait a minute guys remember what my dad said about simplicity?" Yes Ashley and I replied in exhausted unison.

"Let's start with the first three words; 'on morrow's night'. What is happening tomorrow night?"

"I'm supposed to receive the information tomorrow." I said.

"Where?"

"I don't know. I assume at my house."

"That's certainly possible, but where else?"

"The school, your dad's, my sister's, my parents," *Helen's* I wanted to add, but thought better of it.

"The reunion!" Ashley shouted.

"Bingo," Kelly shouted.

"The reunion, what's that got to do with the Garrison project?"

"Maybe nothing, but then again maybe its where the information is going to be delivered."

"So you think this riddle is referencing the reunion?" I asked.

"I think so." Kelly said.

"Then we're back to Ann S. Let me get my yearbook and see if there's an Ann S. in my graduating class." We looked, but as I suspected there wasn't an Ann S. Kelly was a little deflated, but only for a second.

"I've got an idea. Let's take the phrase 'hold Ann S.' and write down as many words as we can." We did as instructed, consuming our papers with a host of two, three, four and five letter words, when Kelly shrieked. "I know what 'hold Ann S.' really means."

"What Kelly?" I said, slightly annoyed at her, drag it out Hollywood style, theatrics; an act which amused Ashley.

"Hold Ann S. is really Landon H.S. or Landon High School. You can find the riddle tomorrow night somewhere in Landon High School." I was impressed with Kelly's discovery, and also struck by a wave of confusion and anxiety. Helen. She seemed to be overly concerned as to whether or not I was going to attend the reunion; was she mixed up in this? Was this why she came back to Landon? Was she the one sending the riddles? No way I thought; it's just a case of nerves and guilt that's causing these crazy thoughts. Still the notion that nothing is impossible flashed through my head and I vowed to watch Helen extra carefully tomorrow night.

"Earth to Alex." Kelly said.

"What?"

"Did you fall asleep or something, I was asking you what you thought and it was as if you were in a trance."

"I'm sorry, I was processing what you said. Okay so we know that the location is the high school, the question is where?"

"Let's take the next sentence." Ashley interjected. "Within the cover of silver and white, the swirl of this mystery will flush to light." It took a few minutes but I thought I figured it out.

"Sounds like a bathroom. The silver represents the handle and the white is the base and bowl. It was easy to figure out because of the second part of the sentence. The words swirl and flush are dead giveaways."

"So you're not asleep after all." Kelly quipped.

"Which bathroom are we talking about?" Ashley asked.

"Two stories above where the air is sweet." Kelly read.

"Since when are bathrooms sweet. I've never been in a public bathroom that smelled sweet."

"And you wouldn't Dr. Marshall."

"Why do you say that?" I asked.

"Because you're a man. The author is talking about the girl's bathroom. Where the 'air is sweet' refers to perfume."

"Very good Ashley." Kelly said with a smile. "Okay, so we know that the next riddle can be found tomorrow night at the high school in the second floor girl's bathroom; all we have to do is stake it out."

"Slow down Jessica Fletcher. We can't just go walking in there. How do we know that Pratt didn't send us this riddle?

Maybe it's a set-up. Maybe the riddle contains the location of the information."

"Alex, listen to what you're saying, if Pratt knew the location of the information why would he send you a riddle telling you where it is and then set you up to take it back?"

"Okay I see what you're saying; it's just something isn't right. And if it wasn't Pratt, then who?"

"Maybe its Lydia Sinclair. Maybe she's double-crossing Pratt." Ashley said.

"It's possible, but for what reason?" I sat silent for a moment. "Okay here's the deal. Kelly call your friend the detective and ask him if he can help us out, you know hang around on the periphery."

"Okay."

"The reunion starts at eight. We'll get there precisely at that time and I'll pretend to take you two on a tour. We'll slip upstairs to the bathroom and get the riddle."

"But how do you know it will be there by eight?"

"I don't for sure, just a hunch."

"And once we find the riddle, then what?" Kelly asked.

I started to answer when my cell phone rang. Who is it, Kelly mouthed?

"Hello?"

"Did you figure out the riddle?" The voice was muffled so I couldn't tell whether it was a man or a woman.

"Who is this?"

"That's not important. Did you decipher the riddle?"

"Yes."

"Good. I suggest you get some sleep Dr. Marshall because you will need it for tomorrow night."

"Why do you say that?"

"You shall see Dr.; you shall *see.*"

"See what?"

"The truth and the light."

"What are you talking about?"

"Good night Dr. Marshall." The line went dead.

"Who was it Alex?"

"The voice was muffled, so I couldn't tell whether it was a man or woman."

"What did the caller say?"

"The caller asked if I'd deciphered the riddle and then said that tomorrow night I would see the truth and the light."

"What does that mean?" Kelly asked.

"Sounds biblical to me." Ashley replied.

"Yes, but what does it mean?" Kelly repeated.

As Kelly finished her question, the large grandfather clock, a present from my late uncle Theodore, ominously struck twelve, and though I'm not a superstitious person I couldn't help but think that it wasn't a good sign; not a good sign at all.

Twenty-one

November8th

Why did I have to wake to a dark cloud filled morning? Why, after the spate of warm, sunny days, did today, of all days, have to look like the intro to the 1960's cult classic 'Dark Shadows.' I stepped out onto the deck, to a symphony of thunder and swirling leaves, a tell tale sign that a storm was brewing. The temperature had dropped drastically, a signal that the eighty degree days we'd been having were now stored away for a long nap. Though my nerves were a little on edge I didn't really feel any different, in fact my primary concern was not the girl's second floor bathroom at my alma mater; no my fear was Kelly and Helen being together in the same room. My father once told me, after I'd strung out for weeks a lie about an incident in school, that *deception always has an end point.* Sooner or later Kelly was going to find out that I'd seen and spoke to Helen twice within the past few weeks, and she'd be pissed that I didn't tell her. For some reason I was certain that sooner would come before later, in fact I was sure that sooner would come tonight. I was also anxious because I honestly didn't know what I was going to do as far as Kelly and Helen was concerned. I called Carol and told her about running into Helen at Hollands last night and of course she said it was a sign. Whether it was a sign or not I wasn't sure, but the one thing I was sure about was that I had to make a decision.

Ricardo awakened to the soothing melodic tones of Mahler's Ninth Symphony, a stark contrast to the violent thunder that boomed angrily at what seemed to be every five to ten seconds. The phone rang and it was the cute young woman who'd checked him in asking if he needed anything, and she meant anything. *If only time permitted*, he smiled to himself. He glanced at the package and knelt silently in prayer. *Tonight our destiny will be fulfilled.*

Lydia Sinclair shifted restlessly in her chair despite its plushness. She along with Timothy and the other key members of Alistair's inner circle had been summoned to his penthouse at six in the morning. She listened as Alistair droned on and on about what was to take place that evening. She started to interrupt him, to ask him why was it necessary to go over and over the plan, but she wisely kept silent. She was already on thin ice and she knew that any questioning that whiffed of impatience or opposition to the plan would seal her fate. So she listened as she watched the dark storm clouds sift through and then settle directly over Central Park. Luke 23:44 popped immediately into her conscious: *It was now about the sixth hour, and the darkness came over the whole land until the ninth hour.* She smiled inwardly because tonight truth would illuminate all.

Carson Lowery was in a celebratory mood because tonight would be the culmination of all that he and the woman had worked for. The fruits of their labor would be rewarded. His only source of disappointment was the weather. For days Landon epitomized the meaning of Indian summer, and now today, the day when truth would reign, the weather refused to cooperate. But his disappointment was only temporal. His cell phone rang.

"Are you ready?" The woman asked.

"Yes." He said ebulliently.

"I share your joy, but you must not let your emotions keep you from the task at hand. There will be plenty of time to celebrate once everything is complete, do you understand?"

"Yes. I'm fine, you don't have to worry."

"Is your team ready?" She asked.

"Yes, ready to move on my signal."

"And the high school?"

"Covered."

"That's what I want to hear. I will see you, afterwards."

"I look forward to it." Carson smiled and snapped his phone shut.

Pope Mark Peter couldn't believe that this day was finally here. After years of planning, of selecting a site, of securing funding to renovate the site, a task that proved difficult despite the immense wealth of his colleagues, who occupied the other rooms. Funding had to be obtained without any trace to his fellow clergy, not because his brethren were engaged in any illegal activity, but for their own safety. If word got out for instance that the Islamic faith was in alliance with the Jews, holy bloodshed, set forth by radical fringes of both faiths, would occur and not just in the Middle East. In addition the choice of location, America, and New York, much less would spur hatred toward the Holy See. Many religious people view America is an infidel, and New York is seen as the bastion of corruption, loose morality, a modern day Sodom and Gomorrah, the last bastion of everything anti-God. Mark Peter dismissed such talk as foolishness, citing the millions of Americans who faithfully confess and serve God everyday. But while the need for secrecy is paramount, in order for there to be true world harmony the conference must be broadcast live, much to the dismay of Cardinal Augustine. Mark Peter was assured that technology would allow him to do so without giving away the location of the Council's headquarters. He walked over to the balcony and stepped outside. The dark ominous clouds instantly flashed Luke 23:44 into his head, and he was taken aback. But it was another scripture that produced dual emotions of joy and trepidation: Luke 12:40, *for no man know the hour when the Son of Man cometh.* Could the dark clouds be a sign? His question reminded him of a conversation he had a few months back with an important Baptist minister from America.

"Why now Holy Father?" The pastor asked Mark Peter in reference to the conference.

"I know it sounds trite, no doubt the product of Hollywood's sudden fascination with the 'end of days', but look around you pastor. Look at the world. It's a cesspool of corruption, greed, scandal and sexual depravity, not too mention the sudden onset of natural disasters. It's Revelation coming to fruition."

"But Holy Father, what you have described has always been with us. When Solomon says in Ecclesiastes that there is nothing new under the sun, he is talking about the things that we see today."

"Your understanding is absolutely correct, but I believe that we are truly in the last days and I believe that we must unite to fight against the coming of the enemy."

"But your Excellency, if man does not believe in Jesus Christ, if he claims that he can be saved by other means, other Gods, then in essence isn't he the enemy?"

"I don't see it that way."

"You don't?" The pastor asked, his eyebrows rising slightly with curiosity at the Pope's response.

"No. In Matthew when Jesus tells the parable of the wedding feast, he talks about how in the end the king ordered his servants to go into the highways and byways and invite anyone he saw, both good and bad, right?"

"Yes."

"What do you think Jesus was trying to accomplish with this parable?" The Pope asked the pastor.

"Jesus was trying to illustrate that God wants us to come to him willingly, to accept his invitation for salvation and eternal life."

"You are correct, but only half correct. Jesus was also illustrating that God's door is open to everyone if they will only believe. But how do you get people to believe?"

"You have to welcome them with open arms." The pastor replied.

"That's right, and that's what I'm doing. If I am to convince some of our brethren, who do not call on the name of Jesus, that he is the truth and the light, then I must create an environment that facilitates change."

"But aren't you being disingenuous Father? I thought the goal was to promote tolerance and respect for others who serve God differently?"

"And that is precisely what we are doing. Think of it this way pastor. If a man comes to your church and he stinks to high heavens, has not had a bath in weeks, not brushed his teeth, are you going to throw him out of the church?"

"No, probably not, unless he's a physical threat to the congregation."

"I gathered as much. Yet while you won't throw him out, you would like to see him cleaned up wouldn't you?"

"Sure."

"The conference operates on the same premise. I accept my brethren, but it's my goal to 'clean' them up so that they have a true understanding of what it means to serve God."

"I see," said the pastor.

"So I can count on you to get on board."

"Let's just say I'll buy a ticket and check things out." Both men laughed.

"Fair enough. Come let's eat."

The thunder snapped the Pope back into the present and he walked to the highest point in the building and looked down at the fruits of his dream. *We will be one and no weapons formed against* us *will prosper. If it is indeed the end of days, if Christ is to return tonight, he will be pleased.* Mark Peter smiled at what he'd accomplished. It would be his legacy, his gift to God.

Jordan Nelson laid the strapless black gown on her bed. Things were going better than planned. It had been her intention to finagle her way into the reunion, but when Helen asked her to come, because she didn't have a date, Jordan happily accepted. She opened her dresser drawer and pulled out her gun, and placed it on the bed. She stared at her naked body and then the gun. *There'll be fireworks in more ways than one tonight.*

Twenty-two

The storm came as expected and it rained heavily off and on all day. It was now seven thirty and I was impatiently waiting for Kelly and Ashley to finish dressing. With what was at stake, I wondered why they were taking so long. Finally they descended down the stairs and I was taken aback with how beautiful they both looked, especially Ashley. I say that because I've only seen her dressed up one time. She was wearing a long black silk gown with spaghetti straps, which accented her perfect shoulders. The dress had a slit up the left side, which was revealing, but tastefully so. Kelly was wearing an updated variation of the dress that she wore when we first met six years ago and she looked even more stunning.

"It's about time," I said, glancing at my watch, which now read seven forty-five.

"Relax Alex didn't you say that your school was only five minutes away?" Kelly said.

"Yes, but."

"No buts, we'll make it in plenty of time."

"Alright let's stop gabbing and go. By the way you both look beautiful."

"Thank you and you're quite handsome." Kelly said.

"Yeah doc, you look good in the tux." I owned four tuxedos, I wasn't satisfied with just one, a fact that grates on my mother's nerves. She doesn't understand why I need more than one tux. The rain had slacked up for the time being, and there was hope yet for the night to become pleasant. It was warmer than I thought, which made me happy, and the streetlights reflecting off the puddles gave me a pleasant feeling. As we approached the school I found myself thinking about those years of my life that I had spent searching for the so-called ancient artifact. The notion that the clue to to its existence was in my old high school was numbing. For ten years I traveled all across the world, became sick, lost friends, and exhausted my savings, all to come up empty. And yet now here I was, right back in the middle of it, possibly in danger of being murdered, placing in harm's way my girlfriend and my assistant, and enjoying every minute of it. What I didn't enjoy, was being in the same room with Helen and Kelly; *that's what scared me!* I pulled up to the front, where the parking attendants met us; but then suddenly I pulled off. The attendants stared in confusion.

"Alex why did you do that?" Kelly asked.

"It occurred to me that if we have to make a quick getaway I don't want to have to wait for our car."

"Oh I see."

We walked into the building and a wave of nostalgia flooded me. I hadn't been back to Landon High School in years, and while it clearly had been updated, in my mind's eye it hadn't changed. It was the same semi-modern structure that I remembered. I say semi-modern because the village elders fought tooth and nail to keep the school's façade in the dark ages, but with a younger mix on the village council, the elders were outvoted. Landon High School was the forerunner to what many city planners now describe as the "pub-priv" institution. Though chartered as a public school, it has the feel and clientele of a pricey, upper middle class private school, along the lines of Exeter or Andover, and despite the school's feeble ministrations about the need for diversity, the school is still pretty much the same. The reunion was being held in the gymnasium, a small bandbox, which can be intimidating to opposing teams, because the crowd is right on top of you. It's a smaller version of Duke University's Cameron Indoor Stadium which was inundated with 'Welcome Class of 1983' banners strewn everywhere. Everything was blue and white, which are our school colors. At the door Kimberly Wallace, the older, and less endowed sister of pert breasted Taylor Wallace, greeted us. Kim, who was very skinny during high school had filled out, and she looked good, though nowhere near as hot as her sister. I hadn't seen Kim since we graduated because she moved to Miami, where she'd made a mint in real estate.

"Alex Marshall, how are you?" She said kissing me on the cheek. "You look good as ever, boy my sister sure messed up when she let you go." *Let me go, oh so that's how the stories been told.*

"Kim, you look good as well. I hear you're the real estate queen in Miami."

"It's been very lucrative. And whom do we have here? Your wife and daughter?" She said with a fake smile.

"No, this is Kelly Van Astor, my girlfriend and this is Ashley Winters, my graduate assistant." I looked down at my watch it read seven fifty-five.

"Well nice to meet you, and please have a good time." Kim said disingenuously. It was clear by the way she eyeballed Kelly and Ashley that she was envious of how they looked. Though the reunion hadn't officially started there were already quite a number of people in the gym, some I recognized and some I didn't. The gym looked the same, small and intimate, plastered in blue and white, with the boys and girls' basketball team's State championship banners hanging from the rafters. Hall and Oates 'Maneater' was blaring from the speakers and everyone seemed to be having a good time. Helen hadn't arrived which was a relief because I didn't want to see her *before* the business at hand, though if she were involved perhaps she were already in the building. It was now seven fifty-nine and we walked back out into the hallway. The steps to the second floor were to the right of the trophy case, a mere few feet from where we were standing.

"Leaving already Alex?" Kim cooed.

"No. Actually I'm going to take Kelly and Ashley on a tour of the building, if that's okay?" I added for effect, to make Kim feel important.

"Of course sweetie. I took George, my husband earlier. Don't stay too long, or you'll miss the Michael Jackson 'Thriller' contest."

"We won't." I replied.

We climbed up the short set of steps and ran to the end of the long and wide hallway. The floor is dark blue and the walls and ceiling a combination of blue and white. On the left side adjacent to the steps is the girl's bathroom. Kelly pushed the swinging door open slowly and checked each stall to make sure it was empty. Once the coast was clear Ashley and I stepped inside. There were five stalls in total and we checked there first; we didn't find anything. Then we checked underneath the sinks; empty. I was getting frustrated, when Kelly suggested that we look inside the soap dispenser, and sure enough there it was, a sheet of copy paper folded in half, held in place with scotch tape. I opened it up and in the same font as the first and second riddle it read:

The apple falls not far from the tree. And so we've come full circle my friend. At ten tonight the answers you seek await you at the Fortress.

"The fortress?" Ashley asked slightly confused. "Dr. Marshall does this mean what I think?"

"I'm sure it does." I replied, alternating between curiosity and fear.

"Can someone clue me in please?" Kelly interjected.

"The fortress is the nickname for the old Armory. It used to be a military enclave, but it's been closed for years. It sits about fifteen miles outside of Landon, and for a long time after it closed, teenagers and college students used to go there to drink and have sex."

"Were you one of those teenagers Alex?" Kelly asked with a sly smile, her hazel eyes sparkling with mischief.

"I plead the fifth."

"So what do we do?" Ashley asked.

"We're going to the Armory at ten just like the note says." I replied.

"But what if it's a trap?" Kelly said.

"I'm not sure, but we've come to far to turn back. Call Patrick and let him know what's going on and I'll call the Chief."

"What do you think the author meant by 'the apple falls not far from the tree. And so we've come full circle my friend?' You think it's from Pratt?"

"That's my guess."

"But why?"

"I guess we'll find out at ten."

"So what now?" Kelly asked.

"Let's go check out Michael Jackson." I said.

We went back to the reunion, to find that the shindig was in full swing. Reese Harrington, now Walters, cheerleader extraordinaire, and village pediatrician, was doing an excellent Jennifer Bealls impersonation to Michael Sembello's, 'Maniac', one of the signature songs from the movie Flashdance. Reese's strawberry blond hair was swinging all over the place and she was sweating profusely. She'd taken off her heels and was really going for it; same old Reese. She was always the life of the party. Like me she never left Landon, setting up shop after medical school and marrying her high school sweetheart, Dr. Jeffrey Walters, the village podiatrist. Reese spotted me and summoned me over. She stopped dancing and after catching her breath gave me a big hug. It's funny how things turn out. Reese who made fun of me when I was a skinny little geek, but once I'd filled out in high school; I was suddenly on her "A" list, a fact that would have gotten to my head if it hadn't been for Carol.

"Alex how are you doing? You know even though we both live here, I never see you. And how are you Kelly?"

"I'm well Reese. Excuse me Alex but I'll leave you two to catch up, I'm going to get something to drink."

"So Alex, how've you been?"

"Reese don't you really mean how's Helen?"

"Am I still that transparent?" She said, locking her arm through mine.

"Only when you want to be."

"You know you and Helen are meant to be, I mean you were voted 'Couple Most Likely to Be Happily Married for Eternity.' "

"Life had other plans."

"You mean her?" She said pointing at Kelly, who was talking to Hadley Willis, who no doubt was flirting with her. Hadley's always been the best-looking guy wherever he's been. Tall and dark, with a head full of unruly curly hair, Hadley's always possessed a look that's part model, part intellectual, which drove women crazy. He liked to give the impression that he was above the fray, above the rest of us, and yet he once confided, in a drunken stupor, that it was all an act to get laid. Hadley lives in New York City, working piecemeal as a model, an actor, and piano player. His uncle left him a mint, so he just sort of works when the mood hits him. He and I keep in touch because he says that I'm the only person from school that he really trusts. Why that is I don't know, but I feel honored. I wasn't worried about him pressing the issue with Kelly because he respects our relationship.

"Kelly is here and now, Helen was past, besides she dumped me; remember?"

"It's complicated Alex. If she had to do it over again, she'd do things differently."

"Why is it that everyone knows the real story but me?" I said.

"It's complicated, that's all I can say."

"Whatever Reese."

"Well, well, speaking of the devil." Helen walked in along with Jordan. *Jordan?* No, it can't be, I thought. Has Helen become a lesbian? Reese, who was watching my reaction when Helen walked in, seemed to read my mind and quickly squelched whatever I was thinking.

"No she's not a lesbian Alex. She told me that because Jordan is relatively new in town it would be something for her to do. But so what if she were a lesbian, this is the twenty-first century Alex, get with it."

"I'm all for changes Reese, but there are some things that I'll never *get with.*"

"Oh Alex." Reese said, squeezing my arm. Helen looked magnificent. Her dress was a replica of the black number Audrey Hepburn wore in 'Breakfast at Tiffany's'. I was looking around for Kelly, but I didn't see her. Jordan was her usual sexy, sensual self. "So tiger what are you going to do. From the way you stared at both Helen and Jordan, it appears as if you've got a three-way dilemma, or shall I say four-way, I forgot all about the pretty young thing that came with you and Kelly." Reese said with a snicker.

"Reese that's sick." I said with a chuckle.

"No tiger, that sounds like fun. Good luck big guy, I'm going to find my *one* husband." There I stood in the middle of the dance floor, oblivious to everything around me. "Sweet

Dreams' by the Eurhythmics was playing and I wondered if I was in a dream or a nightmare. Where was Kelly I wondered, as Helen and Jordan were walking towards me. Fortunately Helen was cornered and she stopped to talk. I felt like a child. I was trembling on the inside, part nerves, part not wanting Kelly to make a scene once she saw Helen and I talking. I know that sounds crazy, because Kelly has too much class and dignity to turn her displeasure into a street brawl, but when you're scared all sorts of crazy thoughts float through your head. But I think the real reason I was nervous is because of the guilt I felt in lying to Kelly. Though I was certain that Helen would not say anything about our prior conversations, the fact is *I knew* they took place. That's the type of guilt that destroys a man. It's like Raskolnikoff, Dostoyevsky's protagonist in 'Crime and Punishment.' Raskolnikoff was eaten alive by the guilt he felt for murdering the old woman, even though he knew that the inspector didn't have any tangible proof that he'd committed the crime. That's how I felt as I searched the gym for Kelly. At that moment Hadley came over, walking arm-in-arm with Ashley.

"Alex my boy, where have you been keeping this lovely creature?"

"Hadley don't even think about it." I said.

"Dr. Marshall, he's harmless, besides he's not my type." Ashley said.

"See Alex, you have nothing to worry about." He said flashing the smile that's disarmed many women. "You're the talk of the reunion my boy, showing up with two beautiful women, now all we need is Helen." Ashley's face flashed a quizzical look.

"Speaking of beautiful women did you see where Kelly went after she left you?"

"No I didn't."

"Well I need to find her, the Deejay promised to play 'You and I' for us," I lied. It was now almost nine-fifteen.

"I'm sure she's around somewhere. Why don't I keep the lovely Ms. Winters company while you look for her?"

"The offer sounds inviting Mr. Wills, but I think I have to go to the lady's room, I'll see you later."

"Don't stay too long my dear or I'll be snatched up."

"Oh well it will be my loss," Ashley replied, blowing a kiss as she walked away.

"I'm sorry about Hadley," I said when we were out of earshot.

"He's okay, a bit full of himself, but he's cute in an old sort of way."

"Gee thanks, I'm the same age." I said in mock anger.

"You know what I mean doc. So who is Helen?"

"What? Oh Helen. She's an old fling from days past." I said.

"Is she here?" My stomach moved.

"Yes she's here. She came with Jordan Nelson."

"Oh, I see." Ashley said as we made our way out of the gym.

"No it's not like that at all. Where could Kelly be?"

"Maybe she stepped outside to get some air, or maybe she's in the bathroom." We walked outside and sure enough there she was standing in front of the building.

"Why are you out here, I've been looking all over for you?"

"Why didn't you tell me that your little girlfriend would be here?" Kelly was angry, and her eyes looked like fire.

"I'm going back inside." Ashley said.

"How, how do you know she's here?"

"Your slimy friend told me."

"Hadley?" I could kill him.

"What's going on with you and her Alex? Why couldn't you tell me that she would be here?"

"How was I supposed to know, I don't talk to her," I'd just stepped deeper into the abyss. If there was anytime to come clean, that moment was it, and I chose to keep on lying. *Deception has an end point.*

"Maybe not, but she was your high school sweetheart, she graduated the same year you did, for Christ sakes, you had to know that she just might possibly come."

"What's the big deal? I'm here with you, not her. It's not as though I still want her."

"Dammit Alex, can't you see how I feel? Let your sister tell it, everyone in this fucking backwater town, loves Helen. I feel like all those little bitches are snickering at me."

"They're not."

"How the fuck do you know? You're an asshole Alex, a fucking asshole, you fucking humiliated me, and for what? That bitch left you, or did you forget?"

"Well hell Kelly, you've left me too, so what's your point?"

"That's different and you know it." It was now nine thirty-five.

"Why the fuck are you glancing at your watch?" Her voice was getting louder and angrier, fortunately everyone was inside, and the music was loud enough to drown her out.

"It's getting close to ten o'clock." I said.

"Well you better work fast." She said.

"What are you talking about?"

"I want to meet her, so you better work fast at introducing me."

"Kelly, do you think that's wise?" I asked as my stomach moved again.

"Let's go Alex, get your ass inside and do it." She grabbed me by the hand and dragged me inside. Ashley was standing by the door talking to Kim Wallace. Kelly composed herself, but I'm sure I looked like a deer caught in the headlights. I could feel my pupils expanding, and my stomach was moving at a rapid pace. It was approaching nine thirty-eight, and we had to leave soon, because the drive to the Armory would take at least ten minutes even exceeding the speed limit. "Where is she?" Kelly whispered venomously.

"I don't see her." I was telling the truth. "I'll ask Jordan." Jordan was standing at the Deejay booth working her charms on him.

"You do that."

"Jordan, have you seen Helen?"

"She left."

"Left, why?"

"I don't know, said something about not feeling well." The Deejay put on 'You and I', but this definitely wasn't the time to ask Kelly for a dance, besides it was now nine forty-two. We had eighteen minutes.

"Let's go." Kelly said. "Lucky for you she's not here."

"Now what?" I asked.

"You and Ashley can go on your little adventure. I'm staying here."

"And do what?" Images of her flailing butt naked on top of Hadley flashed instantly into my head.

"I don't know Alex. I'm just not going with you."

Ashley came running over to tell me we had less than fifteen minutes.

"Kelly you can't stay here, you don't know anyone." I was grasping. Images of Hadley thrusting like a wild animal were consuming me.

"I'm not going Alex. Right now I don't want to be around you; so go."

"Don't do anything we'll both regret." I said.

"You mean your friend Hadley? You're such an asshole Alex. This isn't about revenge, it's about you and your presence sickens me right now, so please go. We'll talk tomorrow." With that she turned and walked back inside. The time was nine forty-nine. I started to go back inside and say the hell with the Armory, but I didn't. Kelly or no Kelly I realized that I had to know, and I owed it to Ashley, but most importantly, I owed it to myself.

Ashley and I ran to the car and tore out of the parking lot. We had less than ten minutes to get to the Armory. Fortunately the drive was on country roads with no stoplights, but on the flip side, there weren't any streetlights. I tore down Old Landon Road at ninety miles per hour. As we approached the Armory we saw a host of signs that warned, No Trespassing, Government Property Please Keep Off. As we approached the entrance, which was fenced in, we were met by two ominous characters dressed in military fatigues and they motioned for me to pull the car around to the left side of the building. I was surprised to see six helicopters parked in two rows of threes. *What the hell is going on?* I put the car in park and the two men motioned for us to step out of the car. They were carrying machine guns and we nervously complied.

Ricardo watched the whole scene unfold from a path some twenty yards from the Armory. Armed with the package he was instructed to wait a half hour after the gatekeeper was led inside, then he was to make his entrance. *What about the armed guards, he queried?* Everything will be arranged, just make the delivery as instructed.

Carson Lowery had his team assembled as per the woman's instructions. She assured him that nothing would go wrong, but he was nervous. He went over the plan of action with his team several times until he was certain that they understood every minute detail. He crouched in position, some forty yards from the entrance to the Armory. When the messenger made his move, that's when he would make his.

Twenty-three

Kelly was still fuming, but she'd vowed to forgive Alex. Let him stew she thought. As much as she wanted to go with him, she felt that she had to stand her ground. I'll have some fun at this little affair, do some dancing, kick back a few drinks. She must have had too many drinks because the urge to pee seemed to be coming every few minutes. I'll go to the bathroom on the second floor this time. So the bitch got sick? Kelly mused as she walked up the stairs. And what's up with that Jordan chick? She looks like she'd fuck every guy in the place. I'm sure Hadley will get his hands on her before the night is out. In fact didn't I see her leave with him? She realized she was a bit drunk and her thoughts were rambling, incoherent. She walked into the bathroom and sat down to pee. And then everything went black.

"Welcome everyone, welcome," said Pope Mark Peter from the dais of the expansive conference room. This is such a momentous occasion. Who would have ever thought, especially after the horrific events of September 11, that we could come together as one, united in our service to the almighty God, willing vessels to his bidding to bring about peace and harmony amongst us all. I am so honored to be in the presence of such great and honorable men, and it is my prayer that when we leave here, we will have broken the bonds of intolerance and embraced the olive branch of peace and harmony." The other leaders stood up and applauded vigorously. "As you know we've taken painstaking measures to pull this off, under the cloak of veiled secrecy and I want to take just a second to thank each and everyone of you for putting your lives on the line for such a worthy, honorable and necessary cause." More applause. "In just a few moments, the entire world will know what is transpiring and again I applaud each and every one of you for your willingness to show the world your commitment to this process. I know that each and every one of you, myself included is running the risk of alienating and angering many who look to us for leadership and guidance. But it is my prayer that anger will turn to acceptance and appreciation. I would now ask each and every one of you to pick up your candles and come to the dais, so that we may light the ceremonial flame of peace. The television hookup will be ready in a few minutes. This is what we want the world to see, men of the cloth united in the light of God."

Kelly woke up only to discover that her hands and feet were bound to a chair and Jordan was pointing a gun in her face. *Is this the same chick from the party?*

"Where am I?" Was she at the school, in a classroom?

"Shut up bitch, I'm asking the questions."

"What? Kelly asked. She was still groggy from the alcohol and her nose smelt like chlorophyll. *Chlorophyll?* Jordan then smacked her in the face with an open palm. Kelly had never been smacked before. It didn't hurt as much as it startled her.

"I told you I'm asking the questions. The next time it'll be the gun. Do you know who I am?"

"No, I don't, but I assume you're working for Pratt."

"Pratt, what are you talking about? I don't know any Pratt."

"If you say so," Kelly replied. *It had to be Pratt. If it wasn't then who? Could it be that bitch Helen, did she put this girl up to this? No, she wouldn't be that stupid. It's got to be Pratt, Kelly decided. Dammit, you should have gone with Alex!*

"If I say so! If I say so! You're damn right I say so. Now I'm going to ask you again, do you know who I am?"

"No I don't, why don't you tell me."

"You must think I'm stupid. If I tell you who I am, you'll be able to identify me. Wait a minute, what does it matter, you'll be one dead, whoring bitch." *Let her go*, said the voice, she didn't do anything to you. "*Shut up I said, I told you this is my time.*" Kelly wondered what was going on. She surmised that Pratt had instructed the kidnapper to act crazy, in hopes of scaring her.

"I didn't say anything," Kelly answered nervously.

"What are you talking about?" Jordan screamed.

"You just told me to shut up. I was just saying that I didn't say anything."

"Do you know who you're dealing with?" Jordan asked.

"No I don't, why don't you tell me."

"Are you hungry?" Jordan asked.

"No, but I'm a little thirsty."

"Okay I'll bring you some water." What was going on, Kelly thought. Just a second ago she was raving like a lunatic. *Was this an act, or was this chick really crazy?*

"Are you still thirsty Ms. Van Astor?"

"No I'm not."

"You know what? I think it's time that you know who I am and what you've taken from me."

"What I've taken from you?"

"Yes. I warned you to stay away from him, but you wouldn't listen. All of this could have been avoided if you would have just listened and obeyed. Well *you will* obey me now."

"I'll do whatever you say."

"Bullshit! That's what Harold said after I caught him with that slut. They're both dead you know."

"Harold, what are you talking about?"

"Why did you have to sleep with him? You could have any man that you want and you had to have him." Kelly was racking her brains trying to figure out who she was talking about.

"If I did anything to hurt you I'm sorry."

"*If I did anything to hurt you I'm sorry*", Jordan said mockingly. "You're not sorry. If you were then you wouldn't have stolen him from me."

"Stolen who?"

"Don't play with me bitch, you know who."

"No, I don't."

"Let me spell it out for you bitch; A L E X M A R S H A L L. Does that ring a fucking bell?"

Twenty-four

"Where are we going?" I asked the two men, but they said nothing. We were whisked inside, blindfolded, taken down a flight of stairs and then put in a room. Was this Seville all over again, I wondered? It was then that we heard loud voices, angry voices and gunshots.

"Everyone calm down," Pope Mark Peter was saying, but the other members of the clergy were not listening. They were in a state of panic as their worst fears had come to fruition; to be murdered by terrorists. The room was in disarray, with dead Swiss Guard littered everywhere. How could this happen Mark Peter wondered, the grounds were secured, no one knew we were here, no one but the men in this room. Wait, the Pope screamed silently, where is Cardinal Augustine? The Pope sunk in anguish at the thought that his best friend, his confidante, had sold him out as had Judas done to Jesus. It was then that Alistair Pratt appeared and ordered his men to clean up the mess. The room had to be pristine because in a few moments the world would be his stage. The world would not see the carnage that had taken place just moments ago. Alistair stood smugly as he surveyed the dead Swiss Guard. *Fools!* Did they really think that they were a match for me! As he watched his men remove the dead bodies and clean up the blood he marveled at how easy it had been to take the vaunted Swiss

Guard down. Alistair then quickly dismissed his feelings of pleasure; this was only the first phase, he reminded himself; now my real purpose begins.

Ricardo heard what he thought to be gunshots, but he wasn't sure. If that is what I think it is, *how can they be right? How will I complete my task?* He looked at his watch. In fifteen minutes he was to enter the fortress.

As the gunshots rang out Carson Lowery anxiously tapped his right foot on the moist grass. He was ready to move his team in, but he had his instructions. He unsnapped his cell phone and dialed the woman's number. "It has begun," he said, staring simultaneously at the messenger and the armory. He was nervous, but he was ready. He knew this moment was coming and he was prepared, but he knew that one mistake could spell disaster.

"Relax, I told you this is how it would happen."

"I know but still."

"Unfortunately it had to play out this way. Are you ready?"

"Yes I'm ready."

"Good."

Twenty-five

"Alex, what are you talking about? You and Alex had a relationship?"

"Yes," said Jordan.

"When?"

"Forever."

"What?" Kelly was completely confused.

"We have been together forever."

"When was the last time you two were together?"

"Last night?"

"Last night?" What is she talking about, Kelly thought?

"That's what I said, are you deaf?"

"He was at your house?"

"Yes he was and we made love for hours and hours."

"Last night?"

"Isn't that what I said?" Kelly realized that this was all a fantasy in the girl's head, but she couldn't let on.

"So if he's been yours forever, then how could I have stolen him from you?"

"Do you think I'm stupid?"

"No."

"Then stop acting like you don't know what I'm talking about."

"But I don't."

"You liar! You stole Alex and now I'm going to get him back."

"Are you a student at Landon College?"

"I was, but that was a long time ago, I left."

"Why?"

"I'm asking the questions bitch."

"Okay calm down."

"Don't fucking tell me what to do? You've got a lot of nerve, stealing him like you did."

"But you were with Alex last night so how could I have stolen him?"

"Bitch you know what I'm talking about!" *"Let her go Jordan,"* the voices said. Kelly shuddered. *"Shut the fuck up!"* Jordan replied as she paced the floor frantically.

"But you said that you made love to him last night."

"You stupid bitch, Alex doesn't even know I exist, not that way at least."

"But you said."

"You stole him from my mind, can't you see. He was my safe haven and you stole him and now you're going to die." Jordan was calm now, the gun at her side.

"If you kill me you're going to go to jail and then you'll never have him."

"Oh but I'm not going to kill you."

"You're not?"

"No, you're going to commit suicide."

"Suicide?"

"Yes, ingenious, isn't it?"

"You'll never get away with it."

"Oh yes I will."

"Alex knows that I would never kill myself."

"Well you're going to call and convince him."

"Look, you can have him. I'll never see him again."

"Lying bitch! Here call him now!"

Is that my cell phone, I wondered? I hesitated because I didn't want to get shot.

"Answer it, and don't say anything about where you are or you'll both die." Said one of the men.

"Hello, Alex?"

"Kelly, where are you?"

"Alex," she said, reading from Jordan's script, "it's over, I can't take it anymore. I'm not happy."

"Not happy, what are you talking about, Kelly can we please talk about this later? I." She cut him off and kept reading.

"I'm not happy."

"It's not you Alex. I'm not happy with my life and I don't see the point in going on." Kelly purposely sounded choppy as she read the note. She was hoping that Alex would pick up on the fact that she was reading against her will.

"Kelly, what are you talking about?"

"This is best for everyone. You'll be happier in the long run. Goodbye Alex." I heard a loud noise that sounded like a gunshot, and the line went dead.

I was instantly thrown into a state of shock and panic. Was Kelly dead? I couldn't believe it. I must be dreaming. Yes this is all one horrible dream, all of it. There is no Alistair Pratt, no Lydia Sinclair, and no Sir Arthur Garrison. This is a dream and when I wake up, Kelly will be right next to me.

Alistair Pratt strode to the dais, triumphant and proud, adorned in a long cape, knee high boots and black riding pants. His hair was slicked back and he carried a large satchel, which he placed on the floor. The room sufficiently cleaned to his liking, he instructed the seven men of the clergy to sit at a long table that was adorned with an array of food. It was Minister Hamed who immediately recognized what this madman was doing.

"You are replicating the last supper." Hamed offered.

"Yes you are very wise my Muslim brother, the only difference is that this will literally be your last supper." Alistair said with a wicked grin. He then turned to Timothy. "Is the television feed ready?"

"Yes." Timothy replied.

"What is it that you want?" Mark Peter asked.

"Only what is rightfully mine."

"Who are you?" the Pope asked.

"The feed is ready." Timothy shouted.

"You are about to find out." Alistair grinned wickedly.

"You should have been an actress Kelly, because you had me convinced that you wanted to take your own life."

"You sick, pathetic bitch, you'll never get away with this."

"Just a while ago you were so understanding, now you've turned on me," said Jordan with a wicked smile as she placed the end of the gun on the bridge of Kelly's nose.

"Fuck you."

"Sorry sweetie, but I only like men."

"Why don't you just kill me and get it over with?"

"Oh don't worry, it's going to happen. I'm just waiting for the exact time," Jordan removed the gun and stepped back.

"The exact time, what are you talking about?"

"At approximately 11:58 am, I will celebrate the anniversary of my emergence from my mother's womb. At that precise moment, as I'm eating my birthday cake, I'll be putting a bullet into your head, sort of a symbiosis of life and death."

"You're sick."

"Aren't we all?"

Ricardo's watch read ten-thirty and as instructed he began to walk towards the entrance to the fortress. He felt a few drops hit his back as he began the final leg of his journey. The sweet smell of the falling rain was pleasing to his nostrils. He approached the entrance to find that it wasn't guarded, just as he was told. The huge steel door was left slightly ajar and he stepped in, where he was immediately met by two men, whose dress was familiar, and who bore the mark of the order, the **cc**. Still Ricardo was wary, what if this were the enemy, The Light of Hellas disguised as members of the Chamber. The men sensed his concern. "Don't worry, we are with you," they said in unison. Ricardo clutched the package and followed the men as they led him up a steep set of stairs and into a large windowless room that was bare, with the exception of a gray folding chair, a coffee table, a lamp, a pitcher of water, a glass and a fan. "We will return shortly, if it gets stuffy turn on the fan "one of the men said. They left the room and locked the door.

Carson Lowery gave the signal and his team moved into position. He expected opposition, but it never came. The woman had told him that entry would be easy, but his instincts told him otherwise. He did a double take, not sure of what he saw lying before him. There were dead bodies everywhere; clearly Pratt's men. But when, how, he wondered? And there isn't any blood, so how were they killed? The woman, she's behind this. He shook his head in amazement; the things she could do! He moved his team into the Armory and phoned the woman. 'We're in, have you alerted the others?" he asked the woman.

"Yes, we're all set. Was entry just as I said?"

"Yes, but the men in the hanger, they were Pratt's men, who took them out and are they with us?"

"Yes they are with us."

"Who are they and why didn't you tell me?"

"I will explain after everything has been completed. You must go now."

Carol had just gotten out of the shower and was preparing for her nightly routine. She popped some popcorn and turned on the news, but the person she saw wasn't familiar at all, nor was the background. It looked like a hotel. At first she thought it was a commercial, but when the image didn't leave the screen, she checked the channel to see if she'd turned on the wrong station. When she realized that she hadn't she was perplexed. She went to get up to change the station manually because the remote was missing again, a fact of life when there are children in the house, when she froze. *Did I hear correctly? Did he say what I thought? And isn't that the Pope? Oh shit, where's Alex?* She dialed his number, but didn't get an answer. Then she tried his cell phone, but all she got was his voice mail. *He's safe, he's okay,* she tried to convince herself. All I can do is watch and see what's going on.

"Richard," she screamed, "Come quick."

"For those of you who've just tuned in, let me repeat, my name is Alistair Pratt, Grand Marshall of the Light of Hellas, the true and rightful servants of God. Ladies and gentleman these men you see sitting before me are the true enemies of

God. They are blasphemers of God's word and tonight they will be dealt with as all infidels are dealt with. These seven men, the so-called spiritual fathers are nothing but liars, thieves and idolaters and tonight they will suffer their just fate. But that is just the beginning, for tonight the antichrist will be exposed and destroyed, and mankind will be free. Tonight I will end the hopelessness that has clouded man for centuries. Hopelessness that began, not in the Garden of Eden, as these infidels would have you to believe, but with the shame and humiliation brought to my forefather, whose name I shall reveal in just a short time. As you can see, I have prepared a sumptuous feast for my guests, because it will indeed be their last supper. It will be the last supper for the hypocrisy of the church, as we know it. After tonight, but before tomorrow, before the clock strikes twelve, I will possess the true and rightful symbol of power and I will set you free."

"Oh my God," Carol exclaimed.

All over the world the word had spread that a man named Alistair Pratt and an organization called the Light of Hellas was going to expose the antichrist. The Vatican by orders of the Carmerlengo, an elderly Cardinal by the name of Vincenzo, who was in charge in the Pope's absence, did something that one would never envision in St. Peter's Square; he had a wide screen television placed in the middle of the square so that onlookers could see the events as they unfolded. This scene was played out in the holy land, in mosques and temples, and in churches all over the world. Who is this man, was the phrase on the lips of people all over the world, and more important who is the one he claims to be the antichrist?

"In a few minutes," Alistair continued "we will expose the enemy of Christ and you shall see for yourselves the one the bible has said would come. The antichrist along with the seven infidels before you will meet the destiny that was promised to them by God's holy word."

I was still in a state of shock from Kelly's suicide. How could this have happened? I knew that if I survived I would never be the same. It was my deception that caused her death, my lies that caused her to end it all. Ashley tried to comfort me but I was totally distraught. "Dr. Marshall it's time," someone said.

"What?" I asked my voice barely above a whisper.

"I said it's time."

"Time for what?" But he didn't answer. "What about Ashley, what are you going to do with her?" I asked nervously.

"She is coming too." He said. Someone opened the door to our room and we were taken up a flight of stairs where we heard talking, but then the talking stopped. Our blindfolds were still on, but the room was noticeably brighter. Then a voice that I was intimately familiar with spoke, and said: "*The apple falls not far from the tree. So my dear Alex, it seems as if we've come full circle.*"

Twenty-six

Kelly looked at the clock, and it read eleven fifty-three. If she didn't do something in five minutes, she'd be dead.

"That's right Kelly, in five minutes, you will be dead and Alex will be mine. Of course he will grieve your death, but I will be there to comfort him, and then he'll be mine."

"Aren't you forgetting someone?"

"Who?"

"Helen."

"My boss, she doesn't want him, they just went to high school together." Jordan was totally confused.

"Oh really? Why don't you ask your boss who her high school sweetheart was, who she's been talking too lately." Kelly cringed, but she had to keep up the offensive. I think that's who will take my place once I'm dead, and you'll be left out again."

"No, that's not going to happen, you shut up." Kelly sensed an opening, not to mention that she had managed to work her hands and legs free, though she gave the illusion that they were still tied up behind her. "Yes it will. She still loves him, you'll see."

"Shut up," she was screaming, "It's not true." Jordan turned her back and slapped herself in the face with her gun, while repeatedly screaming "it's not true." If Kelly was going to live, this was the moment of truth. She jumped up from the chair, dove and grabbed Jordan by the legs, causing her to drop the gun. She then rolled on top of her and hit her with a solid right to the jaw. Jordan was fazed, but not out. She kicked Kelly in the stomach and made a beeline for the gun, but Kelly managed to grab a hold of her leg and pull her down. Jordan tried to get away, but Kelly had a firm grip. Kelly then bit Jordan on the ankle, and as Jordan writhed in pain Kelly was able to grab the gun.

"Kill me, please kill me," Jordan pleaded.

Kelly was tempted to pull the trigger, but she didn't, she saw the pain of her own life, her own past flash before her. She didn't know this girl's past, but she was sure it was the cause of her pain and despair. She knew that Jordan was no longer a threat. All she could think about was getting out of there and getting to Alex.

Twenty-seven

"You don't look surprised," Alistair said as he removed my blindfold.

"Why should I be surprised," Alex said, as he tried to readjust his eyes to the bright lights.

"Here we are just as it has been ordained, full circle if you will." My vision back in focus, I couldn't believe what I saw. Sitting just inches away from me were the most powerful religious leaders in the world. *What the hell was going on?*

"What do you mean by the 'apple falls not far from the tree, we've come full circle?'" Alex asked.

"I will explain in a second, but first I must speak to the world. Ladies and gentleman standing before you is the one I have promised, the messenger of death, the antichrist, Dr. Alex Marshall." For a second my entire body froze, locked up. *Did he say what I thought he said?* I looked over at Ashley and she stood there, her mouth agape. My head was spinning and as I stood there I thought I was in some kind of weird dream. There were a group of men sitting around a table filled with food and one of them looked like the Pope. But it wasn't a dream, and as my head cleared and my eyes adjusted to the lights, I was convinced that I was in the lair of a madman.

Carol couldn't believe her ears *did that bastard say my little brother was the antichrist?* All around the world the question on everyone's minds was: *Who is Alex Marshall?*

Pope Mark Peter looked as though he was about to have a heart attack, and the other leaders stared in disbelief.

"Did you say I was the antichrist? I asked Alistair. As I watched him on the dais in his long cape and riding boots I couldn't believe this was the same person. Ashley shot me a glance of similar disbelief.

"Yes, you heard me correctly. You are the harbinger of death, the forerunner to the evil one, and tonight, you and your seven minions will be destroyed."

"Why do you say I'm the antichrist?"

"Because my friend you are following in the footsteps of your legendary ancestor." *What?*

"Ancestor, what are you talking about? Are you saying that I'm a descendant of Satan?"

"In a manner of speaking, but aren't all of you who distort God's word, spawns of Lucifer himself?" As he said the words he looked straight at the men sitting at the table.

"Well if you're not talking about Satan directly, then whom are you talking about?" I asked.

Carol and Richard were staring straight at the television, as were Alex's parents, and the entire world. St. Peter's Square was so quiet it was as if the Pope himself had died.

"Why I'm speaking of the original antichrist, the one who foretold of Jesus' coming, I'm speaking of none other than John the Baptist."

Twenty-eight

St. Peter's Square was aghast, and for a second no one said anything, then everyone began to speak at once, it sounded like the Vatican had been infiltrated by millions of bees, the words no longer audible but sounding like one large human buzzing.

Carol slumped back in disbelief. *The Marshall's are descendants of THE John the Baptist, and this lunatic is calling him the original antichrist?*

All over the world people were in shock. The notion that there was possibly a living descendant of John the Baptist was shocking enough, but the other part, *the original antichrist*, that was too bizarre to comprehend.

"What did you just say?" I didn't know what was more shocking; that I could actually be a descendant of John the Baptist or the part about him being the original antichrist.

"You heard me correctly."

"Are you saying that I'm related to John the Baptist and that *he* was the original antichrist?" I asked.

"Yes. If you want proof, just check the genealogical archives at the Mormon headquarters in Salt Lake City, their records go back to before Christ, isn't that true Elder?" Alistair asked. The elder nodded in the affirmative.

"You're saying that John the Baptist was the original antichrist, that's ludicrous."

"It's only ludicrous to people like yourself, people who distort God's word."

"And what you're doing here, kidnapping these men of the cloth, threatening death, that's following God's word?"

"Yes we are doing just that." He said.

"We, who is that, you and Lydia Sinclair?" Lydia smiled at me, but I looked away in disgust.

"Who are we? We are the Light of Hellas, the only true followers of Christ's word."

"The Light of Hellas, I've never heard of you."

"You utter that sentence with such arrogance. Of course you've never heard of us, we have craftily concealed ourselves for centuries. But you know that from which we've spawned."

"The Chamber of Cyrenaic?" I guessed.

"Yes my dear Alex, you win the prize. I promised the world that I would reveal who we were. Alistair then recounted to the world the history of the Cyrenaic. He paused, looked around and then continued.

"So Sir Arthur took Jesus at his literal word when he said 'Seek and you shall find, knock and the door will be opened.' Sir Arthur also used the Songs of Solomon as proof of God's intentions towards pleasure. Sir Arthur rightfully believed that God encouraged man to seek pleasure, to express himself through sexual purity, which meant man and woman coming together in the purity of sexual union, the highest form of worship. Sir Arthur believed that the Protestant church in fifteenth century England repressed followers of God by telling them to deny the very sense of pleasure God had given them. But then Sir Arthur became soft, gutless. He sought to gain favor with the Protestant Church in order to keep the church off his back. Jeremiah Pratt tried to convince him to remain strong and resolute, but Sir Arthur being the coward that he was, refused to listen and Jeremiah founded the Light of

Hellas. It was Jeremiah who said that the infidels who distorted God's word had to be destroyed. He hatched a plan to rid the world of the religious hypocrites who claimed to believe in God, but taught their flock to deny the very thing that God allowed them to have, the ability to experience pleasure at its highest level. These were the same hypocrites who engaged in all types of sexual deviant behavior, isn't that right Mark Peter?" He smirked at the Pope.

"On November 8, 1503," he continued, "Sir Arthur murdered Jeremiah and another man to prevent them from doing God's work, but that didn't stop the brotherhood of the Light of Hellas, and now here we are five hundred years later, and this time destiny will be fulfilled."

"Interesting, but what does this have to do with John the Baptist and me for that matter?"

"You are here to distort God's word just as your ancestor did, and for that reason you must be stopped and destroyed."

"How did John the Baptist distort God's word?"

"How you ask? I'll tell you how. Look at John the Baptist, he wore rag tag clothing, he lived in the wilds of the jungle, he ate, nuts and berries, he denied himself pleasure. He taught man to believe that was the way to follow Jesus. He was the precursor to the hypocritical Protestant church. When Christ came he ate and drank with sinners, he wore fine garments, he accepted all men and he never told them to disavow pleasure. Show me one piece of scripture where Christ tells man to deny himself sexual pleasure. It was that hypocrite Paul who administered rules regarding sexual pleasure, not Christ. John the Baptist, your ancestor was the beginning and now you've come to take up where he left off, but I will not allow it to happen."

"So what are you going to do to me?"

"I'm going to do what my *ancestor* should have done from the start."

"*Your ancestor*, what are you talking about?"

244

"If my ancestor would have taken care of John the Baptist as soon as he began spouting his anti-Christ message, Christ's legacy would be different."

"You're not making sense."

"Let me make it plain for you then, when I say my ancestor, I'm talking about none other than King Herod himself." I thought I'd heard it all now. So that's what he meant by 'we've come full circle.'

Pope Mark Peter fainted; St. Peter's Square was like a tomb, and then the buzzing began again. Carol just sat there immobilized.

"Enough talk Dr. Marshall it is time for the world to be rid of you and the infidels. Timothy please hand me that bag on the floor." Timothy did and inside was seven gold tipped swords, which Timothy placed on the lap of each clergy. "Now bring Ricardo out." Timothy made the call. Alistair stepped off the dais.

"And now the moment that we have waited for has finally arrived. In a few moments I will have in my possession the ancient artifact; the true symbol of power and truth. In the right hands this artifact represents all that is good, but in the wrong hands it will cause destruction of such seismic proportions that mankind will be destroyed. This man, Alex Marshall, the antichrist was to receive the artifact tonight. But I will stop him and in the process save all of you. It was his people, the Chamber of Cyrenaic who stole the artifact from the brotherhood, but tonight God will restore order, He will restore Eden. God has appointed the brotherhood to destroy the antichrist and the seven headed beast that sits before you."

Alex watched in sheer horror as Alistair spouted on, rambling like a raving lunatic. Somebody had to do something. Where were the police, the FBI, Patrick, somebody! Surely the world knew what was going on, why wasn't anybody doing anything. He had to do something, but what. He looked over at Ashley and her eyes belied the same sentiment, but she had no clue as to what to do.

"They're ready, bring him out," another caller relayed to the men standing guard over Ricardo. The men brought Ricardo out of the room and took him upstairs. When he reached the main conference room, Alistair smiled. This was it, the moment he'd been waiting for, the crowning achievement.

Jordan was balled up in a corner sobbing and muttering incomprehensively. Kelly glanced at Jordan and for a split second contemplated trying to comfort her but thought better of it. Kelly ran from Jordan's. She didn't know where she was and she didn't care. She tried to call Alex again, but she only got his voice mail. She tried Patrick, but got his voice mail as well. She kept running until she began to see familiar landmarks, Hollands, the college. She decided that it would be best to go to Alex's house. She was exhausted when she got there. She tried Alex's phone again, but still no answer. Panic flooded her. Was he in danger? Was he dead? *Was he with Helen*? She called Carol.

One of the guards shoved Ricardo over to Alistair. He snatched the case from Ricardo's hand. Alistair's hands were shaking but he composed himself. Slowly he opened the case as the world watched with baited breath. Though my death was imminent I was thankful that I would get to finally see the ancient artifact. Ashley who'd been standing next to me the whole time was hyperventilating. Then suddenly Alistair screamed: "*This isn't it!*" He threw the package on the floor and lunged violently at Ricardo, but Ricardo sidestepped him and jumped off the dais.

Then everything became a blur, I saw men cascading from everywhere, dressed in funny clothing and it looked like they had the letter c, twice, on their foreheads. I saw Alistair try to run, but he was tackled to the ground by what looked like the "dead" man from Seville. I saw Patrick and the Chief. There were gunshots and bodies flying everywhere, and the clergy were ushered out and I think the Pope was hit in the leg, but I'm not sure. I was on the ground underneath the table trying to take cover and Ashley was crouched behind the dais. Then I heard a familiar voice tell us to come with her. It was Lydia Sinclair. The next thing I knew police were everywhere, and more were coming as the sirens pierced the night. Lydia ushered us outside into a waiting vehicle and we were whisked away, by police escort. For a brief second I was happy to escape, but immediately my thoughts turned to Kelly. As we drove away from the Armory down Old Landon Road I began to cry. My cell phone rang. Could it be? Was I dreaming? I wasn't. It was Kelly, she was alive and at that moment I'd made my choice.

Twenty-nine

St. Peter's Square was raucous with joy and relief; though the Pope had been injured the early reports were that his wound wasn't serious. The rest of world breathed a sigh of relief, but felt shortchanged because they wanted to know what was in the mysterious package. I felt the same way. Maybe there wasn't any information; maybe there never was an ancient artifact. Maybe this gatekeeper stuff was a ruse by Alistair and he was just plain crazy.

When we reached my house all I wanted to do was see Kelly and get some sleep, but there were still a lot of unanswered questions that had to be addressed. When I found out that it was Jordan who kidnapped Kelly I was shocked. Lydia asked us to sit down and as soon as the others arrived, everything would be explained. I picked up the phone to call my family and Felix, when I heard voices outside my door. I opened the door and standing in front of the house was what seemed like the entire village, with my sister leading the flock. It was the most moving experience I'd ever had in my life. We were outside for hours until one by one they all went home. I went back into the house where Lydia ushered all of Kelly, Ashley, Felix, Carol, my parents, into the living room. Then one by one the "others" filtered in standing shoulder to shoulder, each with the funny little cc on the forehead. When Ashley and I saw their faces, our mouths flew open.

"What is it?" Carol asked guardedly, fearing that maybe we were still in danger.

"I will explain," Lydia said.

"To begin, my name is not Lydia Sinclair. It is Kathleen Garrison and this is my sister Louisa." It was the woman in the castle in Seville.

"So you were telling the truth." I said addressing Louisa.

"Yes."

"Then why did the man who snatched us say you were Alexandria Pratt?" I asked.

"Let my sister continue." She said with a smile.

"My sister, my late brother Archibald and I are direct descendants of Sir Arthur and it was our duty to keep the Chamber alive. My brother, unfortunately, was weak and greedy and because of his betrayal he was murdered." My stomach knotted up and a palpable sense of uneasiness enveloped the room.

"You murdered your own brother?" Carol asked.

"I didn't say that. What I said was that his betrayal caused him to be murdered. Archibald loved money, in fact so much that he would do anything to get it. He was already rich beyond his wildest dreams, but it was his thirst for more that caused his demise. As a Garrison he was privy to the legend of the ancient artifact, an artifact that is worth billions of dollars. He knew that Alistair Pratt wanted the artifact and so he cut a deal with him to deliver it. But when Alistair refused to give him what he asked, he broke the deal off. Alistair then had him killed."

"Did you know all along what your brother was up to?" I asked Kathleen.

"Yes I did, we all did."

"And you were going to let him strike a deal with Alistair?" I asked

"I didn't say that."

"Then how do I know that you didn't kill him yourself?" I asked; my pulse quickening. I still wasn't sure if we were safe.

"I assure you Alex; the Chamber did not kill my brother. We had other means to stop him."

"What do you mean?"

"None of that matters now," Kathleen said calmly, but firmly, her cold blue eyes reminding me that she was one not to anger, I thought best to let *that* line of questioning drop.

"Why did your brother agree to talk to me?"

"Do you recall your conversation with my brother?"

"Yes."

"And did he really tell you anything?"

"No, he didn't." I replied.

"And he wasn't going to because there wasn't anything you could do for him." Kathleen said.

"But once I had the artifact he could have tried to cut a deal with me?"

"That's true, but Archibald couldn't take the chance of waiting until November 8. He was involved with some unscrupulous characters to which he owed a great deal of money, so he needed cash right away."

"But that's a moot point because you wouldn't have allowed him to cut a deal with me anyway, right?"

"Right."

"Archibald's wife and children, are they really sequestered somewhere here in the country?"

"Yes they're safe and will be taken care of for the rest of their lives." Kathleen said.

"Why did you pose as Lydia Sinclair?" I asked.

"It was my role in the Chamber."

"Your role?" Ashley interjected.

"Yes. The Chamber of Cyrenaic is an extremely organized unit whose sole purpose is to protect and honor the legacy of Sir Arthur and to make sure that the ancient artifact was preserved so that it could be handed to the gatekeeper. For centuries we have existed under the veil of secrecy in order to protect ourselves not only from the Light of Hellas, but the traditional church as well. As you well know Alex, our beliefs are antithetical to traditional religious doctrine, be it Christianity, Catholicism, Islam, Mormon, you name it. The notion that Christ was an advocate of sensual pleasure is blasphemous to the traditional church and the fact that we possess the ancient artifact made us targets, so we had to stay underground. Like any well oiled machine, we are comprised of different cogs, each separate within itself, but necessary for the functioning of the Chamber. My role was to develop an alliance with our chief enemy, Mr. Alistair Pratt. The others that you see hear, some of which you already know had different roles. The "dead" man from Seville and Mr. Carson Lowery are the military arms of the brotherhood and Louisa was in charge of them."

"And the man who snatched us away in the castle, was he part of this too?"

"Yes, he works for Louisa."

"And how did you get by Alistair's men, did you kill them?"

"We did what was necessary to ensure that you and the package would be safe."

"What does that mean?" I asked wondering about whether the seven of us sitting on the couch were safe.

"It's not important Alex, I will only say that our actions were just."

"But how can you profess to believe in God and kill at the same time?" Ashley asked.

"If you study your bible you will see that God used violence when necessary, we were only emulating our teacher." Kathleen Garrison said.

"But why did you put us through all of this? Why not just tell me the truth?"

"We had to test your mettle?" Louisa said. "Remember when I told you in the castle that we wanted to see what you were made of?"

"Yes, I remember something to that effect."

"We had to make sure that you were worthy of protecting our legacy, so we put you through all of this to test your resolve." Kelly exploded off the couch and stood right in Louisa's face.

"You put their lives in danger to see if he was worthy of protecting your fucking legacy! Are you fucking serious?"

"Ms. Van Astor I truly understand your anger, but please know that Alex and Ashley were never in any real danger. Carson and his team were always in the vicinity just in case something were to happen."

"That still doesn't make it right." Kelly said, her anger dissipating slightly.

"Maybe not, but it was what had to be done."

"What about the Pope and the other members of the clergy, what was that all about?"

"It's only by coincidence that the Council for Religious Unity chose to hold its conference in the same place on the same night as the transfer of the artifact." Kathleen said.

"The Council for Religious Unity?" I asked.

"Yes, it is the brainchild of the Pope in an effort to bring together all of the world's major religions. The goal is to promote peace, harmony and unity."

"Was this public knowledge?" Carol asked.

"No, you can imagine the type of danger they would have been in. They would have attracted terrorists and fanatics opposed to a union such as this."

"Then how did Alistair find out?" I asked.

"He was able to secure the services of his own personal Judas; Cardinal Augustine, the Pope's most trusted confidante." Kathleen said.

"If Alistair was so sure that I was the antichrist, why did he wait until tonight to try and kill me?"

"Because he had to wait until the transfer of the artifact. We had it so well protected that he had no choice but to wait until the appointed date of delivery to you."

"And the suicides?" Felix asked.

"The suicides were borne from Sir Arthur's rightful elimination of Jeremiah Pratt and his partner Richard Black. Sir Arthur lured them to a remote area outside of London and convinced them that they must take another blood oath. Pratt and Black, not wanting to raise the suspicion of Sir Arthur agreed, only Sir Arthur had other plans. The blood oath that they took was with a gold tipped sword, which was laced with poison. From then on it was ordained that whenever the ancient artifact was transferred to the next gatekeeper, he or she would kill themselves via the gold-tipped sword."

"Why would someone agree to kill themselves?" Carol asked.

"Because of their oath and loyalty to the Chamber. There are some people who believe so deeply in a cause that they are willing to sacrifice themselves for the greater good. The suicides that you read about were for that good. Let me assure you that not one person was forced to do so, they were willing participants."

"And the last suicide has it taken place already?" I asked.

"Yes." Kathleen said.

"Then how come I don't have the artifact?" I asked.

"Oh but you do," She smiled.

"Where?" Everyone simultaneously leaned forward as if doing so would make a difference.

"It is in your bedroom." Then Louisa summoned the group to follow her out of the room. We sat on the couch wondering what was going on. Was it another set up, another test?

"In my bedroom, when, how? I thought the young man at the Armory was the messenger. If that's true then when did he get the chance to deliver the artifact to my house?"

"My dear Alex, Ricardo delivered the artifact to your house shortly after you left for your reunion. What was taken from him by Alistair was all part of our plan."

"But something doesn't make sense. As meticulously as Alistair planned for tonight, wouldn't he have made allowances for a switch?" I shifted my feet uneasily, and my stomach moved again. *Alistair wouldn't have missed such an important detail.*

"We were prepared for an attack, on Ricardo, at your home. We knew that Alistair would have your house watched, and so my men were positioned all throughout your house, just in case. If Alistair thought of trying something, he must have reconsidered, because Ricardo wasn't touched." Carson Lowery said.

"And he left it on my bed, just like that?"

"Yes it was safe because someone was always here to guard it."

"This is unbelievable."

"No Alex, it is your destiny, serve it well." Louisa said.

"And Ricardo, where is he?" I asked.

"He has gone on to be with the Chamber in another world. He has fulfilled his duty and for that we will be forever grateful. And now you must fulfill yours. We will leave you now." I couldn't believe what was happening, and yet it wasn't over, for upstairs in my bedroom, was the culmination of a long journey.

"You can't leave yet, there's so much more I want to know."

"Another time, I promise, now your destiny awaits you, we pray that you serve it well."

I walked upstairs slowly, and I swear I could hear each floorboard creak. I left the others downstairs because I felt I needed to do this by myself. I had to see it first, alone. I opened the bedroom door and there it was sitting on my bed. It was a rather large leather case. Dark brown with maroon borders it was surprisingly lighter than it looked. The case appeared to be hand woven, each stitch meticulously woven by the hands of a master craftsman. So this is it, 500 years of secrets encompassed in this beautiful leather case. Every moment that occurred throughout this strange and exciting journey consumed me as I stared at the case. My heart began to race as I opened it. The house was deathly silent, everyone downstairs waiting and wondering. I was puzzled and disappointed at the same time. This is it, I sighed, *a sword?* The sword appeared to be an antique, about four feet long and extremely light. It looked like it may be valuable but hardly worth the number of lives that had been lost. That was until I read the enclosed note.

The sword that you now possess is the sword that was used to behead John the Baptist. As the last and final gatekeeper you will make all decisions as to its destiny. You will find all theological records enclosed in this package.

RICARDO THE CYRENAIC

I picked up the sword, put it down, then picked it up again and walked down the stairs. It was now morning and the sun was filtering slowly through the windows. I didn't say a word when I reached the bottom, I simply handed the note to Kelly, which she read aloud. No one said a word, which was only fitting, because what more could be said.

Thirty

So how does a story like mine end? Is it my decision concerning the sword; is that it, then chapter closed? Frankly I don't know if the story of one's life ever ends, even in death, and so I guess it's more about how the story continues.

It's now May, the eighth to be exact, my birthday. Kelly and I are aboard a cruise ship whisking along the Atlantic Ocean, celebrating our engagement, but more about that in a minute. A lot has happened since that strange night in November. Where to begin? Alistair Pratt's trial, as you can imagine, was a media circus, but taking into account *what had occurred* I don't suppose it could have been anything else. Many times throughout the trial the Judge had several of Alistair's loyal Hellas members thrown into jail for contempt of court because of loud outbursts always ending with the phrase; *truth and power.* Alistair's attorneys tried the insanity defense, but the jury didn't buy it, even though it was evident that he was indeed crazy. Later I found out, through one of Kelly's contacts that the members of the jury were really punishing Alistair for shooting the Pope, and even though they did think he was off his rocker, shooting the Pope had to be dealt with harshly. Alistair, defiant the very end, was sentenced to life in prison for attempted murder and kidnapping. He hung himself three weeks after being jailed.

Jordan Nelson is recovering in a mental institution in upstate New York and Kelly visits her twice a month. At first I couldn't understand why Kelly would do that, but she said she felt sorry for Jordan. She said that Jordan, like herself, was abandoned by her mother but to make matters worse, was sexually abused by her father, until he mysteriously died in a boating accident. Kelly believes Jordan killed him, but she doesn't pass judgment. She said that Jordan told her that her obsession with me was because I was the only man who ever treated her with respect; the only man she felt could ever really love her, if I'd given it a chance. I didn't know what to say to that and I felt guilty in a strange sort of way.

Cardinal Augustine was excommunicated from the Catholic Church and sentenced to twenty years for kidnapping; he was more distraught about being kicked out of the church. The Pope made a full recovery and is more popular than ever. The Council is alive and well though now because of the publicity they have to change their meeting location. The Armory was demolished with plans for upscale housing to be built on the site.

My sister is pregnant, she's hoping for a boy, though it's too early to tell; Felix and Carmen are expecting their third child as well, and the Chief's daughter had another girl; Hadley Willis landed a regular role on a reality television show and is currently living with his twenty-two year old co-star. Grace is just as rude as ever, though after our little episode she doesn't bother me anymore.

Ashley and I are closer; a near death experience will do that. And she's still wearing that ponytail.

Helen, what about Helen? I've seen Helen, in fact I took Kelly to her shop and ironically they managed to get along well. I'm not saying that they hang out with each other, but Kelly doesn't have a problem attending an affair that Carol is throwing if Helen is there. I still don't know what Helen's "complicated" situation was, but I suspect that she'd had an affair while she was in Milan and I have a sneaky suspicion that it was with Hadley. He was in Milan at the same time Helen was, but at the time I didn't think anything of it. But now I think that is what she's been hiding all of these years, and it explains why Hadley's been extra nice to me over the past fifteen or so years. But of course this is all conjecture. I asked my sister about it and she swears that Helen never confided anything like that to her; says that if she did she and Helen would be through as friends. Frankly at this point it doesn't really matter. I guess I should have asked her, but I didn't. Does that mean that I've forgotten what we once had, and that I don't think about her? Of course I haven't and of course I do. I could never forget Helen, but I don't need to *remember* Helen. I don't need to live on fantasy and romantic notions of starry filled nights and stories of days past, because that's all Helen and I really had. It was real, but it's not *real*, and I see now that Helen had accepted that fact a long time ago. It was me who kept hanging on and for what, I can't really say because I can't honestly say that I was still in love with her. I was in love with a memory, which is not what I have with Kelly and it took the notion of Kelly's "death" for me to see that. It's the philosophical question for the ages: *Why does it take a tragedy, or in my case, a near tragedy, to appreciate what you have?*

As for the sword, I thought about keeping it but to do so would have been selfish, so I "donated" it to the Smithsonian, where they gave me a hefty finder's fee.

The legacy of my great ancestor has meaning whether or not one is a Christian. His is the story of a great man who came to serve his fellow man, even at the expense of his own life and that legacy belongs to the entire world.

I know I should have more to say about the sword and about my famous ancestor, but I don't know what. Its not as though I take what happened to me cavalierly, it's not that at all. Maybe it's because I've talked so much about it over the past months that there's nothing left to say. Without a doubt it's an experience that I will never forget and one that has changed me, for the better, at least that's what I've been told, but other than that it's something that happened and now its time to move on.

The warm breeze billowing off the Atlantic was made even more inviting by Kelly's touch as she wrapped her arms around my waist. As we looked out silently at the ocean as the ship skipped through the waves, I smiled. Not a broad smile, but a smile of contentment and as Kelly squeezed me tightly her grasp a reminder that our love, warts and all is inseparable. It occurred to me that Alistair was right about one thing, I had indeed come full circle.

About the Author

Anthony Jemison, a native of Mount Vernon, New York, resides in Baltimore, Maryland with his wife, Dr. Shawnol Jemison and their two children, daughter Morgan and son Miles. Anthony earned a Juris Doctorate from the University of Maryland School of Law in 1991 and a B.A. in Liberal Studies from Salisbury University in 1987.

Though the *Garrison Doctrine* is his first novel, he has had several works of non-fiction published in various magazines. He has also completed two other manuscripts and is currently working on a psychological thriller tentatively entitled *Cranberry Hill.*

Printed in the United States
67352LVS00001B/31-48